W9-BNX-724

POISONED PINS

A Claire Malloy Mystery

Joan Hess

AN ONYX BOOK

ONYX
Published by the Penguin Group
Penguin Books USA Inc., 375 Hudson Street,
New York, New York 10014, U.S.A.
Penguin Books Ltd, 27 Wrights Lane,
London W8 5TZ, England
Penguin Books Australia Ltd, Ringwood,
Victoria, Australia
Penguin Books Canada Ltd, 10 Alcorn Avenue,
Toronto, Ontario, Canada M4V 3B2
Penguin Books (N.Z.) Ltd, 182–190 Wairau Road,
Auckland 10, New Zealand

Penguin Books Ltd, Registered Offices:
Harmondsworth, Middlesex, England
Published by Onyx, an imprint of Dutton Signet,
a division of Penguin Books USA Inc. Previously published in a Dutton edition.

First Onyx Printing, May, 1994
10 9 8 7 6 5 4 3 2 1

To Dominick Abel

I would like to thank Lieutenant Mike Terry of the University of Arkansas Police Department for sharing his time and expertise with me. I would also like to thank Barbara Rose for some of her amazing sorority stories, and several other sources who prefer to remain anonymous (for obvious reasons). Also, Sharyn McCrumb and Les Roberts were kind enough to offer specialized information and deserve my thanks.

1

Summer can be deadly. Oh, it's got some positive points, I suppose, such as not having to shovel ashes out of the fireplace or drape innocent conifers with tinsel. No sleet, no arctic breezes, no bouts of the flu. On the down side, however, there are virtually no customers in the Book Depot, which leads to no income for its proprietor, who is then obliged to stare gloomily at the pedestrianless sidewalk and think longingly of the other nine months of the year, when Farber College students are burdened with reading lists and a thirst for the sort of analytical insights available from slim yellow study guides.

I was doing just that, rather than battling the piles of paperwork that awaited me in the cramped office at the back of the renovated train station. I'd bought the bookstore more than a decade ago, only a few months after my husband of the moment had a most unfortunate encounter with a chicken truck. Business was never what I'd describe as brisk, but I knew with bleak certainty that the next three months would feel like an eternity as my bank balance dwindled, my spotty old accountant hissed about my delinquent quarterly tax payments, and my spirits inversely reflected the temperature.

The bell above the door tinkled, and I looked up with what optimism I could muster. After a brief struggle with the door, a girl with a towering armload of textbooks staggered across the floor and crashed into the counter with a muted gurgle.

"Let me help you," I said as I came around the

counter and began to unload her. A face emerged, framed by wispy bangs and dull brown hair that needed to be washed. Her eyes were small and yellowish, her nose broad, her lips almost puffy. I continued taking books from her and piling them on the counter until we'd completed the task and the rest of her was visible. The rest of her turned out to be skinny to the point of angularity, with no discernible bust, waist, or hips. Beneath the hem of a wrinkled brown skirt, thick calves provided the only convexity.

She was watching me so nervously that I went back to my stool and sat. "What can I do for you?" I asked in the dulcet tones of a mild-mannered bookseller intent on a sale.

"Do you buy used textbooks?"

I inwardly winced at the nasality of her voice, but merely shook my head and said, "No, I don't, but Rock Bottom Books does. It's about four blocks past the tracks, on the opposite side of the street."

"Four blocks? I barely made it this far. I was scared my arms were gonna fall off." She tried to smile, but her enthusiasm must have fallen off along the way, too. "Are you sure you don't . . . ?"

"Very sure," I told the witless wonder. "I do, however, sell books, and you're welcome to look around."

"Thank you." She drifted behind a rack of science fiction paperbacks. "You sure have a lot of books, ma'am."

"Bookstores are like that," I said as I glanced at the spines of the textbooks. Titles ran the gamut from computer technology to medieval poetry to botany, an impressively varied array for someone amazed by the presence of books in bookstores. "What's your major?" I asked the top of her head.

"Elementary ed. I'm going to be a teacher when I graduate. There's something really special about kids, isn't there? I mean, they're so young and everything, like little sponges ready to soak up everything they can."

Was a sale so important? It was well past the middle

of the afternoon, and not a completely unreasonable hour to close the store, meet Luanne at the shady beer garden across the street, and drown my financial sorrows while gazing numbly at the desultory old hippies who came out only while the majority of Farber College students were gone for the summer. Pabst, pretzels, and piteous whining—not an unappealing combination for a summer's eve.

Or I could call Peter Rosen, a man of considerable charm with dark, curly hair, eyes as deceptively guileless as puddles of molasses, a hawkish nose, and an uncanny talent in matters of passion. In other matters he could be somewhat irritating, alas, along with tedious, humorless, dictatorial, and blunt. Cops can be like that. As can men in general, I amended.

"I guess I'd better try to find that other store," the girl said as she reappeared. I helped her pile the books in her arms, escorted her out the front door, and watched her for a few minutes as she reeled up the sidewalk, oblivious to the potential peril of the uneven pavement. Entertainment's not easy to come by in Farberville, a mundane place made tolerable only by the slight infusion—or illusion—of culture from the college.

I was reduced to reading the local newspaper when the bell again jangled. This time the door banged open and the sunlight splashed on my face as my daughter Caron careened into the room with the finesse of a runaway locomotive.

"Mother!" she shrieked. "I have this absolutely incredible way to earn thousands and thousands of dollars! That way I can buy a car at the end of the summer! Aren't you excited?"

Caron is fifteen, an age that precludes pleasantries. Although we are similarly equipped with red hair, green eyes, and freckles, she has such an aura of intensity that I feel obliged to offer a disclaimer when I introduce her to the unwary. She's capable of the brightest explosion or the darkest implosion, neither remotely predictable and both equally alarming. Before she was deluged by demon hormones, she'd not been an unreasonable person with whom to converse. I fully intend to resume such mother-daughter intimacy when it's no longer a life-threatening proposition.

Following more sedately was her best friend, Inez Thornton, also fifteen but without Caron's melodramatic flair. Inez is drab and soft-spoken, a perfect counterfoil to my burgeoning Broadway star. Her hair is brown in an oddly colorless way, her face rounded with the vestiges of childhood. The thick lenses of her glasses give her an expression of mild alarm, but if I were in Caron's wake, I'd look that way, too.

"Thousands of dollars?" I said cautiously.

"Thousands and thousands of dollars!" Aglow with greed, Caron began to dance disjointedly in front of the counter, twirling on one foot and then the other, snatching invisible bills from an invisible money tree. "I think I'll get one of those foxy little red convertibles. Rhonda's getting some really stupid car that her brother used to drive. She'll Absolutely Puke when I pull up in front of her house. Can't you see her face when she realizes Louis Wilderberry is in my passenger seat?" She wafted away between the racks, lost in this consummate vision of revenge. "Oh, Rhonda," she continued in a syrupy simper, "Louis and I are going to the drive-in movie. We'd invite you, but it's too cozy for three. Bye-bye, Miss Cellulite Thighs!"

"Caron's kind of mad at Rhonda," Inez contributed with a sigh. "We called to see if she wanted to go to the mall, but she said she had to stay home and babysit for her nerdy little brother. We went by anyway, and Louis's car is parked in her driveway."

"Oh," I said wisely. "How does Caron intend to chance upon enough money to exact this retribution?"

Caron capered back into view. "I'm going to be a consultant for My Beautiful Self, Inc. It's this unbelievably brilliant opportunity for me to make as much money as I want this summer." Her smile vanished, replaced by a look of sheer agony. "But wait! I can't have a red convertible!"

An observer who might assume I understood any of this would be severely overestimating my maternal acumen, which, as usual, hovered near zero. I wasn't about to ask any questions or demand any explanations, however, and merely watched as she slumped against the self-help books and rubbed her face.

"I can't have black, either," she said in a dull voice. "I'm Friendly, so I suppose I'll have to get a bronze or forest-green convertible. I just can't risk red."

"I'm Elegant," Inez said to me. "I could have a raspberry-colored car, but my parents probably won't even let me drive until I'm twenty-one because of the insurance rates."

I waited for a moment, but both of them seemed lost in despondency. Despite the innumerable occasions when I should have kept out of it and suffered accordingly, I said, "Friendly and Elegant? I suppose that's better than being toady and dowdy."

"Oh, Mother," Caron said, lading the words with contempt as only a seasoned teenager can do, "nobody's toady or dowdy. There's only four categories: Sophisticated, Elegant, Lively, and Friendly, as in S-E-L-F. That's to help you remember them when you're doing a My Beautiful Self analysis."

"And this leads to thousands—and thousands—of dollars?"

"My sixteenth birthday is the week before school starts, so you'd better hope it does. I have to have a car, you know, and not some ugly old pickup truck with dents all over it and a gun rack and horrible splotches of mildew."

"Mildew?" Inez said, then slithered behind a rack as Caron glared at her.

"Who said anything about a pickup truck?" I asked.

"Were you planning to buy me a new Camaro?"

I closed the ledger and locked the cash register. "Frankly, my dear, I wasn't planning to buy you anything more complex than new loafers. We cannot afford a second car, especially in a recession. We'll be lucky to survive the summer, and I'm going to have to figure out a way to increase inventory for the fall semester without selling you into white slavery."

Caron's lower lip shot out. "I am not going to be the only person at the entire high school without a car. Everybody'll have a car this year, except maybe the nonentities who take welding and home nursing and disgusting things like that. Maybe I should forget about Honors Algebra and sign up for Teen Living? That's the course where you carry around an egg all year, waiting for it to take its first step and call you Mama."

"Allison Wade fried hers in the middle of the semester," Inez said, "and the teacher flunked her."

"How about omelets for dinner?" I suggested, then locked the store and herded them up Thurber Street toward our duplex across from the lawn of Farber College. Sally Fromberger's café was closed for the summer, I noted unhappily, as were the renovated theater and pricey sportswear store. Their proprietors had acknowledged the inevitable, and if they were starving, they were doing it without the daily humiliation of silent cash registers.

"Don't you want to know more about how I'm going to get rich?" Caron asked, the lip having retreated for the moment. I nodded. "Well, one of the girls from the sorority house next door came by while I was putting out your garbage and—"

"My garbage?"

"It's certainly not mine. Anyway, she asked if I was interested in making a whole lot of money this summer. Then she told me all about how I could become a My Beautiful Self consultant, and how by the end of the summer I'd probably need a stockbroker and a bank account in Switzerland and—"

"A My Beautiful Self consultant?" I interrupted before we moved into the realm of treasury bonds and retiring the national debt.

We were in front of the sorority house, an imposing white brick structure reminiscent of a plantation with its pillars and green shutters. It would have been imposing, that is, had the paint not been peeling, screens missing from some of the windows, a shutter hanging crookedly, the sidewalk cracked, the shrubbery brittle, the lawn yellowish-brown and crisscrossed with worn paths. Although I'd walked past it numerous times a day for years, I'd never so much as paused to study it. It took me a moment to interpret the Greek letters on the sign: Kappa Theta Eta.

I heard rock music coming from an open window on the first floor. "I thought all the fraternity and sorority houses closed for the summer."

"Not this one," Caron said impatiently. "Anyway, Pippa's going to train me, and when I'm a certified consultant, I can charge people for sessions and make as much money as I want. I can even recruit new consultants and train them myself. Then when their clients order cosmetics and stuff, I get ten percent."

I tried to keep my voice light. "And this sorority girl spotted you clutching a garbage bag and realized you were the ideal candidate?"

"She said she's always looking for potential trainees, and she's noticed me walking past the house and thought how perfect I'd be. There are a few consultants in the dorms and other sorority houses, but there's no one working the high school market. It ought to be a gold mine."

"And she gets ten percent of the gold you dig up at the high school?" I asked. "Is this legitimate?"

Inez nodded. "It's this big company with regional supervisors and catalogs and brochures and everything. My mother had some of her friends over one night—"

"Of course it's legitimate!" snapped Caron. "The founder is this Hungarian aristocrat who wanted to share her beauty secrets with the world. The training's very involved and you end up with a certificate and a card to carry in your purse. You have to sort of make an investment in the beginning, but you earn it back right away, and after that, everything's clear profit."

The last sentence had been said in a fast mumble, but I caught it nevertheless. "How much of an investment?"

"Not that much," she said in such a defensive tone that I knew I was going to hear a real whopper. "You have to order the official My Beautiful Self kit, but it's no big deal and it's totally necessary for when you do the sessions. I'll be able to pay you back at the end of the—"

I stopped in the middle of the sidewalk. "Pay me back?"

The long-suffering martyr rolled her eyes in a heavenly direction. "We're talking sixty dollars or so, not a zillion."

"Don't forget the shipping and handling charges," Inez added. "That adds another twelve dollars and eighty cents, for a total of seventy-two dollars and eighty cents."

Caron did not sound pleased with this display of arithmetic astuteness. "So there's shipping and handling. The point is, Mother, that I'll pay you back within a few days when I sign up all my friends. I can charge whatever I want, but Pippa says I should get a minimum of ten dollars for the basic analysis, and as much as twenty for an accessory awareness session. I get twenty-five percent of all the orders I generate, and ten percent of the orders of my trainees for the first six months."

Before I could share my feelings about what might well be immoral, a silver Mercedes parked at the curb. A battered green truck pulled up behind it, and both drivers emerged from their vehicles. One was a slender middle-aged woman in a beige silk suit and matching heels, who moved with the brisk self-assurance of a Junior League president. The other was a shambling man with a stubbly face, thick wet lips, red-rimmed eyes, hair that might have been styled with pruning shears, and paint-spotted overalls. They started toward the sorority house.

I tried to nudge Caron and Inez into motion. "We will continue this discussion when we get upstairs," I said in a cold, curt voice. I was actually rather proud of myself, in that my stomach was twisted into a cruel knot and I was having difficulty breathing. Clouds had not crossed the sun, but everything seemed to glow in an eerie way.

"Did you see who that was?" gasped Caron. Apparently Inez was too flabbergasted to do anything more than goggle at the figures on the porch of the sorority house.

"It's none of our business," I said.

Inez finally found what there was of her voice. "It's Arnie. You remember him, don't you, Mrs. Malloy?"

"Yes, I do." I grabbed their arms and propelled them through the door and up the stairs to our apartment. Once we were safely inside, the door locked and the chain in place, I abandoned them and headed for the kitchen to make myself a stiff drink. Minutes later, I made myself another.

"Arnie?" Peter choked on the name, spraying the coffee table with a mouthful of beer. "Not Arnie, please. Seeing him was just some form of recurrent hallucination brought on by—"

"Lack of sales?" I leaned my head on his shoulder and stared at the living-room ceiling. "The girls recognized him, too. He's driving a disreputable green truck instead of that hideous Cadillac he used to have, but he's the same Arnie right down to his neon nose and slobbery lips. No better, no worse—just good ol' Arnold Riggles. Can't you keep him in jail for more than ten minutes?"

"He was in the county jail, and your estimate of ten minutes is apt to be accurate. The facility's crowded, and someone charged with a misdemeanor hardly qualifies for a lengthy period of free room and board. All he did was steal a couple of dogs and a cat, Claire."

"And the other times? Drunken driving, drunken hiking, car theft, fleeing the scene, being a nuisance, accusing me of being—"

"All misdemeanors, I'm afraid," Peter murmured, trying to sound soothing despite the edge of amusement in his voice. "We almost nailed him with a felony a couple of months ago, but the prosecutor decided to ignore the small fry and go after the big fish."

I was not in the mood for piscatory puzzles. "What are you talking about, Peter? Rigging a bass tournament?"

"Nothing that interesting. We learned that the man who had the pawnshop out in the strip mall east of town was a fence, and we finally got around to busting him. Arnie was one of the regular customers."

"Why wasn't he hanged?"

"We couldn't prove that he was bringing in stolen property. He claimed a certain necklace had belonged to his mother, and it wasn't on any of our lists. He also brought in a portable television set that might have been taken in an apartment burglary, but the student hadn't recorded a serial number and Arnie swore he'd won it in a poker game."

"And you were gullible enough to believe him?" I rolled my eyes as Caron had done that same afternoon. "Surely you could have found evidence that would be adequate to keep him off our streets for a few years—if you'd tried, that is."

He patted me on the shoulder as if I were a faithful dog curled in his lap. "Let's not talk about Arnie anymore, okay? I had a call from a guy I trained with. He owns a cabin about fifty miles from here, and he offered to let me use it anytime this summer. It's fairly rustic, but it's got a fireplace, a great view of the lake, and a king-size brass bed. We can sit on the deck all day and watch the birds and the bees, and then at night . . ."

He was in the midst of some intriguing remarks concerning other aspects of nature when footsteps came pounding up the stairs. Caron flew into the room, took a deep breath, and said, "It really is that Awful Arnie Person!"

I'd moved to the respectable end of the sofa. I wiggled my eyebrows at Peter, then looked at my daughter's flushed cheeks and air of triumph. "What did you learn?"

"He's going to paint the sorority house." She grabbed a handful of peanuts from the bowl on the coffee table and stuffed them in her mouth as she flopped across a chair. "He works for the contractor, some guy named Ed Whitbred who's a real painter but was across town finishing another job. Mrs. Vanderson thought she was meeting Ed, but Arnie showed up, so she had to deal with him. Mrs. Vanderson's what Pippa calls the house corps president, which means she's in charge of the house maintenance and pays the bills and stuff. The house is going to be painted this summer so they can do better at rush in the fall. They had a real crummy pledge class this year because the Kappa Theta Eta house is the nappiest on campus, even worse than some of the fraternity houses. The pledges have to sleep on the third floor, and the roof leaks so badly they're afraid it's going to crash down on them someday."

"Good detective work," Peter drawled.

She gave him an offended frown. "I wasn't snooping around the way Mother does. I merely went over to the house to talk to Pippa about my training. I may have gotten lost on my way to her room, but that's hardly my fault if all the halls look exactly the same."

"You were prowling around the sorority house?" I said, appalled. "Don't you realize that's trespassing?"

"It is not, and it doesn't matter, anyway. There are only four girls living in the house this summer, along with the housemother and her cat. During the regular year, there are over sixty girls in the house and visitors all the time."

Peter had been grinning, but he grew stern. "You really shouldn't wander around the sorority house, Caron. There're always a lot of thefts in the houses, and an unauthorized person is likely to be considered a suspect. I've seen the data from the campus security force; the number of reported thefts has doubled in the last five years. You don't want to find yourself accused of stealing."

"Me?" she said, now the epitome of innocence.

"How could anybody accuse me of theft? I don't have a dollar to my name, and Mother seems to think it's perfectly fine for me to wear shoes with holes, tatty old sweaters, clothes from the Salvation Army—"

"Go away," I said.

"But I'm going to earn money, anyway," she continued. "Pippa says she'll let me use her kit until I can afford my own. All I have to do is line up eight appointments and then I'll have more than enough money. Once I have the kit, I can train all my friends and really start making scads and scads of money. I'd better make some calls." She sauntered down the hall to her bedroom and closed the door.

Peter wanted to talk about the cabin. I didn't, and after a few more efforts on his part, he left. He didn't exactly stalk down the stairs, but I heard every last footstep and the door slammed with unnecessary vigor.

Going away with him was too much like a honeymoon, I thought as I tidied up the living room and took our glasses to the kitchen. My territory was well defined, and I preferred it to be so. I rarely went to his house, and never stayed the night, even when it required a lonely and often chilly drive to my apartment.

I turned off the lights and went to my bedroom. Access to my bed was by invitation only; the concept of anyone assuming a proprietary interest in one of the pillows was disturbing. I'd tried that with a husband, and although the marriage had not resulted in shackles and submission, I felt no need to take on the responsibility of a relationship, to make compromises—especially when the compromises tended to resemble total capitulations.

Then again, I reminded myself as I studied the newest set of wrinkles while I brushed my teeth, Caron was within a few months of turning sixteen, which meant I was in the same proximity to forty. I claimed to be self-sufficient, but I'd wasted the day wondering how to pay the rent all summer and I had to find a way to get in new stock for the fall semester. A few publishers had threatened to cut off my credit; others were making inelegant remarks about delinquent payments. The roof leaked and the cockroaches were a noticeable addition to the office decor. There were unpaid bills piled in the kitchen. In a few years Caron would have to be sent to college, preferably in a remote state.

Peter earned a decent salary as a lieutenant in the Farberville CID, and there was some family money that kept him expensively dressed right down to his Italian shoes. He'd made it clear that he wanted to get married, and would assume the burden of Caron's education and my decline into old age (slated to begin within a matter of months). The Book Depot could become my hobby rather than my source of incipient ulcers.

I was musing over the heretofore hidden mercenary aspects of my personality when I heard a terrified scream.

2

"What was that?" shrieked Caron as we bumped into each other in the hall. Although I was foaming at the mouth, I was still dressed; she'd pulled on her shirt and was fumbling with shorts.

Having envisioned her with blood spurting from a major artery, I slumped against the wall and waited until the gruesome image faded. "It was a scream, and it sounded as if it came from directly below my bedroom window. I looked, but I couldn't see anybody. We'd better call 911."

"Yeah, do that." She veered around me and headed for the living room.

I lunged and managed to catch her shoulder before she could rush into the welcoming arms of the neighborhood ax murderer. "You wait here. I'm going to make the call, and then we'll try to see something from my window." I went into the kitchen, but as I picked up the receiver to punch the appropriate digits, I heard the front door open and close. Caron was going to find Her Beautiful Self grounded until school started, I thought, torn between anger and fear.

When the dispatcher answered, I tersely described the situation and was informed that the grounds of the sorority house were in the campus police department's jurisdiction.

"Can't you notify them?"

"We're only allowed to respond to emergencies within our jurisdiction. I can give you the proper number, ma'am."

I was back to envisioning Caron drenched in blood,

so I eschewed further debate, noted the number, and dialed it with an uncooperative finger. "Someone screamed at the Kappa Theta Eta house," I announced, then hung up in the middle of a demand for further details, righteously assuring myself I had none. I hurried downstairs and out to the porch. Caron had vanished. The street was dark and still, as was the sidewalk. The ground floor of the sorority house was lit up as if in anticipation of a Shriners' convention, however, so I cut across the adjoining yards, growling Caron's name with every step, and went to the front door.

It was ajar, and from within I heard hiccupy sobs interspersed with murmurs and silky assurances that "she" was safe. I wasn't sure if "she" was the screamer or Caron, but it seemed likely that I'd found the origins of the crisis, whatever it was. I went inside and paused in a large reception room with pink flocked wallpaper, a parquet floor, a small desk with a telephone and a solitary plastic rose in a bud vase, and innumerable group photographs of young women endowed with more than their fair share of glistening white teeth and moist pink gums.

The voices were coming from a room to the left of a staircase. Unlike Caron, I was not pleased with the opportunity to trespass in the Kappa Theta Eta house, but I continued in the direction of the voices and found myself in a lounge with several groupings of shabby furniture.

The most central one was occupied by a huddle of women—and by Caron Malloy, who was soaking up the potential drama with a facade of sympathy. She looked dismayed by my entrance, but managed to say, "There was a prowler, but he's gone now."

I pointed at her. "Go outside and wait for the police. They should be here any minute, but they won't know to come in here." She hesitated, then realized that anything short of prompt obedience would result in a lengthy sentence that precluded a car, a telephone, and everything else near and dear to her. Once she was gone, I approached the occupied sofa and tried to sort out the players. Without a scorecard.

A girl was sprawled in the middle, her face hidden by her hands and her shoulders twitching. The sobbing, although somewhat tempered, was still audible. Three young women surrounded her, all patting her shoulders, stroking her head, and assuring her that she was safe.

A much older woman, dressed in a robe and slippers and carrying a glass of water, came into the room. She halted as she spotted me, her forehead creased harshly and her lips puckered with confusion. "You . . . you look familiar, but I can't quite place you," she said. "I know I've seen you somewhere. I'm so sorry that I don't remember your name, dear."

"I'm Claire Malloy. I live next door, so it's probable you've seen me walking by the house. Several minutes ago I heard someone scream. I've already called the police. They ought to be here soon."

"The police?" She gave the glass to one of the girls and came across the room. She was significantly less than five feet tall, with frizzy gray hair and a smooth, pale complexion that belied her age only with a webbing of fine wrinkles around her eyes and the slackness beneath her chin. I would not have been surprised to learn she'd been born somewhere over the rainbow.

She continued, her voice still high and uncertain, "I'm Martha Winklebury, but the girls call me Winkie. I'm the Kappa Theta Eta housemother. It's so very nice to meet you, Mrs. Malloy; you must stop in for iced tea and cookies some afternoon. But as for now, I'm afraid I don't understand why you called the police. As I'm sure all of us can see, the girl is simply upset."

"She screamed," I said evenly. "I'm accustomed to a certain amount of noise from this place, but this went beyond girlish squeals and shrieks. What happened?"

"It's quite silly. Debbie Anne was coming in from the library and thought she saw a prowler in the shrubbery. I've told the girls again and again not to cut through the side yard when it's dark, but to stay on the sidewalk where there's plenty of light, even if it means going an extra few feet. Her imagination ran away with her."

"If it did, it ran into me and knocked me down," said the accused from the middle of the sofa. Despite her splotchy, tear-streaked face and tremulous voice, I recognized her as the girl who'd tried to peddle used textbooks at my store. She blinked as she realized who I was, but looked down at her tightly clenched hands and let out a groan punctuated with a loud hiccup.

"Couldn't it have been a fraternity boy?" the house-mother asked. "Those dreadful Betas are forever trampling down our grass on their way to the bars on Thurber Street. I've complained numerous times to their housemother, but she cannot control them. They . . ."

She dribbled into silence as two uniformed officers came into the room. Neither looked old enough to be a policeman, but they were burly and armed—and therefore exactly what I'd ordered.

"I'm Officer Terrance," one of them said, "and this is Officer Michaels. What's going on?"

Despite her shortness that put her at a disadvantage of more than a foot, Winkie managed to peer down her nose at them, although with a slightly cross-eyed effect. "Oh my goodness, men are not allowed in the back of the house. If you'll come with me to the living room, I'll explain what happened so you can be on your way."

"Did you make the call, ma'am?" asked Officer Terrance. His partner seemed to prefer to enjoy the view of nubile young bodies, two of them clad only in skimpy gowns.

"I made the call," I said, wiggling my fingers, "and the girl on the sofa is the one who screamed."

"Her name's Debbie Anne Wray," Winkie said with a sputtery sigh. "This has been blown entirely out of proportion, but I suppose we'd better get it settled so the girls can go on to bed. All four of them are carrying full schedules this summer. Come along, Debbie

Anne, and do stop that sniveling. Kappas do not snivel." She went out of the room. Debbie Anne trailed behind her, sniveling more quietly but with no appreciable lessening of drippage from her raw red nose.

Officer Terrance looked at me. I shrugged and said, "All I know is that I heard a scream about five minutes ago. I called the emergency number, then came over here to"—I saw no reason to indict Caron—"find out what happened. I didn't see anybody in the yard or running down the sidewalk. No cars in the street."

Terrance scratched his chin while he tried to grasp what he must have felt were the unspoken complexities in my story. He apparently had no success, in that he said, "You'd better wait here until we've questioned the girl."

I considered my chances and realized they were naught. "Okay, but be quick about it, please. All I did was my civic duty, and I'd like to go back to bed before dawn."

"Wouldn't we all?" he said as he left the room. Officer Michaels reluctantly followed him.

The three girls on the sofa were regarding me with dark suspicion, if not outright alarm. After a muted conference, the two in gowns left through a doorway and the third stood up and approached me with an outstretched hand. She had dark hair cut in a short wedge, flawless if uninspired features, a trim body marred only by overly broad shoulders, and the bright appraisal of a lioness contemplating a crippled eland. Her pale pink sweatsuit had not come from a discount house; her expensive athletic shoes had never so much as walked through the doorway of one.

On her chest was a glittery pin adorned with tiny chains that led to smaller glittery pins. For a brief, stunned moment, I thought it was meant to be symbolic of a skull and crossbones, but as she came nearer, I realized it was nothing more sinister than her sorority pin. I also realized it was much too late to be gadding about the neighborhood.

"I'm Jean Hall, Ms. Malloy," she said as she shook

my hand with the precise degree of firmness for the occasion. "I was the house committee president last year, and I'd like to welcome you to Kappa Theta Eta, even though this is not how we prefer to have an open house." She gave me a pearly smile that went no deeper than the sheen of makeup on her face. "It seems as though we'll be up for a while. Please sit down and make yourself at home. May we offer you coffee or tea?"

"No, thank you." I sat down on the nearest chair and willed myself not to be intimidated by her aura of determined congeniality. "What exactly happened to Debbie Anne?"

Jean's smile tightened. "It's impossible to say. Debbie Anne's a nice enough girl, considering her background, but she's a teensy bit unreliable. We've had a problem or two with her during the year, and I've made a point of doing everything I can to help her adjust to the Kappa Theta Eta way of doing things. I hate to say it, but this may be nothing more than another manifestation of her ... insecurities."

"Insecurities?" I echoed.

"I don't quite know how to phrase this tactfully. She's hardly the shining beacon of scholarship in the house. In fact, she's the only one in her pledge class that we didn't initiate during the year. Even though she took intellectually demanding courses like bulletin board design and kiddy lit, she was put on academic probation second semester. I personally made sure she attended study hall every night, and even excused her from pledge duties so she could spend extra time at the library on weekends. I finally had to tell her that if she can't get her grade point average up this summer, she ought to consider switching to history in the fall—because as far as the Kappas are concerned, that's what she'll be."

I was a little disconcerted at the lack of compassion between sisters. "But what about tonight?"

Jean sat down across from me, folded her hands in her lap, and crossed her ankles. "She was incoherent, which is nothing novel, but her story was that she came up the side yard just as a man stepped out of the shadows. She screamed, and he knocked her down as he fled." She paused as if hesitant to further malign Debbie Anne, and made a pretense of choosing her words ever so carefully before going in for the verbal kill. "She attended some little country school where she actually was a majorette. And there was something about being secretary of the Future Farmwives of America, but I don't recall the details. She's had a great deal of difficulty fitting in with the others. Her clothes aren't quite right, so all year long I've lent her mine and done what I could to instill a sense of fashion. Somehow, she always looks as if she's stepped off the pages of a Sears catalog. Andrew, bless his heart, was in tears after he'd worked on her hair. I've tried and tried with her, but I simply cannot get through to her that Kappa Theta Etas are a special breed. Several times last year, she pulled pathetic stunts for the attention."

"Like screaming bloody murder at midnight?"

"Not exactly," Jean said with a bloodless little chuckle. "Once she claimed someone had stolen her mother's diamond earrings. Her roommates finally got tired of listening to her whine and searched her things while she was in study hall. The earrings were at the bottom of her laundry bag—and they were rhinestone. Another time she was accidentally locked in the chapter room after a meeting. She was in absolute hysterics by the time I found her all of five minutes later. You'd have thought the room was haunted by hundred-year-old alumnae staggering around like mummies. It was too funny."

"And you think this alleged encounter tonight is another stunt to get attention?"

"Well, we all dashed out to the yard and carried her into the house. Winkie was fluttering about like a dazed moth, alternately suggesting cold compresses and hot tea. Now you're here, along with the police. I'd have to say she certainly is getting attention, although, of course, it's not exactly the kind to which Kappas aspire."

The housemother came into the lounge. "Jean, the officers think we should have a locksmith come by tomorrow and check the security system. I have something on my calendar. Will you take care of it?"

"Of course, Winkie. What about Debbie Anne? Are they done with her?"

"I've sent her to bed. There was so little she could tell them that it was hardly worth their coming." She looked at me as if I'd just popped up from the upholstery. "They're waiting for you in the foyer. I do hope you'll avoid causing any more disruptions, at least for tonight. Katie and I would like to get some sleep."

"Katie?" I said despite myself.

"Katie is the house cat," Winkie said. "It's traditional for all Kappa houses to have cats named Katie. Please lock up, Jean, and turn off the porch lights. Good night, girls." She veered around the sofa, barely avoiding an end table, and weaved out of the room.

I glanced at Jean, who was watching the housemother's retreat with a faint sneer. She appeared to be enjoying whatever condemnatory thoughts she entertained, so I did not wish her sweet dreams on my way to the foyer and the local version of the Spanish Inquisition.

I repeated my succinct story, and after a few avowals that I'd seen no one in the vicinity, I was escorted to my door and thanked for my overly zealous call. The adjective was mine, but the snickers were all theirs. This may have resulted in my unnecessarily elaborate expression of gratitude for their prompt arrival and subsequently thorough and piercing investigation, but in the midst of it, I realized I hadn't seen Caron in over an hour and went upstairs.

The child was nestled and snug in her bed, snoring gently while visions of convertibles danced in her head. I thought about waking her long enough to tell her she was grounded in perpetuity, but finally went on to bed, where I devised even more intricate forms of

torture. In the middle of scheming to adopt Rhonda
Maguire and make Caron share her bedroom, I fell
asleep.

The next morning she was gone. The fact that her
bed was made and her room marginally tidy, coupled
with the neatness of the kitchen and lack of toothpaste
smears in the bathroom sink, led me to believe she
knew what lay in store for her. Smart kid, although we
both knew she couldn't dodge me indefinitely.

I started coffee, then went downstairs to fetch the
morning newspaper. This usually required a rigorous
search under shrubs, behind trees, and more often than
not in the gutter, where it could soak up grime or be
flattened by cars. To my surprise, it lay in the middle
of the porch, with a pink construction-paper cutout
propped against it. I gathered both and returned to the
kitchen. The cutout was that of a fat, stylized cat, and
the printed message read: "Katie the Kappa Kitten
Says Thanks!" Handwritten below that was: "For being such a good neighbor!" It was signed by Jean Hall.

Somehow or other, this was all Caron's fault, I decided as I drank a fast cup of coffee, tucked the newspaper under my arm, and headed back downstairs.
Even though it was two blocks out of my way, I turned
right and took the long route to the Book Depot, unwilling to be confronted by a single Kappa, much less
by a pink apparition that purported to be overwhelmed
with gratitude. I felt queasy, and I doubted it was because of the coffee.

No one disturbed me all morning, I'm sorry to say,
and I was packing up returns when the first tinkle of
the day lured me out of the office. A young woman
with an ash-blond helmet of hair and glittery blue eyes
was waiting for me, her plump cheeks dimpled with
anticipation. Had she not been wearing a pink
sweatshirt emblazoned with the Greek letters kappa,
theta, and eta, I might not have recognized her. Had
Caron Malloy not been hovering behind her, an exceedingly leery expression on her face, I might not

have leaped as swiftly to the conclusion that I did, albeit regretfully.

"Hi, Mrs. Malloy," the woman said, dimpling madly. "I'm Pippa Edmondson, and I wanted to come by to thank you for being so swell last night. We were all so stunned by what happened to poor Debbie Anne—or what she said happened—that we didn't even think to call the police. I can't remember when we've ever had them at the Kappa house."

"You're more than welcome," I said pleasantly to her, although I shot a vexed look at my darling daughter. "I was relieved to find out no one was harmed. That's all that matters, so I suggest we let the matter drop and go on about our separate ways."

"No way," Pippa protested, widening her eyes as if she were choking. "We talked it over with Winkie, and we want you and Caron to come for dinner tonight. It won't be anything fancy, since the cooks are off for the summer and we take turns in the kitchen, but National stresses the importance of being on friendly terms with our neighbors, and right now you must think we're dreadfully rude to disturb you so late at night. We really, really would like to prove to you that we're not the least bit that way, and that we're grateful that you cared enough about our safety to call the police."

I edged back into the office doorway. "All I did was dial a total of ten digits, which hardly entitles me to a medal of valor or even a free meal, and someone else would have called if I hadn't. As I said, I'd prefer to forget the incident."

Pippa advanced like a rabid cheerleader, flecks of saliva gathering in the corners of her mouth and her voice rising in pitch. "Oh, please come for dinner, Mrs. Malloy. We have this darling pin that we present to special friends of Kappa Theta Eta, and a little song we sing about the importance of good neighbors."

It was getting worse with each sentence she uttered. Was I to be dressed in a pristine pink robe and required to hold a candle while they crooned to me? Would I be rewarded with a pastel cat to take home and nurture?

Did they plan on a ritual involving the letting of blood and some sort of irrevocable lifetime relationship?

"I'll ... uh, I'll be back in a minute," I stammered, then ducked into the cramped office and closed the door before she could sink her sororal fangs into my neck. I'd attended a large university with numerous fraternities and sororities, but I'd done so during the early seventies, when political radicalism overshadowed the dubious rewards of communal living among the reactionaries who were more concerned with future country-club membership than with the war in Vietnam. While we picketed all day and stayed up all night grinding out primitive pamphlets denouncing almost everybody, they participated in sports, filled the positions on the Homecoming court, and posed for yearbook photos. I don't seem to recall any great animosity between the two factions. They went about their business, which was to find suitable spouses, complete degrees that would result in good jobs, establish bonds for future networking, and have elaborate parties at which either bedsheets or tuxedos and formals were proper attire.

And now I was trapped by one. I, a woman approaching forty, equipped with her own business, apartment, car payment, overdue quarterly tax estimate, and stretch marks, was leaning against the door, holding my breath as I strained to hear any sound, even the tiniest squeak, that might indicate Pippa and my treacherous daughter were leaving.

There was a back door that led to the weedy parking lot. On more than one memorable occasion, I'd fled through the door, dashed along the railroad tracks, and eventually climbed up the overgrown banks. But those flights had been necessary to avert such petty annoyances as being arrested. Surely I was capable of dealing with a lone sorority girl, even if she was burdened with a cute nickname and dimplemania.

I inched the door open and heard Caron say, "I used to adore those dopey romances by Azalea Twilight, but that was a long time ago."

"Me, too," gushed Pippa. "Did you ever read the one about the gorgeous nuclear physicist who falls in love with the Russian spy who's actually a double agent for the CIA? I thought I'd die when he . . ."

I went out the back door and stood in the parking lot. The railroad tracks stretched into the distance and finally curled out of sight beneath an overpass. The brush on the banks was pale green, dotted with small yellow splashes of hawkweed and lacy white yarrow. What thorns and thistles I knew were there were invisible; the growth looked as innocuous as a pastel baby blanket. There was a path near the overpass that zagged up to a street not more than three blocks from my apartment.

Was I a woman or was I a wimp?

More pertinently, was I willing to risk running into good ol' Arnie or yet another Greek bearing a construction-paper gift? I finally squared my shoulders and went back into the office, rehearsing polite if fanciful refusals in my mind. My favorite involved ministering to lepers in the basement of the hospital, but it proved unnecessary when I again inched open the door and ascertained that Caron and her mentor were gone.

Feeling as if the commandant had canceled the firing squad at the last nanosecond, I made sure they weren't hiding behind a rack, then went to the counter to see if Caron had pilfered the pitiful contents of the cash register. There, propped on the keys, was another pink paper cat. The printed message still read: "Katie the Kappa Kitten Says Thanks!" This time the handwritten one read: "For coming to dinner at seven o'clock tonight!"

Cursing under my breath, I searched the store and made sure I had the only perfidious pink cutout. I considered the pleasure I could find in ripping it into a fine pile of pink flakes and scraping them into the wastebasket, set it back on the cash register, and called Peter at the Farberville Police Department.

When he came on the line, I dismissed the idea of accusing the Kappas of terroristic activity and said,

"Let's go to the cabin tonight, okay? I'll grab a couple of steaks, salad, and a bottle of red wine. All you'll have to do is—"

"I can't waltz off in the middle of the week," he said, sounding rather grumpy considering the graciousness of my invitation. "Neither can you, for that matter. You spent two hours last night telling me how poor business is in the summer. If you close the bookstore, it's liable to be worse than poor."

"I didn't say I would close the bookstore. Caron can handle it for a day or two."

"Well, she can't handle this mess I'm into this week—and don't get any wild ideas about mysterious deaths caused by poisonous South American tree frogs or blunt objects. Things are so slow around here that I'm temporarily on the community relations and crime prevention squad."

"How exciting," I said with a yawn. "What crimes are you preventing?"

"The one we're not preventing is shoplifting. Now that the kids are out of school, they seem dedicated to stealing the contents of the mall, one piece of merchandise at a time. Some of them are happy with a cassette or a pair of sunglasses, but we're dealing with some slick professionals, too."

The Kappa Kitten leered at me. "Surely you can get away for one night," I said, lapsing into a despicable female wheedle. "It doesn't get dark until after nine, so we don't have to leave until you're off duty. We'll be there in time to sit on the deck and watch the sunset, then broil steaks while the stars come out."

"Last night you were more concerned with mosquitoes than starlight. I distinctly remember some caustic remarks about the menace of Mother Nature and your unwillingness to risk what was apt to be a saggy bed and a dearth of hot water."

I'd been pretty damn eloquent, too. "I've changed my mind, Peter. I think we really need to get away, if only for one night, to discuss our relationship."

"Do you?" he said in an infuriatingly mild voice. "I

have to meet with mall security at nine, but I can come by after that to ... discuss our relationship."

The Kappa Kitten licked its lips. "That's too late. We need to leave for the cabin no later than six o'clock. We can't discuss anything when Caron might barge in with some new scheme to make her first million. I don't understand why you can't tell Jorgeson or somebody to meet with the mall cops."

"Because I can't. Listen, if you're so frantic to go to the cabin, let me call my buddy and see if we can use it this weekend. We can have a couple of lazy, peaceful days to discuss whatever it is that you find so urgent, and Caron won't have the slightest idea how to find us."

"Then you refuse to go today?" I asked coolly.

"What's wrong with this weekend?"

"Nothing at all. I suggest you warn Jorgeson to stock up on bug spray. I'm sure he'll be great company for you in the brass bed!" I slammed down the receiver, and when it rang seconds later, I grabbed the feather duster and stalked around the counter to attack the classics with serious dedication.

3

"Welcome to Kappa Theta Eta, Mrs. Malloy," said the girl who must have been hovering just inside the doorway of the house. I'd seen her the night before, but only briefly before she and the one I now knew as Pippa had retreated. She was a beautiful girl, with waist-length black hair, deep blue eyes, dramatically sculpted cheekbones, and a dusky complexion that hinted of exotic forebears. "I'm Rebecca Faulkner," she continued in the mellifluous voice of a well-trained singer. "It's so kind of you to accept our invitation, and I'd love to show you the house."

"Is Caron here?" I said as I forced myself to step over the threshold of a residence that produced pink paper cats with the efficiency of a factory line.

"She's in Pippa's room." Rebecca took off like a tour guide, and I followed like a tourist plagued with blisters. I admired the foyer and the living room, which were the only rooms in which men were permitted, and then the lounge, the dining room (apparently busboys were a subspecies), the door to the kitchen, and a short hallway lined with closed doors. All of it was decorated in pink, since, as Rebecca told me, their official colors were pink and white. I was not surprised. I subsequently learned that their official flower was a pink rose, their official mascot the beloved Katie the Kappa Kitten, and their official chapter name Delta Delta. Fearing I was on the verge of learning the brand of their official toothpaste, I declined an invitation to explore the two upper floors and asked to speak to Caron.

"But we haven't been to Winkie's suite," Rebecca

said, visibly dismayed by my presumptuous intrusion into the itinerary. "All guests have to be formally introduced to the housemother. It's a rule from National. I escort you to her suite and introduce you, then you and she come to the dining room together." She looked over her shoulder nervously, as if a spy from National might be lurking in a corner, grimly recording this unseemly deviation from procedure. "Then you'll have a chance to meet Katie, Mrs. Malloy. Don't you want to meet Katie in person?"

I did not point out the oxymoronic reality that one does not meet an animal in person, nor did I mention my animosity toward the species. It was clear to me by now that there was no hope of winning a battle, or even a minor skirmish, with an organization that dictated the color of the toilet seats.

"By all means, then," I said, "let's visit Katie."

Rebecca led me across the foyer and knocked on a door. "Mrs. Malloy is here, Winkie," she called, almost reverently.

Winkie opened the door and invited us in. "I'm so pleased you accepted our invitation, Mrs. Malloy. Kappas should be on friendly terms with their neighbors, and the girls should have invited you and your daughter to visit us years ago."

Her tiny living room was decorated in pink (surprise, surprise), and there was a dusty arrangement of pink silk roses on a coffee table. On the sofa was a long-haired cat; its white fur was the only relief thus far from the relentless pinkness. It gazed at me without interest, and I reciprocated in like.

"May I offer you a glass of wine?" Winkie said in a conspiratorial voice. "Alcohol is forbidden in the house, but since there are so few girls this summer, I decided it might be all right to have a little nip now and then."

I realized that Rebecca had faded away. "That would be lovely, Mrs. Winklebury."

"You must call me Winkie. Sit there right by Katie and I'll get the glasses and the decanter." She moved out of view, but continued talking. "I do hope you were able to get to sleep last night after that minor bother. Debbie Anne never stops to think what effect her actions may have on others. We had a long talk this afternoon, and I feel confident that she'll behave more appropriately in the future."

"Did the police officers catch the prowler?" I asked as I sat down at the opposite end of the sofa from Katie, bleakly suspecting my dark slacks would be covered with cat hair forever after. That particular kind of magnetism seems to be the tribulation borne by non–cat fanciers.

Winkie returned with two glasses and a chipped decanter. "Is burgundy all right? I have a little chablis, but it's old and might not be any good." She served the wine and settled into a rocking chair, her shoes barely touching the worn pink carpet, her dress smoothed over her knees, her face crimped with pleasure in anticipation of a cozy chat. She reminded me of a child playing in her great-grandmother's parlor. "Frankly, Claire—if I may call you that?—I doubt there was a prowler. The girl has a vivid imagination, to put it kindly, and on other occasions has disrupted the house and caused scenes."

"That's what Jean said last night. It's none of my business, but why was Debbie Anne invited to join the sorority if she's so disliked?"

"It's unfortunate that we're obliged to take girls who aren't Kappa material, but it's based on economics. We cannot afford to have vacant beds, much less vacant rooms. The budget's so tight that we have to fill the pledge class as early in the fall as possible; the alumnae and members spend most of their summer having parties and luncheons for potential pledges. All the girls are required to live in the house for a minimum of six consecutive semesters, and we encourage them to stay here all four years."

"I've noticed most of the other houses are closed for the summer," I said.

"We usually close, too, but our house corps president, Eleanor Vanderson, raised enough money for us to do some much-needed redecorating in preparation for rush and for a visit from the financial adviser from National. She's coming in August to audit the books, and we dearly hope she can offer some suggestions to improve our situation. When I agreed to be here to supervise the workmen, the girls asked if they could stay. Two of them are taking graduate classes, and the other will be a senior. Debbie Anne's technically a freshman and I was opposed to having her." A dark look crossed her face, then vanished as she gave a rueful laugh. "But Eleanor determined that we needed four monthly residence fees to cover the utilities, and Debbie Anne was the only other girl in summer school."

"Well, good," I said lamely, not at all interested in the subject or much of anything else, with the exception of surviving the ordeal and achieving the sanctuary of my own sofa. Winkie was swirling the wine in her glass, apparently content to sit in silence for what might be a very long time. To cover the sound of my rumbling stomach, I asked, "How long have you been the housemother?"

"Three years. After the divorce, I worked in an exclusive dress shop for almost ten years, but then my back began to trouble me and I was forced to give up my job. This position rescued me from a very bleak situation. A year from now I'll be eligible for social security and a nice pension from a fund established by the National Board. I'll miss the excitement, but it will be a relief to have my own apartment where I can do as I please. Here, I must admit, I'm basically on duty twenty-four hours a day, supervising the kitchen and custodial staffs, handling deliveries, counseling the girls, attending training and social functions for the campus housemothers, and serving as hostess for the house. There are so many restrictions that I sometimes feel as if I have more rules and regulations than the girls."

"Indeed." I artlessly looked at my watch and then at the cat, which, like any sensible creature, had gone to sleep during Winkie's whiny discourse on her job description.

She caught the hint and stood up. "Shall we go to the dining room, Claire?"

I rose with alacrity. "That's a wonderful idea. I haven't seen my daughter all afternoon, and while Rebecca was showing me around, she mentioned that Caron was already here and in Pippa's room."

"All the girls are staying in the wing off the lounge. It saves on utilities. During the school year, those rooms are used by the house officers, but with just the four . . ." She stopped to stroke Katie's head, then led me out to the foyer and paused in front of two portraits of women clutching white cats. The cats had uniformly bulgy eyes, as did one of the women.

"These are the previous housemothers," she told me. "The chapter was organized eleven years ago by a group of dedicated alumnae. Muffy was the first housemother, and she stayed nearly seven years. She's out on parole now and dropped by to visit just last month. Pattycake was here only a year before she decided to find other employment. She wasn't a Kappa, and the girls did not find her sympathetic. Some of the seniors still remember how detached she was when her first Katie was run down by a garbage truck out back. One of them told me, in the strictest confidence, of course, that Pattycake was never pleased when they dropped by to say good night to Katie or leave little gifts of catnip and squeaky toys."

"Imagine that," I said, trying not to do so myself as we went through French doors to the dining room.

Pippa, Rebecca, and Jean leaped to their feet as if we'd brandished automatic weapons, their ubiquitous sorority pins sparkling madly on uniformly pink expanses. Caron glanced curiously at them but kept her seat as Winkie formally introduced them to me, escorted me to a chair, and told them to sit back down. The majesty of the moment ended with the shatter of crockery from behind the kitchen door, followed by the dispirited wail of someone who was not Kappa material. Eyes rolled like loose marbles, but no one was motivated to go to the kitchen and investigate the disaster.

"I'm so excited that Caron's my new trainee," Pippa chirped, dimpling at me. "She's going to make a swell My Beautiful Self consultant, don't you think? She's got such motivation, and you're going to be astounded at how well she does once she starts working the high school market, where there truly is a need. The school colors are purple and gold, so you can imagine what a challenge it'll be. But I just know she's going to stick with it and become one of my top earners."

"And you do get a cut, don't you?" I said.

Caron gave me a look meant to wither me into silence. "I've already explained that, Mother. I'll get a cut from my trainees, too. It's like a pyramid, but there's all this room at the top."

Unwithered, I said, "Pyramids rise to sharp points."

"I'm using the color analysis theory as a basis for my senior thesis," Pippa continued blithely. "I'm a psych major, and I intend to explore the psychological factors that result from someone's acceptance of her appropriate palette, particularly if that person"—she eyed me critically—"has always worn the wrong shades. It's funny, but the client seems to go through predictable stages: denial, anger, mourning for the lost colors, and then acceptance and celebration of the new beautiful self. I plan to use this in therapy when I go into private practice."

Jean laughed. "Mourning for the lost colors?"

"Woe is me," Rebecca inserted with the same mockery, "no more mauve. However can I go on living?"

Jean and Rebecca grinned at each other. Pippa flushed while she considered her rebuttal, no doubt based on guidelines from National that delineated the amount of violence acceptable in the dining room. Winkie continued to glance at the kitchen door and sigh, and Caron did her best to slither down in her seat and disappear.

I finally tired of the uncomfortable silence and said, "What are you majoring in, Jean?"

"Political history. I've been accepted to law school at Yale beginning this fall. I'm taking a course this summer in economics, and working for the dean at the law school here."

"Mrs. Vanderson's husband," added Winkie, having mistaken me for someone who cared. "She helped Jean attain the position."

Jean gave Rebecca an enigmatic look, then turned to me and said, "In exchange for office duties, I'm allowed to sit in on lectures. Dean Vanderson okayed it with the professors."

"How kind of him," I said. "What are you majoring in, Rebecca?"

She swept her hair over her shoulder, checked to ensure she had our profound attention, and said, "Communications, with a focus on theater. I graduated in May, but I want to be in the productions this summer to enhance my résumé, and darling Carlyle promised me at least one leading role. I do hope you and Caron will come see me."

I'd begun to notice that they were all eyeing Caron in a predatory manner, as if they were crows and she an appetizingly steamy mound in the middle of the highway. Little did they know I planned to send her to college on some remote Canadian island near the North Pole, where she would be more likely to join an organization of feral elves than of sorority girls. I managed a polite smile. "We'll certainly try, Rebecca."

Debbie Anne came into the dining room with a tray piled with serving bowls, mumbling apologies that only I acknowledged. Half an hour later, I made my escape. Caron refused to accompany me, insisting that she was in the middle of her training session and anything more than the short break for dinner would destroy her concentration. I assured her I would wait up for her so we could discuss certain topics, thanked everyone for the meal, and left before any Kappa hymns could be sung in my honor.

As I started across the lawn, a silver Mercedes stopped at the curb and the woman I'd seen the day before stepped out of the car and waved at me. "Excuse me," she called, "but are you Claire Malloy from next door?" She correctly interpreted my grimace and came to the edge of the sidewalk. "I'm Eleanor Vanderson, a Kappa alumna. I serve as the house corps president and local adviser to the chapter. I just wanted to thank you for your concern last night."

As before, she was sleekly and expensively dressed, and if a single gray hair had dared to disrupt her coiffed brown hair, only her hairdresser had been privy to it. She might have been older than fifty, but she had the purposeful look of a woman who went to aerobics classes thrice a week, played golf, and had things tucked and trimmed as needed. Her voice held a trace of a drawl that told me she'd grown up in the southern confines of the state, where country-club candidacies and bridal registrations still dominated the conversations at brunches, luncheons, tailgate parties, and pink teas.

"You're welcome," I said, stopping short of snarling.

"Some of these girls . . . well, in my day it was exceedingly difficult to get into Kappa Theta Eta. If a rushee didn't have at least one legacy, along with strong recommendations from her hometown alumnae, she was cut at the end of the first day. We never considered a girl who didn't have a solid grade point from high school." Her shrug was graceful, rippling down her arms like honey and ending at fingernails that must have been manicured daily. "Now we take almost anyone who shows up at the door, as long as her parents have adequate financial resources. It's simply not the same."

"I'm sure it isn't, Mrs. Vanderson. If you'll excuse me, I'm expecting a long-distance call."

"I won't keep you, Mrs. Malloy, but there's one thing I need to ask you before you go. Yesterday evening I came by to interview the painter, and he claimed not only that you were a dear friend of his, but also that you're a politician. I may have misunderstood him, but he swore that you . . . I believe he said you're a senator."

It would have taken hours to explain why Arnie was convinced I was a senator, and although I had been less than truthful moments earlier, it was possible that someone somewhere was dialing my number. It was apt to be a con man with a foolproof scheme to make a fortune in federal oil leases, but even he appealed. "You misunderstood, and in any case, I'm a bookseller. As much as I've enjoyed our conversation, I really must run along now."

"Then you will vouch for this man's good character? I cannot have anyone in the house who might bother the girls or pilfer the silverware."

"Vouch for Arnie?" I said, startled. "Certainly not. He's worthless, felonious, unreliable, delusional, and a royal pain in the neck!"

"He seemed so very fond of you," she murmured, "and spoke of your friendship at length."

I aimed an unadorned and somewhat gnawed fingernail at her. "As I just said, delusional. I don't care to discuss Arnie further, Mrs. Vanderson. If you decide to hire him, it's none of my concern. I am expecting a call."

Relying on this display of indignation to stifle her, I marched to my porch and through the door. All in all, it was quite as good as anything Caron could improvise, and I was congratulating myself when I heard a scream.

I was not torn by indecision—I was ripped to shreds right there in the middle of the staircase. The dilemma lay not between rushing upstairs to call 911 or rushing downstairs to aid Eleanor Vanderson. It lay between continuing upstairs at a leisurely pace to take a bath or returning downstairs to peek cautiously from the porch before I went upstairs to take a bath. Surely the sorority girls and housemother knew the routine by now, I told myself as I teetered on one foot. We'd had a drill less than twenty-four hours ago.

Reminding myself what curiosity had done to a former Katie, I decided to make sure they were handling the matter and went downstairs, feeling as though I were descending into Mr. Dante's lower rings. The lights were again blazing and figures were darting around in the darkness alongside the house. Jean and Rebecca emerged with Mrs. Vanderson between them. Winkie, Pippa, Debbie Anne, and Caron came after them, their faces pale.

Perhaps, I thought smugly as I headed for a bubble bath and a new mystery novel, they might take Debbie Anne's encounter more seriously now that a real, live Kappa alumna had had the same experience. Dismissing the entire business, I proceeded to immerse myself in more ways than one.

The next morning I staked out the kitchen and waited for Caron to wake up. In that she had not come home until well after I'd given up and gone to bed, she refused to do so and I went to the Book Depot, wishing I knew the details of Mrs. Vanderson's scream. I was reluctant to call Peter, since I didn't know if they'd bothered to notify the police. If they had, he might fall for the argument that it happened in the adjoining yard and be cajoled into calling the campus police to ask for a copy of the report. If they hadn't, he might change the topic to a cabin and a brass bed. I wasn't in the mood for that.

Therefore I was pleased when Debbie Anne trudged into the store, even though the sight of her brought back memories of bad food, a boring and perfunctory conversation during the ingestion of same, and a nearly fatal overdose of pinkness. She was carrying only one textbook this time, and its cover indicated it concerned the psychological development of small children.

I gave her a disarming smile. "Why, Debbie Anne, shouldn't you be slaving in the library?"

"I was there all morning," she said lugubriously. "I was wondering if I could talk to you, Mrs. Malloy. I know we're not friends or anything, but sometimes I get the dumb idea that the girls don't like me very much, and I don't think Winkie does, either. I called my mama last night, but she was mad on account of it being a long-distance call."

"Last night," I said, homing in on the phrase much like a malnourished refugee, "I heard a scream and saw Mrs. Vanderson being helped from the dark area between my house and the Kappa house. That's where you were knocked down, isn't it?"

"Yeah, although you're the only person who believes me. Jean and Rebecca were in the same pledge class, and Pippa was the junior representative to the board, so they all kind of hang around together. During the academic year, I was pretty good friends with a few of the pledges, but now no one bothers to so much as say good morning. We're supposed to take turns in the kitchen, according to Winkie. Somehow every night I seem to be cooking and cleaning up afterward, and all by myself."

I did not want to listen to the complaints of a provincial Cinderella. "You'll have to stick up for yourself, Debbie Anne. I can't oversee the duty roster for you. Now, what happened to Mrs. Vanderson?"

"Not all that much. She saw a figure in the shadows. Thinking it was a fraternity boy, she marched over to give him a piece of her mind. Whoever it was shoved her down real hard and ran away."

"And that's what happened to you the night before?"

"I guess so. I thought the guy was trying to climb in through a window, but Winkie and Jean looked the next morning and they didn't find any scratches on the windowsill. Jean made a point of telling me there weren't any footprints in the mud and the shrubs hadn't been trampled. She made it real clear that she didn't believe me one bit, that she thought I was acting up to get attention." Her eyes filled with tears and she began to snuffle in a most unattractive fashion, not unlike an asthmatic bloodhound. "I didn't make it up, Mrs. Malloy, any more than I did last spring when my mama's earrings disappeared. There're a lot of funny things that happen at the house, not to mention some of the pledge activities. I don't think some of them are right. My preacher back home would have a fit if he knew what all I've done to try to get initiated into Kappa Theta Eta."

"Oh, really? I thought hazing was outlawed on this campus after one fraternity boy jumped off the roof and fractured his leg, and another nearly died of alcohol poisoning."

She stopped snuffling to give me a prissy frown. "We don't allow alcohol in the house, or smoking, either. Some of the seniors smoke in their rooms, and everybody knows Winkie keeps wine in her refrigerator and a bottle of brandy under her bed. One night when I couldn't sleep on account of worrying over my midterms, I went down to get a glass of milk and I could have sworn I heard a man's voice right there in Winkie's suite. I asked her about it the next morning, and she got real peevish with me and told me I'd better stop imagining things and concern myself with my grades. When I told Jean about it, she just laughed and said the same thing Winkie did."

I clucked my tongue. "Let's hope National never hears of this. So, what pledge activities would scandalize your preacher back home?"

"Mostly silly stuff, but sometimes ... well, you know, things that sure might ..." She gulped and turned away, but not before I saw the red blotches on her cheeks. "I shouldn't talk to you about those things. If anyone overheard me, I'd be out on my fanny in no time flat." She promptly discarded her own advice, and dropped her voice to a husky whisper more suitable for secret agents exchanging bomb recipes. "There was one time when I got so upset I thought I'd throw up, but Jean was real sweet and talked to me half the night. She kept repeating how Kappa Theta Eta meant a lifetime of sisterhood and how I'd better learn to accept their ways if I ever hoped to be initiated. Now I don't know if I want to be a Kappa or not!"

I took a tissue from the box below the counter and gave it to her. "If you're so miserable, why not quit and live in a dorm?" I said pragmatically, if not sympathetically.

"Mama would skin me alive if I quit," she said. "I just can't make her understand that most of the girls make fun of me. Jean's been real kind about lending me clothes, and Pippa did that color thing for half price, but it didn't do any good. I don't dress like them, talk like them, have families like them, or drive fancy cars like them. Everything about me's wrong, according to them. My hair, my accent, my major—everything!"

She sank to the floor and began to snuffle with increasing vigor, until she was sobbing and I was trying to decide what to do about her. Since there were no customers, she was not likely to discourage sales, but it seemed rather cold-blooded to simply watch her until she subsided and I could shoo her out the door. On the other hand, I had no desire to cuddle her in my arms and make soothing noises while she splattered my shirt with tears, not to mention less desirable fluids. She was a wet creature, I thought, and inclined to dribble on every possible occasion.

I opted for a middling approach. "Come now, Debbie Anne, it can't be all that bad," I said consolingly, but from a prudent distance. "Your friends will be back in the fall, and you'll have raised your grade point so you can be initiated and you'll feel more like a real Kappa Theta . . . whatever."

She wiped her nose and looked up at me. "I don't see how I can ever be initiated. I'm too scared to go into the chapter room after what happened at the last meeting."

"Jean said you'd been inadvertently locked in the room."

"Inadvertently my foot! Jean asked me in a real sugary voice to put away the candles in the ritual closet, then locked the closet door, turned out the lights, and left. I was there for most of an hour, beating on the door and screaming, but nobody could hear me on account of the chapter room's in the basement. She locked that door, too, and the one at the top of the stairs."

"The ritual closet? What exactly is a ritual closet?" I asked, allowing myself to entertain macabre visions of mutilated cat corpses.

The bell tinkled before she could answer, to my regret. It was a customer of sorts, a whiskery, ponytailed science fiction freak of indeterminate years who resided in a reality that mirrored whatever he was reading. He blinked at Debbie Anne for a minute, then waved a hand at me and shuffled into the netherworld of the racks.

Debbie Anne scrambled to her feet, blotted her nose, and stuffed the wadded tissue in her pocket. "Golly, Mrs. Malloy, we're not allowed to talk about"—she lowered her voice to a twangy whisper—"the chapter room or the ritual closet. That's secret Kappa stuff, like our whistle and handshake."

I was intrigued by the arcanum. "You have a secret whistle? Please, I beg of you, let me hear it. I promise I'll erase the memory afterward and never so much as exhale in any similar way."

"I can't! I'm sorry I bothered you, Mrs. Malloy. I'm desperate for some advice, but I can't tell you about what goes on at the house. You're not a Kappa." Having delivered the ultimate insult, she grabbed her book and fled.

I was disappointed, but I reassured myself that my curiosity might yet be assuaged and turned my attention to this rare and precious commodity—the customer. "Finding anything good?" I called.

He poked his head over the top of the rack. "No, not as of yet. I was gonna buy a copy of *Bimbos of the Death Sun* to give to this lady I've been hanging out with, but you don't have any. She's kind of spooked by science fiction fans, and refused to go to the last World Con with me, even though I assured her that no one's been badly injured in a D&D game for more than a year. It was his fault, anyway, for thinking he ought to challenge a five-hundred-pound Plutonian mercenary with a real sword when—"

"I do have a copy," I interrupted. I was about to give him specifics when it occurred to me that he might not be in a right-left mode. I joined him in front of the gaudy covers. "I saw it several days ago, right . . . in that empty space."

"So maybe you sold it?" he said.

Recalling sales was unpleasantly easy. "No, I didn't," I said with a puzzled frown. "I'm certain I had the one copy and it was there two or three days ago. I've sold some romances, a few classics that are on the high school reading list for the fall, a book on building decks, and a cookbook. That's it for the week. If I didn't sell it, someone stole it!"

I stomped back to the counter, reached for the telephone, and then lowered my hand, and, I hoped, my blood pressure. It was doubtful the police would rush to the scene of the crime to fingerprint the rack and take photographs of the ominously empty spot. Not for a paperback that cost less than four dollars.

"Wow, what a bummer," my SF freak said as he left.

"Wow, what a bummer," I echoed under my breath as the bell tinkled and the cash register stayed mute. "What a bummer, indeed."

4

At some point Caron had groveled and I'd granted a period of probation, although I'd made it clear that I considered her a habitual offender who'd best tiptoe through the rest of the summer unless she wanted to walk through the rest of her high school years. Peter seemed to have tiptoed off to battle larcenous mall rats, which was fine with me.

On Friday I called Luanne Bradshaw and arranged to meet her late in the afternoon at the beer garden.

"A secret whistle, if you can imagine," I said to her after we'd settled down at a corner picnic table shaded by a lush wisteria vine. "I always associated that kind of thing with the male-only clubs where they wear funny hats and play games in the woods. It never occurred to me that I was living next door to it."

Luanne snickered at me, as she so often was inclined to do. She's of a similar age and political persuasion, divorced, and owns Secondhand Rose, a used-clothing store that specializes in outrageously funky clothes from the thirties and forties. This endears her to Caron, who has elevated avarice to an art form, and I regret to say Luanne's not immune to taking advantage of it when she needs help unpacking a shipment or straightening stock.

"And a ritual closet," I added, wiggling my eyebrows. "I've learned they keep candles in it, but for all we know, they've got an altar, hooded robes hanging on hooks, and all sorts of medieval instruments of torture. They seem to go through cats on a regular basis."

Luanne refilled her cup from the pitcher, somehow

managing to light a cigarette in the midst of the process, and leaned back against the rough bench. "Could
this sudden obsession with a houseful of flat-bellied
girls have any relationship to what you perceive to be
impending bankruptcy?"

"There's no need to be vulgar."

"It's characteristic of those of us who are catego-
rized as Sophisticates," she said, letting smoke dribble
out of the corners of her mouth in the style of an aged
Hollywood starlet. "You are no doubt aware of the
ramifications of being labeled thusly, but it had to be
explained to me in great detail. For a small fee, of
course."

"You didn't . . . ?"

"I resisted as best I could, but your daughter is not
only charmingly persuasive, but also more obstinate
than any one-eyed mule in the state. I finally got fed
up with listening to her whine and agreed to a color
analysis, although I was terrified I would be deemed
something like 'anemic.' I'm sure you're vastly relieved to know that because of my milky white skin,
ebony hair with silver highlights, and clear blue eyes
with risqué white flecks, I am definitely a Sophisticate.
This means I'm allowed to wear black, white, emerald,
and navy—but under no circumstances short of my
own funeral am I to be caught dead in brown or orange." She plucked at her shirt and made a face. "I
don't remember if I absolutely must wear green or absolutely must not. What do you think—am I radiant or
muddy?"

"Definitely radiant. At least you know how to avoid
humiliating yourself in public. I've yet to submit, and
based on the number of smirks and snorts aimed at me
daily, I obviously am violating my palette and therefore denying myself immeasurable happiness and admiration. How much did she hit you for?"

"Ten dollars. I resisted the accessory awareness
nonsense, so I do have a smidgen of self-esteem. Why
on earth do you allow her to do this, Claire?"

"Allow her to do this?" I laughed at such naiveté.

"Come on, you raised a couple of teenagers not that long ago. Did you really charge into battle over the misdemeanors, or did you save your energy for the full-fledged felonies? That dippy sorority girl has Caron convinced that there's a bag of money waiting to be plucked out of the gutter by the next My Beautiful Self consultant. My formerly articulate daughter now drifts around the apartment muttering obtusely about the emotional acceptance of one's palette, but only when she's not drooling on the automotive section of the classified ads. She and Inez did a clothes exchange that would have shamed a roomful of commodities brokers. They sustained a disagreement about whether a sweater was cocoa or chocolate until I found myself in the doorway screaming that it was brown and that was that and if I heard one more word about it, it would be reverted to a ball of yarn."

Luanne gazed thoughtfully at a trio of men entering the beer garden, dismissed them for failing to meet an unspecified criterion of hers, and replenished her cup. "And are the big bucks rolling in as promised?"

"She's having a bit of trouble finding clients. She conned Inez's mother and the woman who rents the downstairs apartment, and you, of course, but she hasn't mentioned any others. Oddly enough, her friends aren't eager to fork over ten dollars to be told their wardrobes are total disasters. I heard her arguing with Rhonda on the telephone, and I sat up all night, fully expecting the house to be torched by someone whose unfortunate sallowness could be corrected in a single session. I'm afraid Caron's training was strong on palettes and weak on tact."

"She'll learn eventually," Luanne said as she stubbed out her cigarette and lit another. "I know cradle-robbing's unattractive, but is it truly tacky?"

Having no problem with the non sequitur, I glanced over my shoulder and turned back with a wicked grin. "As long as you don't mind being asked if you're his mother or his baby-sitter."

We debated various male, manly, and macho attributes until the pitcher was empty and the garden began to grow crowded and noisy. The sight of a quintet of shaggy-haired boys setting up mammoth speakers on the stage in preparation to assault our sensibilities was more than enough to send us away. When we reached the sidewalk, Luanne headed for her store and I strolled toward my apartment. There was little traffic in the street alongside the campus lawn, thus allowing me to savor the scent of honeysuckle rather than the stench of auto exhaust.

I was contemplating which frozen entree might best suit my mood when a voice hissed my name from the shrubbery next to the Kappa Theta Eta house. It was enough to jolt me out of my gluttonous reverie, and as I turned, I saw blue lights flashing in the alley behind the house. Static from a radio mingled with the barking of male voices and the slamming of car doors.

A single light glinted in the front room, but the porch light was off and the shadows exceedingly thick on either side. They'd also spoken to me, which was less than heartening. These were the very same shadows that had produced prowlers only a few nights earlier—rude and rambunctious prowlers who knocked down women.

"Psst! Miz Malloy!" the voice repeated beseechingly.

I opted not to rush headlong into potential physical discomfort. "Who is it?"

"I got to talk to you. I think I'm in trouble."

"Unlike Moses, I do not converse with bushes. You have two seconds to show yourself. Otherwise, I shall either scream for the police, who are conveniently situated behind the house, or perhaps merely continue to my apartment to microwave a low-sodium serving of fettucini with a medley of garden vegetables and a tangy cheese sauce. Got that, bush?"

A hunched figure emerged. To my dismay, it was Arnie. He held up a trembling hand and said, "Don't scream, for pete's sake. This ain't none of my doing, Senator, but I seem to be in what some might describe as a sticky situation. What say we go to your place and discuss it over a martini or two?"

He came to the sidewalk, where I had a better view of his wet, slack mouth and a better whiff of his indifference to personal hygiene. "I don't know what all's going on back there," he continued. "It most likely has to do with the body in the middle of the alley, but with the cops, you can't ever be sure what they're up to." He winked at me, although it seemed to require more than minimal effort. "I guess my appointment is canceled, so how about a little drink, Senator?"

I jammed my hands in my pockets before I lost my resolve and punched him in the nose. "You know damn well that I'm not a senator. Just drop it and explain what you said about a body in the alley."

"It's not a pretty sight," he said, shaking his head. "Come to think of it, *Washington Weekly* will be on before too long. Tonight's topic is the impact of the trade agreements with Japan on the American auto industry, which happens to be of particular interest to me. Helluva show, doncha think, Senator?"

"Arnie," I said with all the venom I could muster, "let's get this straight once and—"

"Smile!" He whipped a camera from behind his back. The flash exploded in my eyes, and for a brief moment all I could see were ragged red and purple circles. They'd not yet faded completely as he scuttled past me, climbed into his truck, and drove away, his taillights blinking farewell long before I could concoct a response.

Arnie's repeated avowals of my political position arose from an incident in the past, when he'd been assigned to drive a state senator and a local beauty queen in the Thurberfest parade. He'd shown up drunk and obligated me, the very unwilling assistant pageant director, to play chauffeur (while dodging bullets). In his alcoholic haze, he'd decided I was the senator rather than the beauty queen—a politically correct yet mildly insulting assumption. When Caron had lured me into investigating a pet-theft ring, Arnie'd nearly managed to have me arrested for harboring a fugitive, and shortly thereafter he'd come close to watching me chewed to bits by a trio of enraged pit bulls. All in all, he was not a dear friend. Given the chance, I would have driven a stake through his heart. Cheerfully.

In the alley, the blue lights continued to rotate and the radios to crackle. More car doors slammed, and the beam of a flashlight bobbled on the foliage. There was likely to be an iota of truth in Arnie's statement, I thought as I hesitated on the sidewalk and tried to discern what was happening. The alley ran behind several Greek communes, of both the imposing and the marginally renovated varieties, and it was a handy shortcut from the bastions of academia to the bars of Thurber Street. Although I had to drive a short distance on it to park in the basement garage of my duplex, I rarely promenaded down it, being as averse to miasmatic garbage dumpsters as I was to sweat—and to Arnie.

I finally went past my house, turned at the corner, and turned again at the north end of the alley. There were three police cars parked behind the Kappa house, their lights flashing mutely, and spotlights had been placed to illuminate what I assumed was the cause of the official presence.

An engraved invitation was not likely, nor would I be welcomed into the group and offered details. I knew from experience that officers at the scene of the crime could be blustery and indignant over the presence of a civic-minded citizen who was eager to share her insights into the heinous deed. Peter Rosen, for example, could be quite adamant about what he considered meddlesome intrusions.

There was more going on than a case of a cat flattened by a garbage truck, however, and I was determined to find out what it was. I approached tentatively, pausing every step to scan the crowd for Peter or his minion, Jorgeson. I wasn't at all sure if I'd have more success with them or without them, and I was decidedly ambivalent when I caught a glimpse of Peter's curly black hair as he beckoned at an ambulance creeping toward the scene from the opposite direction.

"Okay," I heard him snap, "where's the medical examiner? You called him—when? Ten minutes ago? Unlike this poor girl, we don't have all night!"

Jorgeson appeared, consulting his watch, and pulled Peter aside to converse. I was keeping an eye on them as I edged forward, and therefore yelped when a flashlight caught me in the face and an unfamiliar voice said, "Hey, Lieutenant, we got a sightseer. You want I should sell her a ticket—or does she already have a season pass?"

This did not amuse Lieutenant Peter Rosen, who shook off Jorgeson's hand and stalked to the edge of the lights. "Claire," he said with petulance rather than the enthusiasm for which I'd hoped, "what are you doing here? Just go to your apartment and wait, okay? I've got enough problems as it is, and the last thing I need is a nosy neighbor lurking nearby."

"I never lurk," I said. "I am merely taking an interest in a crime committed not more than twenty feet from my back door. For all I know, the murderer is lurking in my kitchen."

"No one said anything about murder," he growled.

"You and the gang didn't come out to investigate the theft of a dumpster, did you?" I shaded my eyes and permitted myself a small grimace. "My eyes have been subject to enough abuse tonight. Would you please ask your pyrotechnical expert to give me a break?"

Peter gestured at the officer, then came over to me and gave me a look meant to intimidate me into flight into the nearest haven. "Civilians are not allowed at the scene of a crime," he said in his steeliest cop voice. "We've got the weapon, and in any case, it's unlikely you could be run down in your kitchen by a 1973 Buick. Please, this one time, let me do my job without your assistance. When I can get away, I'll come by and tell you what happened."

"Was it one of the girls from the Kappa Theta Eta house?"

He bit down on his lip in a manner I found incredibly virile, but I left it unspoken. He said, "We don't have a positive ID yet. If she was carrying a purse, the impact knocked it into the brush or it was taken from the scene." He glowered at me. "You don't know them, do you?"

"Yes, I do. I had dinner at the house in the middle of the week, and am capable of identifying any one of them. However, I sense that I'm interrupting, so I'll run along home and have a nice cup of tea while you and the boys get back to business." I took a couple of steps backward to prove I wasn't bluffing. "Call me when you can."

"We're not going to find her purse tonight, Lieutenant," a uniformed officer called. "The undergrowth's a damn jungle. Maybe it'll turn up tomorrow when we can see what we're doing."

Peter was now biting down on his lip hard enough to draw blood, and I could see it took an effort on his part to relent and mutter, "See if you recognize her."

I allowed myself to be escorted between two police cars, and then forced myself to look down at the body sprawled on the eroded asphalt surface. Once I was sure, I spun away and bent over the hood of one of the cars, struggling not to lose the beer I'd imbibed. I squeezed my eyes closed, but the image of the lifeless face and ribbons of blood seemed all the more intense, more vivid than the reality.

Peter rested his hand on my back. "Is she one of the girls from this sorority house?"

I gulped back the bitterness that rose in my throat, and stood up. "Her name was Jean Hall. She was . . ." I harshly rubbed my temples as if my fingers could erase the image. "She was planning to attend law school at Yale in the fall. She was enrolled in one course this summer, and also worked for the dean of the law school here." I moved out of the light and kept my eyes locked on Peter's face. "What happened to her? She looks as though she'd been run down by a fleet of buses."

He pointed at a wide white car that was partially buried in a tangle of brush. "The lab boys are on their way, but we're fairly certain that's the vehicle, and we're running the plates right now. A brown substance on the front bumper appears to be blood, and a headlight is broken."

"But she was . . ." I couldn't find the word, much less say it aloud in the presence of the badly violated body.

Peter put his hands on my shoulders and drew me across the alley, where he could wrap his arms around me without risking grins from his cohorts. "The initial impact most likely killed her instantly, or at least knocked her unconscious. Go on upstairs, Claire. As soon as I'm done, I'll join you for a drink. I have to deal with this, but I don't like it any better than you, especially when it's a kid."

"What about the girls in the house, and the housemother? Why aren't they out here? How could they not see the lights? I don't understand why—"

He dug his fingers into my back until I stopped sputtering at his shoulder. "There's no one home at the moment. It's Friday night, so they may all be out on dates or working late at the library or whatever sorority girls do on weekends. We'll stay here until someone returns and we can get information about the victim. Now that we have a name, I'll send an officer to see if he can roust the registrar. Maybe we'll get lucky."

I was still battling nausea, and the idea of collapsing on my sofa with a cup of tea was enough to make me giddy. I hadn't liked Jean Hall. Then again, I thought with an explosion of frigid anger, my antipathetic opinion hadn't given someone tacit permission to kill her. She hadn't deserved to be run down so brutally, so dispassionately.

It was not yet time for tea. "Listen, Peter," I said, "all four of the girls were staying in a wing off the lounge. I don't know which room was Jean's, but I can tell with a quick look. Maybe you can find an address book or some correspondence that will indicate where her parents live. They should be notified as soon as possible."

"I suppose you're right," he said gloomily. "I'll send for a campus cop to unlock the house for us. They've already made it clear that the alley is city property and in our jurisdiction, but they'll assist us."

"If no one's in the house and it's locked, she must have taken her key with her. Did someone check her pockets?"

"Earlier, for identification. Her pockets are empty, and as you heard while so charmingly eavesdropping, her purse hasn't turned up yet. Campus security can be here in a minute or two." He told me to wait where I was, then reentered the brightly lit arena of activity to confer with the medical examiner, the squad from the crime lab, and the medics.

A disgruntled campus policeman arrived with a key, and shortly thereafter, Peter and I entered the house. Jorgeson followed with a flashlight, which proved necessary when we found ourselves in a dark kitchen. Aluminum pans and bowls glinted dully from hooks along the ceiling, and stacks of plastic glasses reflected slivers of orange and blue. A vast refrigerator droned unsteadily.

I found a light switch, and led them through the dining room to the lounge, and after a moment's consideration, down a corridor replete with a blank bulletin board and tiers of mail cubicles, all empty. When Rebecca had given me the tour, she'd pointed out the hallway lined with four bedroom doors on one side, and on the opposing side a pink-tiled bathroom and a closet used by the custodial staff.

The first door was locked. I stepped back, and Jorgeson fiddled with a pick until we heard a ping. He opened the door and switched on the light. I knew it wasn't a matter of breaking and entering, not with a pair of cops accompanying me, but I felt as guilty as a dieter with a doughnut as I went inside the room.

It wasn't much larger than my office, and contained a narrow bed, a built-in closet, a dresser, and a desk cluttered with all the paraphernalia necessary to produce the flawless face of a Kappa Theta Eta. Clothes were piled on the bed, draped over a chair, and discarded on the floor. Mixed among jeans and shorts were pink cashmere sweaters and pink silk blouses, lacy pink panties, a single fuzzy pink bedroom slipper, pink sweatpants, and a pink-and-white-striped umbrella.

I wasn't surprised to see a stuffed cat on the bed, dozens of pink paper cats taped to the walls and around the mirror, and on the desk, a necklace with a silver cat charm. Beside it was a framed photograph of a group of girls positioned around a cat, all of them smiling brightly except for their hostage, who looked panicky.

"What's with this cat thing?" Peter asked from the doorway, unwilling or possibly unable to encroach on this feline sanctuary.

"You really don't want to know," I said. "This must be Rebecca's room. These are scripts, and the textbooks have to do with theater history."

We went to the next room, which had a distressingly similar decor and a selection of psychology textbooks. On the bed was a My Beautiful Self manual and strips of paper that reminded me of paint sample cards. "Pippa's room," I said as we retreated.

While Jorgeson plied his magic on the third door, I related what little I knew about Rebecca and Pippa. We entered the room. The cat motif was nearly nonexistent, with only a single pink paper cat taped to the wall and nary a kitty on the pillow. The bed was made, the desk surface pristine, the floor bare, the lone photograph that of a middle-aged couple with squinty eyes and unsmiling mouths. The room had the austerity of a convent cell, and perhaps slightly less warmth.

"This is Debbie Anne's room," I said with a sigh. I picked up an envelope and noted the return address. The town was unfamiliar, but the state is riddled with towns that are no more than a few forlorn houses clumped around a post office. "She's the one who's not Kappa material, from all accounts."

In the last room, the cats were back in full force on the bed, the mirror frame, the walls, and the back of the door, and even on the personal computer on the desk. There were dozens of photographs of Jean, each with a different boy wrapped around her and grinning drunkenly at the camera. Slogans on their T-shirts proclaimed the occasions to be such dignified affairs as Purple Cow Madness Night and Sin City. Jean had managed to keep at least some of her clothes in the closet, and her books were aligned on the shelf above the desk. She had a portable television on a plastic crate, presumably out of deference to her exalted position as house president, and an extensive collection of stuffed cats piled on the bed.

Peter and Jorgeson were beyond response by that time. They both looked so intensely uncomfortable that I felt sorry for them. Jorgeson glanced down the hallway as if he were anticipating an attack by a blustery pink coed or a rabid cat. I had no problem empathizing with their disquietude, having experienced it myself.

"This is Jean's room," I said patiently. "Do you want to look for her home address, or shall I do it for you?"

My offer was ignored. While I sat on the bed and watched Peter search through the drawers and Jorgeson paw through the closet, I mentally replayed my conversations with Jean. She would have made a fine lawyer, I thought as I remembered how deftly she'd maligned Debbie Anne with only a few facetiously concerned observations and a delicate sneer or two.

"Here's an address book, Lieutenant." Jorgeson held up a small leather book and flipped through the pages. "She didn't write down her parents' address or telephone number, but there's a number for Aunt Mellie in Little Rock. You want me to find a telephone and try it?"

Peter nodded distractedly, his eyes darting from cat to cat and his forehead creased as if it had been raked by sharp claws. "I don't get this," he said under his breath. "I'd go crazy after ten minutes in this place. It's so . . ."

"Pink?" I suggested, wondering if he was so unsettled that he inadvertently might pass along a few official tidbits. We amateur sleuths must be ever vigilant to take advantage of any momentary weakness. "I didn't know Jean well, but she was the one I'd have said was not a pink person. She had a brittleness about her, and certainly not an easygoing, pastel personality. Either I was mistaken in my judgment, or she's gone to extremes to present herself in a particular light." I paused delicately, then continued in a vague, musing voice, "It wasn't a simple hit-and-run, was it? Whoever was driving made sure she was dead. I suppose we'll find out who it was when you find out whose car it is."

"Yeah," Peter said as he studied the room as though it were a museum reproduction from an extraterrestrial culture. "This sort of thing usually involves a drunk driver who suspects he hit something, backs up for a better look, drives into the nearest tree, and flees on foot. He'll turn himself in at the station in the morning, deeply repentant but nevertheless accompanied by his father's attorney, and eventually be let off with a fat fine, probation, and enough community service to cause minor inconvenience. Even with a suspended license, he'll be driving that same day and drinking that night."

"Who reported the accident?"

"We got an anonymous call, maybe from the driver himself, who might not have been sure the girl was dead."

I looked at Jean's face in one of the photographs, but now saw it dappled with blood, the eyes glassy, the mouth crooked. "How could he not know he'd killed her?"

"It was dark, and he was drunk and frightened. It happens all too often on back roads and even on the better-lit highways. A guy has car trouble and starts walking along the shoulder to find help, or a drunk steps out in front of a speeding car."

Jorgeson came into the room. "Aunt Mellie isn't home, but we've got something on the car. It's registered to James Wray of Bethel Hills, which is a little town in the bottom corner of the state."

"As in Debbie Anne Wray," I said. "The girl who occupies the room noticeably lacking Kappa spirit. She's the one who was knocked down by a prowler several nights ago, or claimed she was."

This was of interest, naturally, and I related the recent events, glossing over my reluctance to be drawn into a quagmire of cuteness. "I can't remember the woman's name," I concluded, "but she's the wife of the law school dean. She's also some kind of alumna adviser, so I suppose she might have the names and addresses of the girls' families."

Peter sent Jorgeson to work on it, then gestured for me to follow him out of Jean's room. "What can you tell me about the Wray girl? Do you have any theories why she'd want to hurt the victim—or where she might be at this moment?"

"Debbie Anne told me that Jean gave her a bad time, but I failed to spot any flicker of diabolical desire to seek revenge in the alley because of it. She's a limp, impassive girl, more likely to sit in a corner and whimper than to do something violent." I shuddered as once again Jean's face forced its way into my mind, and I halted and leaned against the wall to steady myself. "As for her whereabouts, I doubt she's out on a date. You might try the library if it hasn't closed."

"I'll need a description."

I was doing my best to paint a colorful picture of a girl less animated than the faded carpet in the hallway when we heard a scream from the front part of the house. Peter hurried past me, careened around the corner, and vanished. Having become somewhat desensitized to the Kappas' screams, I trailed after him with

more decorum and arrived in the lounge in time to see
Winkie clutch her neck.

"Men are not allowed in the private rooms," she
gasped as her eyes rolled back and she crumpled to the
floor.

5

"Well, at least we know where two of them are," I said as I knelt beside Winkie and patted her cheek. At my request, Jorgeson went to the kitchen and returned with a damp dishtowel; I toyed with the idea of using it on myself, then relented and placed it across my patient's forehead. "You must have scared her pretty badly, Jorgeson. What'd you do to her?"

Peter glared at me as if I were in some way responsible for this most recent disaster, as well as everything else that had occurred of late, including but not limited to the breakdown of the Middle East peace talks and the hole in the ozone layer. Barely able to spit out the words, he said, "And this is . . . ?"

"Mrs. Winklebury, the housemother." Irritated by his unseemly attitude, I sat back on my heels and looked up at him with a bland smile. "But I'm quite sure she'll insist that you call her Winkie. There's some sort of obscure tradition that all the housemothers must have fuzzy-wuzzy nicknames. The cats, on the other hand, are invariably called Katie." I noticed Jorgeson was scribbling notes and added, "That's Katie the Kappa Kitten, to be precise, immortalized on those zillions of construction-paper cutouts plastered on every surface in this residence. If science is unable to meet the challenge, they'll continue to proliferate at an alarming rate and soon we shall be awash in them."

Peter bristled so fiercely I could see the dear little hairs on his neck rise. "Thank you for your insight into sorority traditions. Perhaps it's time for you to—"

"What happened?" Winkie said groggily, thus rescuing me from a temporary eviction, if not a permanent exile.

"You fainted." I helped her to her feet and guided her to the nearest sofa. "Would you like some water?"

She shook her head. "I'll be fine. It was so silly of me to overreact that way, but with all these prowlers outside the house and the problems among the girls and my medication, I'm a nervous wreck. I simply don't"—she dropped her voice to a noticeably fermented whisper—"understand why these men are roaming all over the house. Who are they and how did they get inside?" She pointed a stubby finger at Peter and Jorgeson. "You cannot remain in the lounge! It's not allowed, not allowed at all!"

I glanced at Peter, who nodded at me and herded Jorgeson out to the foyer, where they began to talk in low and, unfortunately, inaudible rumbles.

Winkie deflated into the upholstery, her complexion as gray as her dress. "I do hope I wasn't too brusque," she said dispiritedly. "Because of allergies, I take rather strong antihistamines, and they add to my anxiety. I haven't had a night off since spring break, you know, and I decided to slip out and go to the movies, to be surrounded by people of my own generation instead of these ... girls." Her small, childlike hands shot into the air, and saliva dripped down her chin. "But what should I see as I approach the theater? A long line of high school and college students, all pushing and braying and behaving as if each and every one of them had been raised by wolves."

"Oh dear," I murmured, bemused by her lack of interest in the presence of Peter, Jorgeson, and me in the house. Her initial reaction had been strong enough to evoke a bout of the vapors, but now she seemed much more concerned about justifying her absence than demanding explanations.

"Sitting in the theater with them was out of the question," she continued. "I ended up taking a nice, quiet drive up on the mountain, where I could admire the lights below and enjoy the tranquillity. I can't tell you how lovely it was to be all by myself for a few hours."

"I'm sorry the officer frightened you."

She clutched my arm. "Officer? That man who was here? I heard a noise in the lounge and came to investigate, fully expecting to find the girls playing bridge or studying together. With the exception of the cooks and waiters, men are never allowed in the back of the house. National has very strict rules about that. If one of the girls allows her date to so much as step across the threshold, she'll find herself facing the standards committee within twenty-four hours. One of my most sacred duties is to accompany any repairman who needs to go beyond the public rooms."

Her antihistamines must have been industrial-strength, I thought as I waited for her to return to the issue at hand. Either that, or whatever kind of training she'd endured to become a housemother included a partial lobotomy. "National" was sounding less like a committee of conscientious alumnae and more like a squadron of Gestapo agents in pink silk suits.

I took a deep breath and said, "I think you'd better hear what happened tonight. There's been an accident, and I'm afraid one of the girls . . . was run down in the alley behind the house."

"Run down? What do you mean? I don't understand what you're saying, Claire! Is she dead? Who?"

I gave her a skimpy account of what had happened, admitted we'd been in the four bedrooms in search of information concerning Jean's next of kin, and omitted to mention that the car registration had been traced to someone who coincidentally shared the same last name and hometown of a Kappa pledge.

"Then it was a senseless accident?" Covering her face with her hands, Winkie began to rock back and forth, moaning softly and occasionally flicking away a tear with an impatient gesture. "Oh, that poor, poor girl. She was so intelligent, so determined, so decisive, and a truly outstanding Kappa Theta Eta. She's maintained the highest grade point average in the house since her first semester as a pledge, and it was very likely that she would receive a stipend from the scholarship foundation to help finance her law studies."

I allowed her to carry on for a minute, then eased her hands away from her face and handed her the dishtowel. "The police haven't been able to locate Jean's parents yet. Do you have paperwork with that sort of information?"

"There's a file cabinet in my bedroom. The keys to it and to the suite are in my handbag there on the floor. I'd appreciate it so much if you could see to it, Claire. Never has any of the girls been seriously ill, much less ... passed away while under my care. I feel responsible for Jean's tragedy. If only I'd been here, she might not have walked up the alley but instead chosen to stay on the sidewalk. I don't know how many times I've scolded them for utilizing shortcuts at night."

I didn't know how many times, either, but this was my second turn to hear it. I scooped up her handbag and went into the foyer, tersely explained my mission to Peter and Jorgeson, and stopped at the door of Winkie's suite, all the while digging through wadded tissues, checkbooks, pencils, folded papers, and plastic pill boxes for a set of keys.

There were more than fifty keys on the ring, but I opted for a noticeably worn one and slid it into the lock. A tiny click confirmed my intuitive acuity.

"I'll bring you the files," I said to Peter, then went into the living room and felt for a light switch. All I encountered was the fuzziness of the flocked wallpaper, but I had a decent visual image of the layout and headed for a floor lamp beyond the rocking chair. I was groping for the button when burning needles plunged into my ankle.

As startled as I was pained, I recoiled instinctively, stumbled over the coffee table, and went sprawling headlong into the sofa. I heard shrieks and realized they were my own, but before I could convince myself to stop, Peter and Jorgeson barreled through the doorway with the dedication of Marines, weapons drawn, scowls in place, hands curled into fists.

Jorgeson aimed the flashlight at me. "Are you okay? Did someone attack you?" Peter was saying much the same thing, but he was speaking so rapidly and urgently that he was difficult to understand.

Had I been in a more dignified posture, I would have thanked him for his concern. However, with my knee wedged under my chin, one foot hooked around a table leg, my nose embedded in a throw pillow, and my ankle throbbing, I was not in an appreciative mood. "I'm fine," I muttered. "Turn on the damn light."

As soon as Jorgeson complied, Peter realized there was no one else in the room and lowered his gun before he unwittingly put pockmarks in the flock. "Why'd you scream?" he asked.

"I think the cat bit me. Although it would give me a great deal of pleasure to watch you shoot off its head, I suppose you'd better not until we're sure it doesn't have rabies."

Peter frowned. "What cat?"

"It was here a minute ago, but now it's likely to be cowering under the bed or hiding in a closet." I struggled to a sitting position and examined my ankle. "It didn't break the skin, so I don't have to worry about rabies. Go ahead and shoot it."

"Maybe later," Peter said. "Give me the key ring so that Jorgeson and I can get the files. We've been trained to fight off homicidal kitty cats."

I flung the keys at him. He caught them deftly, and he and Jorgeson left the room. I examined my wound once more for droplets of blood, found none, and decided to track down the beast and if not reciprocate in kind, at least make known my displeasure at its antics. Beyond the living room was a passageway equipped to serve as a kitchen. On one side was a dinette in front of a window with pink-and-white gingham curtains, and across from that a small refrigerator, a sink, and a two-burner stove. There were two wineglasses on the counter; the decanter had been rinsed and left to dry on a rack.

The kitchen had no potential hiding places for the cat, nor did the utilitarian bathroom beyond it. In the bedroom, Peter was seated on the unmade bed, an open file spread across his knees. Jorgeson shuffled through the contents of the bottom drawer of the metal filing cabinet. I crouched to look under the bed (where indeed there was a bottle of brandy), then opened the closet door and found only clothes, shoes, clumps of cat hair, and a suitcase.

"The aunt's her legal guardian," Peter said as he took notes. "There's a work number, but it's an insurance office, and we won't catch her at this hour. I'd better call the local police and ask them to wait at the house until she returns."

Jorgeson plucked a manila file from the drawer. "Here's one with the Wray girl's name, and according to—" He noticed me and stopped.

"I'm going, I'm going," I said with a shrug. "I was looking for the cat to make sure I hadn't kicked it when I fell." I backed out of the bedroom and retreated to the kitchen, puzzled by the absence of the cat, but by no means distressed. It could have run out the door while Peter and Jorgeson goggled at me, or escaped into some obscure niche that I'd overlooked. Although I must have frightened it, I was fairly certain I hadn't hurt it, and it was welcome to stay wherever it was— indefinitely. Hoping Winkie had recovered enough to answer a few questions, I took a step and then noticed the screen beyond the open window was improperly set. When I pushed it, it obligingly fell into the bushes below. Had the cat so desired, it could easily have slipped out the window and scampered away to attack hapless pedestrians.

Pleased with my deductive prowess, I returned to the lounge. Winkie was still ashen, but she had dried her face and was sitting primly, her hands gripped in her lap and her head erect. "I couldn't bring myself to go out there," she said to me, "but I did look through the

window. That poor, poor girl. What kind of person
would do such a dreadful thing?"

"The police will find out as soon as possible." I
went to the window. The body had been enclosed in a
bag and was being placed in the ambulance, and as I
watched, a tow truck pulled up next to the white car.
Turning back, I said, "Where are the other girls tonight?"

"I don't know," she said blankly. "They come and
go as they wish, and there are no curfews anymore.
When I was in school, we had study hall every evening
during the week and had to be in the house by midnight on the weekends. Now they all have their own
keys, although we do have the locks rekeyed at least
once a semester, since one of the girls inevitably loses
hers. I switch on the security system at midnight. This
requires the girl to punch in a four-digit code, as well
as use her doorkey. Very often she'll have had too
much to drink and will forget the code or hit the wrong
button. Either results in the alarm going off, and the
girl has to explain her thoughtlessness to the standards
committee."

I was about to ask if the committee could pass down
the death penalty when I heard increasingly strident
voices from the foyer. Peter's was easy to recognize;
the other was more elusive, and I frowned as I strained
to identify it.

"Eleanor Vanderson," Winkie said without enthusiasm.

Her theory was confirmed as the woman thus tagged
came into the room, her heels clattering like a machine
gun. She was dressed more casually than she'd been
the night we met, but her jacket and trousers were by
no means shoddy and her hair was impeccable. "What
is going on, Winkie?" she asked unsteadily. "Are those
men who they say they are? Has something happened
to one of the girls?"

"There was an accident, Eleanor. Jean Hall was hit
by a car in the alley." Winkie made an effort to stand,

but sank back down and covered her face with her hands.

Eleanor froze as Peter and Jorgeson passed through the room and disappeared into the kitchen. "Jean Hall? Are you sure? I can't believe . . . Could you please explain this, Mrs. Malloy?"

Beginning to feel like a cassette player, I told her what had happened to Jean.

"But that's dreadful," she said as she sat down next to Winkie and patted her back. "Jean was such an asset to the chapter, always enthusiastic and cooperative, eager to organize activities for the pledge class. Do you remember her initiation, Winkie? She looked angelic in her white dress, didn't she? When she sang the Kappa Theta Eta prayer, I nearly cried."

"Why are those police cars parked in the alley?" demanded Rebecca from the doorway of the lounge.

"They strung yellow tape all over the place and wouldn't let us through," Pippa added indignantly, standing on her toes so she could see over Rebecca's shoulder. "When the ambulance came by, we literally had to stand in the ditch."

I waited for a brief moment to see if Debbie Anne Wray might appear over Pippa's shoulder with additional complaints, but she did not. I left Winkie and Eleanor to tell them what had happened, went out the front door, and cut across the lawn to my porch. Only a short time earlier I'd been within forty feet of it, lost in a reverie of food and drink, but I'd been sidetracked into violence and death.

I was halfway up the stairs when I realized I'd forgotten to tell Peter about my encounter with Arnie, maybe because it had had such a dreamlike quality—or nightmarish, anyway. Why had he been hiding beside the Kappa house? He'd admitted he was in what he called a sticky situation, but I couldn't imagine what it was. I doubted he'd stolen Debbie Anne's car and run over Jean as she approached the house. Arnie was an ambulatory catastrophe, but he was motivated by the preservation of his pickled condition rather than by innate wickedness.

I went to my bedroom window and looked at the sorority house. All of the lights were ablaze on the ground floor, including those in Winkie's suite. The top of the screen was visible within a bush. I'd also forgotten to tell her what I'd done or ask Peter to have one of his men replace it. My lapse would allow Katie to sneak back in after a night of terrorizing the town, however, and Winkie would surely notice its absence in the morning.

A campus police car stopped in front of the house. It was too dark to tell if the two officers were the ones I'd encountered previously, but it seemed likely that Peter had sent for them to get a full report about the prowlers. As they disappeared beneath the roof of the porch, yet another car pulled up to the curb. Hoping it might be Debbie Anne returning with a date and an alibi, I waited for someone to materialize.

The driver's door opened and a man stepped out of the car. I caught a glimpse of a round white face and a bald head that glittered in the bath of the streetlight. Massaging his chin and mouth with one hand, he stared at the house for a full minute, then climbed back into his car and drove away.

I went to my kitchen, where I found a note from Caron that stated she was spending the night at Inez's house. I made a pot of tea, heated the fettuccine, and retired to the living room to eat. I wasn't confident that Peter would appear before morning, but I was eager to find out if they'd located Debbie Anne. It could have been an accident, I thought as I envisioned her behind the wheel of the white car. The alley was dark and narrow, but the college kids drove down it as if it were an interstate, and on more than one occasion my hatchback had been imperiled.

However, I had no notions where she might go, nor was I inclined to walk the streets until dawn, plaintively calling her name in hopes of coaxing her out of a shadowy hideout. Assuring myself that Farberville's Finest would do just that, I went to bed.

Peter did not appear at the Book Depot until nearly noon. He hadn't shaved, I noted with a wince as he nuzzled my neck, although he had changed into a fresh shirt and another of his expensive Italian suits. "Let's go away next weekend," he said, displaying a goodly amount of seductive charm. "A loaf of bread, a jug of wine . . ."

"Did you find Debbie Anne?"

He released me and folded his arms. "No, we did not find Debbie Anne, my dear snoop. She didn't return to the sorority house last night, and hasn't shown up as of now. She didn't go to her classes, the library, or her parents' home."

"How could she? You've impounded her car."

"It's one of those official things we do, along with the yellow tape and the fingerprints. The captain saw it on some television show and decided we ought to try it."

"Whose fingerprints were on the steering wheel?" I asked, refusing to react to his sarcasm. I had more important things on my meddlesome mind. "What about prints on the door handle? Did you find her purse?"

"I don't know, I don't know, and no." He gazed at me with an expression not unlike that of a condemned man on the gallows. "All you did was have dinner at the sorority house, Claire. It's evident that you didn't like them then, and I can think of no reason why you might have changed your mind. They've interfered with your sleep, burdened you with their personal problems—and their cat bit you, for pity's sake!"

"So what's your point?"

"Furthermore, as far as we know, we're dealing with involuntary manslaughter rather than a baffling mystery resplendent with red herrings and subtle, provocative clues. Debbie Anne Wray accidentally ran over the Hall girl, and now is sobbing at a friend's apartment until she gets up the nerve to turn herself in. This is not something in a mystery novel."

I contemplated mentioning it was right up my alley, in more ways than one, but instead nodded meekly and said, "I suppose not. Did you reach Jean's aunt?"

He shot me a suspicious look. "She came home around midnight, and the local police officers informed her of the accident. It turns out that Jean's parents live in California, but when the girl decided to come to school here, she filed some papers to have her aunt appointed her legal guardian."

"To save having to pay out-of-state tuition?"

"That's what the aunt said."

"I'm surprised the registrar fell for that ploy, but I must admit I'm not surprised Jean came up with it in the first place. She'd probably been planning to be a lawyer since birth, her little red face aglow with glee at the thought of suing the doctor for malpractice. Is her body going to be sent back to California?"

"In a day or two." Peter managed a smile or two, and had either quit suspecting my motives or was concealing it well. After a brief discussion about dinner the next evening, he left and I sat on the stool and tried to convince myself that he was right, that this wasn't anything more than an unfortunate accident. Debbie Anne would turn herself in, sniveling steadily, and ultimately the judicial system would slap her wrist and admonish her to be more careful in the future.

Then again, her reception at the sorority house might be chilly, to put it mildly, and National would demand the return of her pledge pin and faded pink sweatshirt. No more secret whistles and construction-paper cutouts in her future. No hope of singing the Kappa Theta Eta prayer so sweetly that Eleanor Vanderson would weep.

I was working on a secret whistle that I would share only with regular Book Depot customers when Caron and Inez came through the door. I tried it on them.

"This is not the time for parakeet imitations," Caron said as she slumped across the counter, covering her head with one arm and speaking in a hollow, muffled voice. "My life is in shambles. I might as well die right now and get it over with. Inez, call the funeral home and ask if they're running any specials this week. Tell them I'll need an ivory casket."

"I don't think I have a black dress," I said, frowning, "but I did buy a nice navy one last week."

She lifted her head far enough to glare malevolently at me. "Navy is not one of your colors, Mother. It makes you look like you've got one of those polysyllabic diseases."

"That's right, Mrs. Malloy," contributed Inez. "You really ought to wear earth tones like salmon and peach. For a funeral, you could wear gray, maybe."

"Thank you." I awaited the next development with jaded maternal patience.

I was rewarded with another malevolent look and a string of sighs. Caron at last found the energy to stand up. "Don't you care that my Life Is in Shambles?"

"Not as long as I know what to wear to your funeral. Can I rely on Inez's advice when I take clothes to the mortuary?"

"You're not funny, Mother."

I'd assumed otherwise, but merely said, "What's the cause of the ruination of your life at the tender age of fifteen? Out of deodorant? Expired subscription to *Seventeen* magazine? New pimples?"

Inez blinked sternly at me. "You shouldn't make jokes about it, Mrs. Malloy. Didn't you see the ambulances and police cars in the alley behind the Kappa house last night? There was a horrible accident and one of the girls was—"

"I wasn't making jokes about that. I know what happened, and it's not in any way amusing." I began to realize the source of Caron's eloquent and well-dramatized misery. She wasn't mourning Jean's death by any means. "This has to do with your Beautiful Self, doesn't it?"

"Pippa's thinking about dropping out for the rest of the summer and going with some friends to France or someplace dumb like that. She says she's too upset about Jean to stay in the house."

"And you can't continue doing the analyses without her?"

"Not if she takes her kit with her," Caron said with the long-suffering resignation characteristic of the age. "If you'd lent me the money in the first place, I wouldn't be in this situation, but you wouldn't so much as invest one lousy dollar in my career. Now there's no way I can buy a car at the end of the summer. All along, you've encouraged me to be re-sourceful and industrious, and you're the one who said—"

"That's enough," I said evenly. "I did not tell you to do something that goes beyond the ethical pale by ex-ploiting your friends. If you want to earn money, line up some baby-sitting jobs or yardwork. Run errands for people. Clean houses."

She stared at me as if I'd suggested she rob graves in order to sell the body parts. "You're telling me that I ought to scrub other people's toilets or rake their leaves or wipe their babies' noses? I can't believe it, I really can't! Come on, Inez, let's get out of here before Mother decides I ought to ride bulls in a rodeo."

Inez dutifully followed Caron out the door, and no doubt would nod just as dutifully until indignation faded and some degree of calculation replaced it. In the interim, the pedestrians on the sidewalk could be enter-tained by a lengthy tirade of artistically colorful phrases, explosive sighs, and accusations of parental perfidy likely to provoke a visit from the Department of Child Welfare.

Two uneventful hours later, the telephone rang, and I answered it with some hesitancy, hoping it wasn't a social worker.

"Mrs. Malloy?" whispered a voice. "This is Debbie Anne Wray."

6

"Debbie Anne," I said, clutching the edge of the counter to prevent myself from toppling off the stool to shatter like a cheap vase, "where are you?"

"I can't tell you. I was just calling to ask you to let my mama know I'm all right. They might have her line tapped so they can trace calls. It's long-distance, but I swear I'll pay you back when all this is over. Every last penny of it."

"I'll make the call for you, but you must tell me where you are, Debbie Anne, so that I can come pick you up. You're in trouble, and hiding out is not going to help the situation."

"Golly, Mrs. Malloy, you think I don't know I'm in trouble? I should have stayed home and maybe gone to the junior college like my friends, but my mama insisted I go to school in Farberville, and look where it's got me!"

"Where?" I said cleverly.

"In a passel of trouble, that's where. Please won't you call my mama for me? If the police call her first, she'll most likely have a heart attack right there in the middle of the kitchen." She rattled off a telephone number, waited until I regained a semblance of consciousness and found a pencil, repeated it, and added, "Don't worry about me, Mrs. Malloy. She'll never find me, and even if she figures it out, she'll be too scared to come here. Once she's been arrested, I'll come right to your store and pay you back for the call."

"Who is this 'she' you keep mentioning, Debbie Anne?"

"I'd like to tell you, but I promised I wouldn't. If I did, I'd be in worse trouble than I already am. Why, they could arrest me, you know, and lock me up tighter'n bark on a tree—especially if she lies about it and they believe her. In the end everybody'll know it was her idea, but I don't aim to sit in jail until she admits it."

I closed my eyes and sought inspiration, but nothing was forthcoming (except an embryonic headache). However, I was a wily and well-seasoned inquisitor, and she was but a freshman in more ways than one. I took a wild guess. "I don't think Winkie would want to see you in jail. She'll admit it."

"Huh? I'm talking about Jean Hall, Mrs. Malloy. Somebody just drove up, so I've got to go. Have a nice day."

After I'd grown bored listening to the dial tone, I replaced the receiver and tried to make sense of the conversation. Unless Debbie Anne was terrified by the possibility of being haunted by a diaphanous, chain-rattling law student, she wasn't aware that Jean was dead. On the contrary, she was worried about being locked up "tighter'n bark on a tree" (the quaint phrase did not refer, presumably, to a birch tree) because of something Jean might accuse her of doing, or of having done, or of planning to do in the future. Whatever it was would result in incarceration until Jean admitted her guilt, at which time Debbie Anne would be vindicated.

I knew Debbie Anne's parents had been contacted by the police, but I'd promised to call them and I was a bit curious about their reaction. No one answered, nor did a mechanized voice suggest I leave a message at the sound of the beep. Resolving to remember to try later, I tucked the piece of paper with the number into my pocket.

The police were not usually brought in on cases in which the perpetrator shared the secret whistle with someone outside the sisterhood. Surely Debbie Anne knew that, I told myself as I dialed Peter's office number. He was out, I was informed by a woman with a chilly voice, who subsequently declined to share the details of his destination or his estimated time of return. I left a message for him to call, waited the rest of the afternoon for him to do so, periodically tried Debbie Anne's home number with no success, and locked the store at seven.

I hesitated under the portico that had once protected ladies with bustles from rain when they'd debarked from the train and waited for their carriages. These days the ladies tended to wear jeans and T-shirts, and rarely bustled. Nor, frankly, did I, even during prosperous times when I could afford such behavior.

The beer garden was too rowdy for my taste on Saturday evenings, and my apartment was apt to be occupied by a teenaged tragedienne who'd had all afternoon to drape the living room in black crepe and polish her performance for the final act. Unwilling to be subjected to it, I walked up the hill to Luanne's store to see if I could interest her in fajitas, cheese dip, and speculation.

The "closed" sign hung on the inside of the door, and the windows of her apartment above the store were dark. I couldn't remember if Luanne had mentioned plans for the evening, but it didn't much matter. As I stood on the sidewalk, hands on my hips, frowning at my undeniably comely reflection while I debated what to do, I felt a twinge of sympathy for Debbie Anne Wray. How many nights had she been in the mood for food and chatter, only to be rebuffed by her so-called sisters? She had no place else to go, no one else on whom to rely.

I had my apartment, but I would be forced to listen to Caron's insufferable whines. The Book Depot was bleak and inhospitable after dark, inclined to creak as if trains of bygone days were racing by to the next abandoned station. If Peter were home, we could cuddle on the sofa and watch inane movies, but he might be occupied until all hours. It occurred to me that I'd insulated myself too well, and my insistence on self-reliance would reduce me to a half order of fajitas.

"Ho, Mrs. Malloy," called a familiar voice as a bicycle sailed down the sidewalk on what I felt was a collision course.

I shrank into the doorway and fluttered my fingers at my science fiction hippie. In honor of the weekend, he'd combed the crumbs out of his wispy beard and tied his ponytail with a relatively clean shoelace. His blue workshirt was unsoiled, if also unironed. He braked in front of me and put a foot down to steady himself.

"You ever find that copy of *Bimbos?*" he asked. Behind the smudged lenses of his glasses, his eyes sparkled, either from friendliness or from the recent inhalation of an illicit substance.

"No, but I ordered one for you, and it should be here next week. Would you like to join me for fajitas and beer? My treat, naturally."

"Is this like a date?"

"This is like a dinner," I said firmly, although inwardly I was quivering like an adolescent at a junior high dance. I was on the verge of withdrawing my offer and scurrying away when he nodded, and shortly thereafter I was perched on the back of his bike and we were zooming down the sidewalk.

Several hours later I emerged from the restaurant, satiated not only with food and beer but also with a heady conversation about the manuscript he was writing, well over a thousand pages already and still in the germinal stages of its plot. It was an alternative history that concerned the impact on our modern culture had Napoleon refused to the us (as in U.S.) the eight-hundred-odd-thousand square miles known as the Louisiana Territory.

I was pondering the convolutions of *Nebrasqué* as I approached the Kappa Theta Eta house. It looked innocent, as if the tragedy of the previous evening had never taken place. Lights were on in the front room, and in Winkie's suite. With Debbie Anne still in hiding, only three occupants were left: Winkie, Pippa, and Rebecca. Pippa was threatening to leave for the summer, which meant Eleanor Vanderson might decide to close the house. For her, a *coup d'autorité,* for me, a *coup d'éclat.*

I may have been smiling complacently when I saw a tiny light in a third-floor window. It blinked out, but after a moment, it appeared in another window, illuminating a construction-paper cat on the wall for a brief moment, and then again blinked out. I tried to convince myself I'd had one fajita too many, but when I spotted the light in yet a third room, I dismissed the heresy.

Someone was prowling on the third floor, moving through the rooms at the front of the house, apparently unimpeded by locks. And doing so stealthily, in that a person with a legitimate presence would find it more expedient to switch on the ceiling light fixture rather than risk stubbed toes and bruised shins.

I had no idea what to do. I was barely able to prevent myself from clasping my hands together and fluttering my eyelashes in the timeless tradition of gothic heroines. I had options, but racing upstairs to confront the prowler was not high on the list. There were three people living in the house; one of them might have been doing some sort of ritualistic room check, as required by National. Or Debbie Anne might have been hiding up there since the previous night, I told myself slowly. The police had been told no one currently lived on the second or third floor, and therefore might have searched in a perfunctory manner, ascertaining only that lights were off and doors were locked. If she'd hidden until they left, she could be staying in her old bedroom and using the communal pay telephone in the hall. And creeping from room to room in search of clean towels or pink paper cats.

As I congratulated myself on the theory, a face appeared in a window. It was not Debbie Anne Wray, unless she'd shaved her head and put wadded cotton in her cheeks. I wasn't completely sure, but the man bore a remarkable resemblance to the one who'd driven up to the house the previous evening, parked for a minute, and left. He jerked away from the window so abruptly that I assumed he'd seen me staring at him from the sidewalk.

I forced myself to shrug and stroll toward my apartment, seemingly unconcerned by his presence on the third floor. I was unable to whistle, but I made every effort to look as if I might at any moment. Only when I was in the foyer of my duplex did I go storming up the stairs, gasping in a most unattractive fashion. I pounded on the front door and yelled, "Caron! It's an emergency! Hurry up!"

I'd dumped the contents of my purse on the floor and was pawing through the litter for my key when the door opened. "Mother," Caron said, her lip curled in distaste, "what on earth are you doing?"

I told her to pick up everything, hurried around her, and dialed the fateful three-digit number. "There's a prowler in the Kappa Theta Eta house!" I said. "It's on Campus Boulevard near the corner of—"

"You'll have to call campus security, ma'am. It's in their jurisdiction."

"I don't have time to—" I stopped, lowered my brow, and growled, "Give me the number."

After I'd reported the problem to the campus police, I banged down the receiver and nearly knocked Caron down on my way to my bedroom window, where I did my best to watch the front and side yards for any sign of the prowler.

"Are you having a hot flash?" Caron asked from the doorway. "Most women don't have them until after the age of fifty, but it's not totally unheard of in medical circles. You can look forward to osteoporosis, urinary incontinence, and my favorite, genital atrophy."

"Will you shut up!" I said without turning.

"Irritability is another symptom, you know. Watch out if the doctor puts you on a combination of estrogen and androgen. You may feel great, but side effects include hirsutism and acne. You might turn into a spotty troglodyte."

This time I tried a bit more vigorously to knock her down as I went past her, through the living room, and downstairs to my porch to await the campus police. My two old chums pulled up within minutes, and I trotted across the yard and caught up with them as they headed for the Kappa house.

"Another prowler, Mrs. Malloy?" said Officer Terrance.

"I saw a man in that room." I pointed at the pertinent window, which was black and blank, and then explained the progression of the flashlight and tried to describe the face I'd seen in the window. All I could do was hope it sounded less preposterous to them than it did to me.

He and Officer Michaels exchanged skeptical looks, but continued across the porch to the door. I followed them, praying that the delay hadn't resulted in mass murder in the lounge, and was relieved when Winkie opened the door with a puzzled frown rather than a bloody gurgle.

"Your neighbor here reported another prowler," said Terrance. "This time, according to her, he's up on the third floor, carrying a flashlight and—"

"Men are not allowed on the third floor," Winkie said automatically, then put her hand to her mouth and stepped back. "Don't just stand there—go find him and bring him down here!"

She looked so small and frightened that I edged past the policemen and put my arm around her. "You need to give them the keys to all the bedrooms and storage rooms, Winkie," I said. "Until we're sure he's not hiding up there, you're not safe. Where are the girls?"

"They went out together to see a movie." She glanced at the dark staircase. "How could someone be up there? I made quite sure the back door was locked, and I've had my door open all evening, waiting for Pippa and Rebecca to return just to reassure myself that they were safe. No one came through the front door."

"The keys, ma'am?" Terrence said impatiently.

"Yes, of course, but I'll have to accompany you. Even with no girls in residence, I cannot . . ." She went into her suite and returned with the key ring. The keys clinked and her voice was thin and uneven as she said, "Well, then, shall we go upstairs, gentlemen?"

I trailed along, telling myself I was doing so to give moral support to Winkie. She switched on the lights as we came to the third-floor hall, then began unlocking doors and waiting as the officers searched each room. The storerooms that were used for luggage were empty, as were the pink-tiled bathrooms and the shower stalls. The bedrooms were incredibly small, some jammed with as many as three or four bunk beds, all with built-in furniture, well-worn textbooks, electronics equipment, oddments that had been overlooked during frenzied departures, a plethora of construction-paper cats, and the aura of a shabby hotel that had seen way too many better days.

After the final room had been searched, we repeated the process on the second floor, found nothing more intriguing than a solitary mouse, and returned to the first floor.

"We'd better check the basement," I said.

Winkie stiffened. "This is the door that leads to the basement," she said as she gestured at a door that had been painted pink and was almost invisible. "There is only one key, and it is in my possession at all times. Furthermore, I have a clear view of the door from the rocking chair in my living room. I promise you that no one can go down there without my knowledge."

Officer Terrance glanced at me, then said, "If there was a prowler, he's gone now. Everything's okay, but I would like to say it's not wise to allow the girls to leave things in their rooms all summer. You're asking for trouble."

"Normally, we don't allow it, but since the house is occupied this summer, I didn't insist they remove all their belongings. I didn't realize how many of the girls have computers these days. When I was in school, we shared a portable typewriter."

"We've had a lot of thefts on the campus this month," he said. "Not just in the dorms and houses, but in the departments, classrooms, maintenance sheds, you name it."

"Better get your exterior locks rekeyed," added Michaels.

"I did exactly that three days ago, after Debbie Anne and our house corps president were attacked outside the house. There's no way this man could have a key unless ..."

"Unless he has Debbie Anne's," I finished for her.

"Oh, my goodness," she gasped. "Then we're not safe here! This man could murder us in our beds! My God, Claire, I'm responsible for the welfare of the girls."

The look they exchanged this time was weary, leaving me to be skeptical as Terrance said, "We'll patrol the house every hour. If there was a man on the third floor, he knows he was seen and he's long gone. Besides, you have Ms. Malloy here to keep a surveillance on your house, night and day."

They left, but Winkie seemed so distraught that I offered to stay with her until Pippa and Rebecca returned. I was leery of accepting her invitation for tea in her suite, but she assured me that Katie was curled up on her little bed. I called my apartment to let Caron know what I was doing, but the line was busy and I doubted she'd be overcome with worry about someone who insisted on wearing an inappropriate palette.

"Debbie Anne called me early this afternoon," I said when we were settled with tea in her suite. "She wanted me to call her mother."

"She called you? Are you and her mother acquainted in some way?"

"Debbie Anne's afraid her mother's telephone line has been tapped by the authorities and they could trace her call."

"Where is she?"

"She wouldn't tell me. The odd thing is that she spoke as if she were unaware of Jean's death." I could have added more, but I wanted to assess Winkie's reaction to each tidbit.

"But how could she not be? It was her car, and she must have been driving. Rebecca borrows Pippa's car on occasion, and I've let Jean use mine when hers was in the shop, but I can hardly imagine anyone wanting to borrow Debbie Anne's old clunker. Last fall some of the girls signed a petition to forbid her from parking it in front of the house. They felt that it made the house look disreputable, as if we were on the verge of putting rusty pickup trucks on concrete blocks, scattering broken appliances in the yard, and raising farm animals. Even though I ordered them to forget such foolish snobbery, Debbie Anne cried for days."

"Unless she's a skillful actress, she doesn't know what happened," I said. "When I first saw the flashlight on the third floor, I wondered if she was hiding up there. But it was a man, the same one who parked briefly in front of the house last night while the police were here. He's short and plump, with a round white face and a basically bald head. Does he sound like anyone you know?"

"And he was on the third floor tonight?" Without waiting for an answer, Winkie went into her kitchen, opened and closed the refrigerator, and returned with the decanter and two wineglasses. "This has been too much—all the excitement, the police, the ambulance, prowlers in every nook and cranny. Will you join me?"

"Yes, thank you," I said as I watched her slosh wine into the glasses. She'd withdrawn her emotions and was the epitome of indecipherable blandness, but it was clear she had a good idea of the identity of the man I'd described. And wasn't going to tell me. "Even if this mysterious man"—I gave the phrase a bit of emphasis—"had access to Debbie Anne's house key, he couldn't have used it to open bedroom doors, could he? They're all keyed differently."

She handed me a glass and sat down in the rocking chair. "Yes, they are. Each girl has two keys—one for the exterior locks and one for her bedroom. It doesn't make any sense, and I'm beginning to wonder if you might have seen a reflection in the window, perhaps from a car driving through the campus. As for this face, it was nothing more than the man in the moon shining back at you. You did say you'd been drinking beer, dear."

I took a deep swallow of wine, and when I could trust myself, said, "So I did, and in any case, it wasn't Debbie Anne. Do you have any idea where she could be hiding? Does she have any friends from her hometown who're going to summer school? Is there a professor she might have gone to?"

"The police asked me those questions last night, and all I could say was that we have sixty-seven girls in the house, and I cannot keep track of their friends and confidantes. On the rare weekends when there were no pledge activities, Debbie Anne went home. The pledges are strongly encouraged to involve themselves in Kappa projects in order to strengthen the bonds of sisterhood in anticipation of initiation. Jean was the pledge trainer last year, and she did a marvelous job. She organized picnics, treasure hunts, outings to rest homes and child-care centers, parties with fraternity pledge classes, all sorts of things. I can't remember when a pledge class has been so busy."

It sounded more like isolation to me, an attempt to erase or at least minimalize their individual personalities and mold them into genuine Kappa material. All that enforced togetherness would have driven me into the nearest built-in closet. I'd endured two years in a dormitory, but I'd done so at a civilized distance, eschewing floor meetings and popcorn parties, and moved into an apartment as soon as it was permitted by the *in loco parentis* policy of the college.

The squeaks of the rocker were barely perceptible as Winkie gazed at the wall above my head. Her eyes darted not from flock to flock, but from thought to thought, as if she were filling in a crossword puzzle in her mind.

As tempting as it was, I reminded myself I could not shake her until she relented and told me what she suspected. "Debbie Anne said something else that troubles me," I said conversationally. "Not only was she unaware of Jean's death, she seemed frightened by the idea that Jean might accuse her of something that would end in arrest."

"Jean? I find that impossible to believe. Jean was one of the few girls who never came home drunk, never failed to sign out for the weekend, never was late for our Monday-night dinners, never skipped a chapter meeting or a house meeting. She was so very responsible, unlike Debbie Anne, who more often than not claimed she'd lost track of the time or had a flat tire or some silly excuse." She finished her wine, refilled her glass, and sat back to regard me with the smile of a used-car salesman who'd just closed a deal. "Jean Hall was a girl of impeccable character and breeding. No one ever so much as breathed a word against her."

But someone did run her down in the alley, I considered mentioning, but kept it to myself. Winkie was not going to offer me anything that might explain Debbie Anne's slightly incoherent avowal that Jean had coerced her into something illegal. Girls of impeccable character and breeding didn't do that sort of thing; they simply became Kappa Theta Etas.

The doorbell rang. Winkie patted my shoulder as she went past me and out to the foyer to open the door. "Why, Eleanor," she said, "whatever brings you here at this hour?"

"I'm so worried about all this, and about you and the girls, and even little Katie. I was at a charity bridge party all afternoon, and this evening at a dreary reception for a faculty candidate. I wanted to stop by and find out if the police have made any progress."

Winkie remained in the doorway, smiling politely at her guest but managing to shoot a quick—and noticeably panicked—look in my direction. I grabbed the decanter and glasses and took them into the kitchen, and was relaxed on the sofa by the time Winkie and Eleanor came into the suite.

"Claire," Eleanor murmured with a gracious nod. "How nice of you to keep Winkie company."

"She seemed nervous," I said with an equally gracious nod, "and Pippa and Rebecca are out."

Eleanor accepted a cup of tea from Winkie. "Has Debbie Anne come back? I heard on the morning news that the car is registered to her parents and that she'd obtained a campus parking permit. It pains me to say it, but the evidence is certainly mounting up against her. I wish I knew how to help her, but we don't even know where she is or how to assure her that . . . we want to get this settled as soon as possible. How terrible for her to be alone at this time, no doubt terrified of what will happen to her."

I waited for Winkie to mention the call I'd had, but all she said was, "I was just telling Claire what a wonderful girl Jean was, how enthusiastic and energetic. Some of the pledges must have wondered if she was a drill sergeant, considering how busy she kept them."

"Yes, indeed," Eleanor said in a strained voice.

"And she herself was always so busy," Winkie continued. "With her zealous dedication to classes and to house activities, it was a miracle that she found time for a social life. I spoke to her about it, suggesting that she relax and try to enjoy her senior year, but she assured me that she was enjoying it very much."

"I hope as much as you've enjoyed the year, dear Winkie. All your responsibilities must exhaust you."

I felt as if I were watching them toss a hand grenade back and forth. Either the room was oppressively warm or they were filling it with inarticulated anger, along with their sugary words and thin, meaningless smiles.

Eleanor unexpectedly lobbed the grenade to me. "Winkie's on call day and night, and as the housemother, she must have a reputation and demeanor above reproach. I'm afraid I myself would find it a relentless burden. Don't you agree?"

"Oh, yes," I said, fingering the metaphorical pin and discovering it was loose. "I'd hate to face life without an occasional scotch or a lovely Sunday morning in my shabbiest bathrobe and bare feet."

I thought I'd passed it to Winkie, but it ended up in Eleanor's manicured fingers. "I understand you have a relationship with that handsome police lieutenant who was here last night. Rosen, isn't it?" She laughed as I opened my mouth to protest. "Farberville's a small town, Claire, and you've gained some notoriety with your involvement in those mysterious cases." To Winkie, she added, "Our neighbor is a renowned amateur sleuth, which explains why she was so quick and clever when that awful man was prowling in the yard. She knew just what to do."

It struck me as an opportune moment to mention the most recent prowler, but Winkie again ignored the obvious. "So quick and clever," she murmured. "So quick and clever."

I didn't feel quick or clever, and I was tired of the grenade game. If I'd heard anything worthy of my analytical attention, I had no idea what it was. Smothering a yawn, I bade them good night and left, not caring which of them was blown to smithereens, metaphorically or otherwise.

7

"I hear you went out with another man last night," Peter said as he came into the Book Depot. During the school year, it was closed on Sunday afternoons, but I was too desperate to risk missing a single sale, and at that particular moment I was considering the possibility of adding a section of Greek-related items. Not virgin olive oil and ouzo, but cutesy coffee mugs, visors, clipboards, and pastel stationery, all with appropriate letterheads. Other stores in town carried that sort of thing, but I was the closest to the campus and might do well. Then again, it would be challenging to put on makeup every morning if I were unable to look at myself in the mirror.

"I'm impressed with the breadth of your surveillance," I said evenly. "Where have you been? I was beginning to suspect you and Jorgeson were sharing romantic moments at the cabin. The mere thought of such treachery is what drove me to the arms of another man—that, and the need to avoid my daughter until she regains her grip on fiscal reality."

"That could take years." Peter propped his elbows on the counter. He wore a cotton sweater rather than a suit, but his cheeks were smooth and I caught a whiff of the after-shave I'd given him for his birthday. After a moment, I realized I'd given him the sweater for Christmas. The rest of his clothing was of his own doing; a lady never proffers trousers or underwear, and the cost of his shoes was comparable to my rent.

"Jorgeson's not bad," he continued, "but his ankles are bony and he sweats. So who's this guy?"

"Merely one of those potential millionaires one meets on the street every day. As soon as his book hits the best-seller list, he's going to whisk me away to some swanky resort with an employee whose sole duty is to swat mosquitos."

"I also heard you called 911 last night, and then the campus police, who responded promptly to your latest claim to have seen a prowler at that blasted sorority house. You might as well move in and save yourself the bother of dashing over there every hour."

I told him about the man I'd seen in the window, adding that I was convinced he was the same man who had stopped in the street the night Jean Hall was killed. "And when I described him to Winkie, she reacted as if she knew him," I concluded, doing my best to hide my frustration.

"But refused to share the name with you?" He flashed his perfect white teeth at me. "How uncooperative of her. I'll go by tomorrow and see if she'll be more forthright with an officer of the law. Is there anything else you've discovered and failed to share with us?"

I thought about attempting to strike a bargain with him, but I had a feeling he might interpret my offer as blackmail rather than a display of camaraderie. I related the gist of Debbie Anne's call, and said, "She sounded genuinely worried about something Jean was going to do to her, and I doubt she was bluffing. However, I keep characterizing her as a soggy-nosed ninny, but she did graduate from high school and was accepted at Farber College, so she can't be totally devoid of wits. Those who know her better than I seem to think she's devious and deceitful, and capable of manipulation. For all I know, she could be a contemporary Mata Hari with a secret agenda that forbodes ill for the future Kappa Theta Eta alumnae pool. Maybe she hired this prowler and staged her encounter with him to fool us, gave him her keys, and sent him to the house last night to . . ."

"Plant bombs? Bug the bedrooms? Kill the cat?"

"I don't know," I muttered, unamused by his condescending attitude. There I was, willing to share my ideas and pass along information, and in return, I was rewarded with smirky intonations, delicately arched eyebrows, and those damn teeth. It was time for a new game plan. "What progress have you made? Did you identify any fingerprints in the car?"

"With the exception of some unremarkable smudges, they belong to the person who reputedly occupied Debbie Anne Wray's bedroom at the sorority house, used her toothbrush, and placed the photograph of her parents on the desk. The blood on the bumper, hood, and tires matches that of the victim. A shard of glass from the broken headlight was taken from the body. The prosecuting attorney won't file charges until we have her in custody and can finalize our report, but even if it was an accident, he'll probably opt for negligent homicide and leaving the scene of a personal injury—both felonies. No one admits to having any idea where she is, so we're just waiting for her to get tired of hiding. I suppose we could put a tap on your telephone."

"Not without a court order signed by Sandra Day O'Connor. If Debbie Anne calls again, I'll persuade her to tell me where she is and you'll be the first to know. But I am not going to allow you to eavesdrop on my calls or monitor my private life as if I were a criminal. How did you know that I had dinner with a man last night?"

"One of the desk sergeants was at the restaurant and said something about it," Peter said. He had the decency to look somewhat embarrassed to be caught gossiping, which gave me a measure of satisfaction. "I was teasing, Claire. You're perfectly free to see anyone you want, or date other men, or spend the weekend with them. It's increasingly clear that our relationship isn't going in the direction I'd hoped it might. Maybe seeing other people would help both of us figure out what's for the best."

"Maybe it would," I said without inflection, inwardly appalled at the thought of even a second dinner with my science fiction hippie, who was harmless (when not discoursing on his manuscript) but hardly as stimulating as Peter. Rather than allow the conversation to lapse into something more suitable for a romance novel, I told him I had work to do and he huffed away.

I did not burst into tears, but I admit I sniffled just a bit as I dusted the self-help racks with more than usual vigor. My predicament was of my own making, which made it all the more irritating, and by the time Caron and Inez came into the bookstore, I'd dusted every book, swept the floor, cleaned out the drawer beneath the cash register, and rearranged the racks in order to determine if I could add sorority and fraternity paraphernalia.

"Menopause," Caron explained to Inez. "Her face is red and she's drenched in sweat. Furthermore, she's been behaving very erratically lately, and—"

"Help me move this table," I interrupted in a glacial voice, struggling not to imagine the warm satisfaction I would receive if I throttled her on the spot.

Inez blinked soberly at me. "My mother started having hot flashes in her mid-forties, Mrs. Malloy. She said she felt as if she were wrapped in an electric blanket set as high as it would go. Sometimes she'd start crying for no reason, but the doctor gave her estrogen and it really worked."

The intensity of my scowl provoked them into mutely helping me drag a heavy oak table across the room and situate it in front of the window. "I am not having hot flashes," I said, panting. "Peter and I had a disagreement, and I was perturbed. I'm not even forty yet, for pity's sake, and I do not care for all this unsolicited advice from teenage girls whose knowledge of medical matters is gleaned from soap operas. Do you understand?"

"Whatever." Caron wandered toward the office. "You had a call earlier this afternoon, by the way. Some man, but he didn't leave his name or number."

As the door squeaked, she added with ill-disguised relish, "He said you'd better mind your own business or you'd be sorry."

"What?" I gasped. "Tell me exactly what he said."

"I just did, Mother. A rather poor choice of clichés, if you ask me, but the whole thing was probably a wrong number. I mean, why would some man call you? Do you have any diet sodas stashed in here? I'm about to Die of Thirst after all that work."

Inez had edged behind the travel guides, as if she feared my purported hot flashes might escalate into an incendiary eruption. "We don't have much time," she called to Caron. "You have an appointment in less than an hour and it'll take us a while to walk over there, especially if we go by the Kappa house to get the kit."

"Who's the victim?" I asked her.

"Mrs. Verbena, the art teacher at the high school. I don't think she was all that enthusiastic, but she finally said Caron could come by and explain it."

"She's an Elegant," Caron said as she returned empty-handed. "Of course, I won't tell her until she agrees to pay me. My Beautiful Self consultants have to watch out for sneaky people who try to weasel free advice." Her eyes narrowed as she regarded my jeans and black T-shirt. "Some of us certainly could use some, free or otherwise. Come on, Inez, we have to go all the way to the Kappa house, and then turn around and go all the way back to Mrs. Verbena's house. If I had my own kit, we wouldn't have to walk the extra six blocks, but no one would lend me the money for one crummy week so I could get it. That's why we have to go all the way to the—"

"So Pippa didn't leave?" I asked before we reheard the entirety of the itinerary, which in her mind seemed to require miles of walking barefooted on glowing coals.

"If she'd left, I wouldn't be able to borrow her kit, would I?" She jabbed Inez. "I need to go home and change clothes. This forest green is good, but my royal-blue blouse really demonstrates how effective the analysis is. If you'd stop being selfish about your new earrings, I could probably do an accessory awareness, too. Come on, it's going to take at least half an hour to get the kit and find Mrs. Verbena's house. If we're seconds late, she'll make up an excuse to leave and we'll have hiked All Over Town for nothing."

Inez trudged after her, but turned around and came back to put her hand on my arm. "Why don't you call my mother, Mrs. Malloy? I'm sure she'll be happy to give you the name of her doctor."

"I'll think about it," I said through clenched teeth. Once they were gone, I sat on the table and stared at the cobwebs on the rafters, wishing I'd stayed in bed with the Sunday newspaper and countless pots of tea—or with the blanket pulled over my head. First Peter, then the girls, and to top off the afternoon, an anonymous threatening call.

After another bout of sniffling, I bestirred myself and dialed the number Debbie Anne had given me. This time a woman answered, and I told her who I was and why I was calling.

"I am worried sick about this," Imogene Wray said, having identified herself as such in a twangy drawl identical to her daughter's. "The police calling, and then Brodie—he's the deputy sheriff—coming by to make sure Debbie Anne wasn't under the bed or out in the barn. My husband's ulcer flared up so bad he finally went over to the drugstore to buy another bottle of that gooey pink medicine. I can't imagine what's gotten into Debbie Anne. She's always been so sweet and respectful, never ever in any kind of trouble. You can ask any of her teachers at the school, and they'll tell you the same thing."

"I want to help her, but I don't know where she is or how to find her. Has she ever mentioned any friends who live in Farberville and might let her stay with them?"

"I don't reckon she has any friends outside the sorority," Imogene said promptly. "That's all she ever talks about, how they had a party or played cards or went to the picture show together. They seem to keep her awful busy when she's not studying, but I guess the reason for joining a group like that is to have girl-friends who are as close as sisters."

I told Mrs. Wray that I'd let her know if I found Debbie Anne and replaced the receiver. It appeared that Debbie Anne had failed to communicate the true nature of her relationship with her sorority sisters, but that was understandable and by no means proof that she was generally mendacious.

What I needed was not estrogen therapy, but a clear idea of Debbie Anne's personality. And of Jean Hall's, I added as I wrote each name on a discarded envelope. Presumably, they were opposites, but I had no idea which personified good, which evil. Winkie and Eleanor had made their position known, and Rebecca and Pippa were likely to concur. Imogene Wray dissented, but she was biased. Peter didn't care. I seemed to be the only person willing to defend Debbie Anne, although I wasn't going to do it until I had more evidence about her.

Unable to rally the energy to play devil's advocate, I tried a scenario in which she was nothing more complex than a soggy-nosed ninny. If this persona accidentally hit Jean in the alley, she would have leaped out of the car and dashed inside to call an ambulance. She might have been distressed to the point of hysteria, but if she'd panicked, she would have gone no farther than my apartment to sob on my shoulder (if I let her, and since it was my scenario, I instead made her sit at the kitchen table) and whine about her troubles.

Her telephone call added to my confusion. If she had been telling the truth, she hadn't been driving her car, and had gone into hiding for another reason—one that had to do with illegal activity instigated by that lovely girl Jean, who was in no condition to be questioned.

The anonymous call was equally bewildering. Arnie? The man-in-the-moon prowler? Some unknown figure who lacked the imagination to come up with an innovative threat? After all, I *was* minding my own business, or at least what business there was on a Sunday afternoon in June; it was hardly my fault that prowlers kept popping out of the Kappa shrubbery like possessed prairie dogs.

A growing sense of petulance provoked me into closing the bookstore several hours earlier than I'd intended. I took the long route home in order to avoid passing the sorority house, although I couldn't prevent myself from glancing at it as I approached my porch. Rebecca and Pippa sat on the top step, surrounded by unopened textbooks, notebooks, bags of chips, and cans of soda, clearly more interested in painting their fingernails than in the quest for knowledge.

I veered across the lawn and said, "Have you heard from Debbie Anne?"

Rebecca shook her head. "I'm not sitting here waiting for her to walk up the sidewalk so I can give her a welcoming hug. After what she did to Jean, she'd better have taken the first bus home to her little redneck enclave amid the pigsties and chicken coops." Her lovely blue eyes brimmed with tears, and her lovely voice with bitterness. "Jean and I were best friends since our first semester, and we shared a room until last year when we both moved into private rooms. It was going just great—until that pious little bitch pledged Kappa Theta Eta and ruined everything!"

"Pious?" I echoed.

"She didn't approve of anything, not even some of the boring public relations stuff the pledge class has to do every year. Apparently in her hometown, nobody ever smoked a cigarette or drank a glass of decent French wine, much less partied past midnight. Right before spring break, Jean bribed one of the Betas to take Debbie Anne out and get her good and drunk, but she drank half a martini, gagged on the olive, and threw up all over his front seat. What's that supposed to do for our reputation?"

I had no answer for that. "Debbie Anne did tell me that she was pressured to do things she felt were wrong."

"Such as?" Rebecca said with a faint sneer that reminded me of Jean.

"She said she couldn't tell me because I wasn't in
the sorority. Her faced turned red, however, and she
implied they were things that would upset her
preacher."

Pippa giggled. "She was probably thinking of the
Bedroom Olympics weekend. What a prude!"

"You have to consider her background," I said, hoping I didn't sound prudish. "But you're convinced she
was driving her car when Jean was struck?"

Rebecca leaned back and regarded me coolly.
"Winkie tried to convince us it was an accident, as did
Mrs. Vanderson, but I won't buy it. There's light in the
alley, and it's too narrow for someone to be driving
very fast. It's obvious that Debbie Anne did it on purpose. She murdered Jean out of jealousy."

Trying to mask my surprise, I said, "I would have
said it was more a case of wistfulness than of jealousy."

"Everybody in the house knew how jealous she was.
She stole silk blouses from Jean on at least two occasions, and she pretended to be overcome with astonish-
ment when Jean's tennis bracelet just happened to turn
up in *her* desk drawer. Maybe in the beginning she just
wanted to be like Jean, but became so obsessed that
eventually she had to be Jean. When she realized she
couldn't, she slandered her and finally killed her."

I certainly had no need to probe delicately to ascertain her opinion of Debbie Anne. I shifted my attention
to Pippa, who was not dimpling.

"It might have been an accident," she said in response to my implicit question, "but Debbie Anne's
awfully moody and reserved. She never contributed to
the conversation or told jokes, and it was like a total
waste of time trying to teach her to play bridge. One
night I found her hunkered in the shower as if she were
in a catatonic stupor. A real spook, if you ask me."

"A real bitch," growled Rebecca.

"And neither of you has any idea where she might be?" I asked with faint optimism.

Pippa gave me a facetiously sad look. "And neither of us cares. Mrs. Malloy, I don't know if Caron's said anything to you, but you really shouldn't wear black. It tends to emphasize all those wrinkles around your nose and chin, and it makes your complexion look ashy."

"How nice of you to notice," I said as my fingernails dug into my palms. "Caron mentioned that you were thinking about dropping out of school for the remainder of the summer. I presume you've changed your mind?"

"You what?" Rebecca turned on her so abruptly that fingernail polish splattered on her knee and dribbled onto the porch like viscous pink blood. "You're damn well not going to split for the summer, honey! We're both going to stay right here at the Kappa Theta Eta house for the duration, especially after what happened to Jean." She caught my bright-eyed look and forced a melancholy smile. "I lost one of my best friends, and I cannot bear to lose another so soon."

It sounded like a line from Tennessee Williams, and the setting was appropriate: decaying mansion, dusty summer afternoon, sisterhood gone awry, tumultuous emotions poorly disguised. All we needed was a surly male in a stained undershirt and a clattering streetcar.

I hesitated, but Rebecca was wiping the polish off her knee with a tissue and Pippa was shriveling into the woodwork. To the latter, I said, "It was kind of you to lend Caron your color analysis kit."

"Oh, it was nothing, and I feel sorry for her. I know what kind of psychological damage can be caused by feelings of economic deprivation, and it's important to feel a part of one's peer group at such a vulnerable age. I just hope she can make enough money this summer to buy a car and successfully integrate herself into her self-perceived community."

I repressed the urge to point out that Caron was neither economically deprived nor noticeably vulnerable, despite her incessant complaining to the contrary. Her

relationship with the infamous Rhonda Maguire was
the root of all evil, and I was disinclined to listen to a
spate of psychobabble from someone who dimpled—
sympathetically, no less.

"Please let me know if Debbie Anne comes back," I
said and headed for my apartment. I was halfway
through the downstairs door when a cacophony of rumbles, rattles, wheezes, and clanks caught my attention.
The green truck pulled to the curb, and visible through
the bug-splattered windshield was none other than
Arnie Riggles. He lurched across the passenger's seat
and disappeared, but after a moment the window on
that side began to descend in tiny jerks.

I had several questions for him, and it seemed an
auspicious moment to pose them. Before I could rally
sufficient enthusiasm, however, Rebecca hurried down
the sidewalk and began to converse through the window. She spoke rapidly and urgently, pausing for what
had to be responses from the pit of the passenger's
seat, and then reacting with increased urgency.
Stunned, I could only watch as she stepped back and
Arnie resurfaced behind the steering wheel and drove
past my house and around the corner. I looked back in
time to see Rebecca and Pippa entering the sorority
house. What on earth could strikingly beautiful, perfectly packaged Rebecca have to discuss with someone
as vile and oily as Arnie?

This was the second time he'd slipped away before
I could inquire into the parameters of his involvement,
and I decided it was high time to have a little talk with
him. The mere thought was enough to make my skin
itch as if I'd rolled in poison ivy and the pustules were
emerging. Rather than retreat to the bathtub, I reminded myself that I was the only person with any
desire to help Debbie Anne, whether or not she deserved it.

Arnie was not listed in the telephone directory. The
last time I'd been unfortunate enough to encounter
him, he'd been living in a storage room at the city animal shelter. He'd subsequently been fired—for just

cause—and I had no idea where he currently lived. I could have spent the remainder of the afternoon turning over rocks in the woods or crawling under bridges in hopes of finding him, but even I had limits (although Peter Rosen would be the last to acknowledge it).

I made a pot of tea and sat down on the sofa to rely on deductive prowess rather than physical exertion, being a fan of the armchair-detective genre. Reading about the women private eyes with brass bras and testosterone for brains had always left my fingers gritty and my eyes dazed with images of violence. Tea and intuition were . . . my cup of tea.

Arnie was employed by a remodeling contractor, more specifically a painter whose name I'd heard and dismissed as unworthy of notice. If I asked Winkie for his name, Rebecca might hear about it and realize I'd seen her talking to him; I wanted to confront him before he could be warned. Under no circumstances would I ask a certain cop to track down Arnie's address.

In the middle of the second pot of tea, it occurred to me that Eleanor Vanderson would know the painter's name, if not the details of Arnie's squalid personal life. There was only one Vanderson in the directory, and she herself answered on the third ring.

"This is Claire Malloy," I said, "and I was hoping—"

"Did Debbie Anne call you again? Do you know where she's hiding?"

"Sorry, but no. This has nothing to do with the horrible accident in the alley. I've been thinking about having the interior of my apartment painted, and I wanted to know the name of your painter—if you've found him competent and reliable, of course."

There was, as Caron would say, A Distinct Lull. "Why, I suppose I could give you his name, but thus far they haven't started painting. I'm afraid Winkie overstepped her authority when she promised the job to him and his assistant. National requires that we take bids in order to choose the most competitive rates, and I'm waiting to hear from several other contractors before I can finalize anything. Based on my one conversation with that man who claimed to know you, I'm as reluctant as you were to offer a recommendation. He's quite a character, isn't he? He's so"—she hesitated to find a phrase suitable for a dean's wife—"earthy and uninhibited."

Or dirty and crude, some of us might say. I instead said, "I might as well take bids, too. His name?"

"I'll have to find the folder." Papers shuffled in the background as she continued to talk. "My husband is forever complaining about the piles of paperwork and the amount of time I dedicate to the chapter, but now that my children have moved away and married, it helps to fill the void. Sometimes I wonder if it's immature of me to engross myself in what's basically a college activity, but it was so vital to me then and I want to do everything I can to ensure that the girls still have a memorable experience. And it is something for which I have a talent."

Serial killers had talent, too. "As long as you enjoy it," I murmured inanely, having agreed with her supposition that it was immature to devote one's energy to something that was indeed a college activity. It wasn't simply the response to a vacuum, I suspected, but a need for power. Her children grown, she'd replaced them with a group of girls who were depleted each spring but replenished each fall during rush.

"Here it is," she said with a laugh. "I feel as if I've been scuba diving through the paperwork. The primary contractor is Ed Whitbred." She spelled it for me, gave me a telephone number, then said, "Bear in mind I've not yet hired him, although his bid is the lowest I've received. Winkie has attested to his character, but as house corps president, it's my obligation to interview him personally and assure myself that he's reputable and honest."

"I don't suppose you have Arnie's address?"

"I believe I do. I needed to send some bidding forms

to Mr. Whitbred's office, but Arnie didn't know that
address and gave me his." Papers again began to rustle
like dried leaves; it was easy to imagine towering
stacks of folders, each emblazoned with Kappa Theta
Eta and of a uniform color. She made little noises of
exasperation for a long while, then congratulated herself and said, "It was in the wrong folder. He lives at
the Airport Arms Motel, which one can only assume is
in the vicinity of the airport."

"One can only assume." I thanked her for her time
and wished her a pleasant afternoon. Mine was less
likely to be that, especially if I spent it tracking down
and interrogating Arnie. Then again, if I stayed where
I was, Caron and Inez were apt to appear to share medical insights about my deteriorating body or regale me
with the details of Mrs. Verbena's analysis. Peter certainly wouldn't come by to visit.

Anyone who could find the airport could find the
Airport Arms Motel. I picked up my purse and went to
look for Arnie.

8

The Airport Arms Motel sat far back from the highway, fronted by a gravel parking lot that was sparsely populated by squatty cars, pickup trucks with gun racks, and an enormous motorcycle with improbably high handlebars and enough chrome attachments to intrigue NASA. The building, weathered to gray and as bleak as a military barracks, was a two-story structure with six apartments on each level. As I pulled into the lot, an airplane came thundering over the treetops and continued its descent onto the runway across the highway. Several seconds passed before I was able to sit up, lick my suddenly parched lips, and park near a battered car that was similar in breadth to Debbie Anne's lethal weapon.

Arnie's green truck was not there, but I'd driven several miles on my mission and it would be silly—all right, cowardly—to leave without any attempt to find him. Hoping there was a parking lot behind the building, I climbed out of my car and went to the double row of rusty mailboxes. Although the numbers of the boxes had been written in crude numerals, the few scrawled names were too faded to be legible.

It was, I decided uneasily, a bit like Russian roulette. Behind the splintery doors were twelve apartments; any one of them might be Arnie's. The eleven others belonged to the owners of the vehicles in the lot. I looked back at the motorcycle, squared my shoulders, and knocked on the nearest door.

The woman who opened it was less than excited by my presence. She had a beer in one hand and a half-eaten sandwich in the other, and kept her eyes on the television blaring across the room and filling the room with flickery blue shadows. Only one side of her mouth moved as she said, "Whaddaya want?"

"I'm looking for Arnie Riggles, and I was told he lived at this address."

"Why you lookin' for him?"

"I want to discuss a job," I said semitruthfully.

She cackled at something on the screen, drained the beer and crumpled the can in one fluid motion, and said, "Never heard of him."

The door closed inches from my nose. No one was home in the next two apartments, and from within the fourth I heard sounds of marital discord heading for a crescendo that might drown out the next incoming airplane.

Surely no one would cohabit voluntarily with Arnie. I continued down the row, interrupting another woman who was watching the same television show and had never heard of Arnie, and a swarthy Middle Eastern male who trembled in response before he slammed his door.

I returned to the middle of the building and went up the creaky staircase to the balcony, where six more doors awaited me. I knocked on the end door, perhaps with less vigor than previously, and backed into the railing when my worst nightmare opened the door.

Dressed as he was only in boots and faded jeans that rode low on his hips, I had an overwhelmingly excessive view of his body hair, all black and curly on his chest and belly, straggly and streaked with gray on his head, and sprouting in thickets on his jaw and upper lip. His nose and cheeks were rosy, his mouth almost feminine. There was nothing feminine about his arms, however; they were so densely tattooed that virtually no flesh between his wrists and his neck retained its original hue. He seemed to realize I was taken aback, and with a wry smile he said, "Be careful, ma'am. The railing's rotten and it's a long way down. Something I can do for you?"

"I'm looking for Arnie Riggles," I said, desperately trying to prevent myself from gaping at the colorful swirls on his arms. I was not at a sideshow, and I hadn't paid a quarter to justify rudeness. Then again, he could have put on a shirt before he answered the door.

"He lives in the next apartment, but he's not home. He came by a little while ago to see if I wanted to shoot some pool. I didn't. You want me to give him a message?"

"No, I don't think so. Do you have any idea when he'll be back?"

"He didn't say, but he's only down the road at the Dew Drop Inn. You can catch him there." Clearly amused at my demeanor and having little difficulty interpreting it, he turned around to expose his back, which was more ornate than a medieval tapestry. When he held up his arms and flexed his biceps, a mermaid rippled as if swimming amid purple and blue fish, and a dragon swished its silver tail. "Pretty neat, huh?" he said, grinning over his shoulder at me. "I've got more, but I usually don't show them to ladies unless we're . . . intimate."

The railing bit deeper into my back, and my voice may have risen as much as an octave as I said, "Please don't. If you could be so kind as to point me in the direction of the place you mentioned, I'll—I'll be on my way."

"Tell you what, let me grab a shirt and I'll go with you. The Dew Drop's not the sort of place for a lady to go by herself." Before I could decline his offer, he disappeared into the apartment. When he returned, carrying a translucent black helmet, he was more pedestrian (and a great deal less colorful) in a long-sleeved shirt and black leather vest. "Why's someone like you looking for someone like Arnie?" he asked as we went downstairs.

"I need to ask him a few questions about some recent events," I said vaguely. "That's my car. Shall I follow you?"

"You're welcome to ride with me, and I'll bring you back whenever you're ready." He spoke politely, with no edge of challenge in his voice, but his mustache quivered as he struggled not to smile. "It's only a mile or so. Nice, warm evening like this, you might enjoy it. 'In those vernal seasons of the year, when the air is calm and pleasant, it were an injury and sullenness against Nature not to go out and see her riches, and partake in her rejoicing with heaven and earth.' Milton, *Tractate of Education,* of course."

"Of course." I wasn't nearly as intimidated by him as I'd been when he opened the door. He was no taller than I, and although he was built like a barrel, he was hardly a massive monster seething with rage and likely to rip apart live chickens with his teeth. There was no skull emblazoned on the back of his vest. Except for the facial hair and that which I, like the Shadow, knew lay beneath his shirt, he was rather ordinary, perhaps as old as fifty, a benign, middle-aged version of Santa Claus. Ordinary, that is, except in his ability to quote Milton.

"Shall we?" He gestured at the motorcycle.

Changing my mind was one thing, but losing it was another. I stayed where I was. "I don't even know your name."

" 'What's in a name? That which we call a rose by any other name would smell as sweet.' Or, in my case, would be as willing to escort such an attractive woman to a dive like the Dew Drop, if only because I'm curious why you want to find Arnie. You game or not?"

That was the question, all right. Approximately twenty-four hours earlier I'd decided that I had insulated myself, that I needed to expand my boundaries, meet new people, experience new things. At the time, I hadn't counted on being offered a ride on a motorcycle, particularly one that could have come screaming out of a futuristic movie that featured heavily armed cyborgs with poor attitudes. But hadn't Peter Rosen, Mr. Propriety himself, encouraged me to go out with other men? There was no doubt about it: this was about as far out as I could go.

"Sure," I said, "I'm game. What do I do?"

He gave me the helmet, helped me onto the padded seat, and showed me where to rest my feet. "All you have to do is hang on and flow with it," he added as he straddled the seat in front of me, did something mysterious, and leaned back as the machine bellowed to life with a fury not unlike a rabid buffalo's.

Just hang on and flow with it, I told myself as we squealed out of the parking lot and shot down the highway, easily passing a pickup truck on one side and a tractor trailer on the other. I'd expected to be stoic yet terrified, but after a minute, I loosened my death grip on his waist and acknowledged that I was enjoying the speed, the wind that stroked my skin and ballooned under my shirt, the vibrating power, the continual roar that isolated us from our surroundings. The traffic moved; we were motion itself.

I was a little disappointed when we slowed down and pulled into a parking lot. My chauffeur cut off the engine. The abrupt cessation of sound was unnerving.

"So what'd you think?" he asked.

I took off the helmet. "A memorable experience, unlike anything I've ever done."

The Dew Drop Inn was shabbier than the Airport Arms, if possible, and held together with splintery sheets of mismatched siding, indecipherable metal signs, spit, and a goodly amount of prayer. There were more than a dozen vehicles in the lot, and as I passed over the helmet, another car pulled in.

"Today's Sunday," I said as we started for the door. "Why is this place doing a brisk business when it isn't even supposed to be open?"

"The Dew Drop's more of a social club than your ordinary tavern, and the NBA playoffs are on this afternoon. Last year Mulie put in a big screen. It's a male rite of spring to congregate and watch the game over beer and bullshit. There's plenty of both here."

All the NBA signified to me was the National Book

Award, but it was hard to envision the literati slinging
quotes at each other across a net. If they were to do so,
sophistry and sherry would be their accouterments of
choice. Mystified, I entered the Dew Drop Inn.

The room was dark, and the smoke was as perni-
cious as the skies of Los Angeles. There were only two
sources of light: a swaying rectangular fixture above a
pool table and a large television screen on which men
in boxer shorts cavorted in pursuit of an elusive ball.
Most of the twenty or so men were seated at tables,
watching the game, but three or four stood in the shadows beyond the pool table. Oblivious to the ashes drib-
bling from his cigarette, a man in a cowboy hat was
bent over the table, the tip of his cue stick resting on
the worn green felt. Competing with the outbursts of
laughter, good-natured curses, and inanely bright chatter from the game announcers was the persistent
ringing of unseen telephones.

"Ho, Senator!"

I located Arnie at one of the tables. It was not challenging, in that he was waving his arm above his head
while pounding on the table with a beer bottle. "I
guess we found him," I said to my companion. I'd gar-
nered enough attention, some of it curious and some of
it smirky, to be glad to have him beside me, and unless
I'd misjudged him a second time, I was safe from the
advances of the rednecks in the room.

"Come join us, Senator!" Arnie yelled, still carrying
on as if we were at a pep rally rather than a seedy tavern. "I got something I want to ask you about this trade
imbalance with the Pacific Rim."

Uncomfortably aware of the incongruity of my presence (there was not so much as a female barmaid), I
went to his table and said, "Could I speak to you in
private?"

Arnie swatted the man in the next chair. "Jesus,
McDooley, were you raised in a barn or what? Give
the lady your seat before I cram a beer bottle up your
lovely snout."

"In private?" I repeated emphatically.

"Anything you want, Senator, as soon as the game's over. I got some serious interest in the outcome, about a hundred dollars' worth." He began to wave again, violently enough to rattle the small copse of bottles on the table. "Hey, Ed, whatcha waiting for—an invitation? Come sit with the senator and I'll buy you both a beer. Arnie Riggles is a-rollin' in dough today!"

I raised my eyebrows as my swarthy driver sat down in the hastily vacated chair on the other side of Arnie. "Ed?"

He mimicked my expression. "Senator?"

Arnie slapped his simian forehead, by pure serendipity with the hand not holding the beer bottle. "Wowsy, Senator, I thought you two knew each other, coming in together like you did. This lovable guy here's Ed Whitbred, my boss and my best friend in the whole damn world." He hiccuped as he leaned over to throw his arm over Ed's shoulder. "In the whole damn world, he is my best friend. I can't tell you the number of times he came down to the can to bail me out, then scolded me all the way home about how I oughta do this detox thing. Ol' Ed Whitbred's meaner than my first wife and uglier than my second, but I love him just the same."

Arnie rested his face on Ed's shoulder and began to cry. From the lack of interest shown by the other occupants at the table, I deduced that the maudlin display was unremarkable, and, indeed, no one remarked on it.

A man in a dirty apron set down two beer bottles and stomped away. I frowned at the bottle, then at Ed. "You didn't mention that you and Arnie are such dear friends."

"You didn't ask," he said. He tried to pry Arnie off his shoulder, but Arnie's grip was stubborn. "I'm not sure he's in the mood for conversation."

A door at the far end of the bar opened to admit two men, and the sound of ringing telephones intensified. Even with the door closed, I could hear what seemed to be at least a dozen of them. "What's with the tele-

phones? Are they running some kind of telethon in
there? This hardly seems the place for Jerry's kids."

"A hundred dollars," Arnie said, lifting his face.
"You wanna little action, Senator? You don't have to
bet much, and it makes the bisketbell ... that is to say,
the basketball game more exciting. Nickel or dime
bet's okay."

I took a nickel from my purse and put it on the table.
"I'll bet you this that you can't sit up and answer a few
simple questions, Arnie. If you can, it's all yours."

One of the men cleared his throat. "It's kinda traditional in gambling circles that a nickel means five dollars, a dime means ten. Considering the state he's in,
maybe it don't matter."

"Do you mind?" I glared until he looked away, then
shook Arnie's arm. "I am not interested in absorbing
the local traditions. If it takes five dollars, then so be
it!" I took out a bill and slammed it on the table, feeling quite as bold as a poker player in a Wild West sa-
loon. "Do we have a bet or don't we?"

Arnie wiped his nose on Ed's shoulder and managed
to sit up. "Yeah, no one ever accused Arnold Riggles
of shying away from a bet, no matter what. It seems to
me, though, that a senator ought to be willing to go
higher than a measly five bucks. What's the defense
budget these days? How about Medicare and Medicaid
payments? You raised your salaries last year—" He
suddenly slumped forward, his head bouncing off the
table several times before coming to rest.

"I am not a senator," I said to Ed, who understandably seemed perplexed. "Whoever said it was impossible to underrate human intelligence must have been
thinking of Arnie. The smoke and the stench and those
telephones are too much for me. Could you please take
me back to my car?"

"Sure, and then I'd better come back and drive
Arnie home. He's surpassed his limit for the evening."

I politely nodded at the occupants of the table and
pushed back my chair, but before I could stand up, the
front door opened and the room swarmed with men.

Men in coats and ties, holding up identification badges. Men in blue police uniforms. Men in khaki police uniforms. More men in overalls and caps. Young men, old men, enough men to take to the football field. For the most part, men with guns. And they were saying, not in unison but in a great babble of confusion ranging from tenor to bass, from strident to coldly authoritarian: "This is a raid!" "Everybody stay put!" "Put your hands on the tables where we can see 'em!" "Stay away from the door!" "You there—put down that cue stick!" "Up against the wall, bubba!"

I sank back into the chair as more of them stampeded through the door at the end of the bar. From within the back room came spurts of official phrases that referred to illegal possession of gaming equipment, violations of federal statutes concerning interstate racketeering, operation of an establishment that operated gambling devices, and more.

"What's going on?" I asked Ed in a strangled whisper.

Before he could answer, a uniformed officer loomed over us. "Hands on the table, all of you! Keep your mouths shut! This is a raid, not a damn tea party!"

I looked up with a cool expression meant to chide him only a bit for his presumptive error. "There's been a mistake, Officer. I merely came by to have a word with someone. I know nothing whatsoever of any illegal activity, and I've never made a bet in my life. I think it would be for the best if I slipped away quietly."

"That your money?" He pointed at the five-dollar bill.

"No, it most certainly is not. It belongs to the comatose gentleman beside me. Now, if you don't mind—"

The comatose gentleman rolled his head to one side. "Damn straight it's mine. The senator here and I have a little bet, and in a minute I'm going to—" His head went back down, flattening his nose. He began to snore.

"Politician, huh?" The policeman gave me an icy smile as he recited the Miranda warning to me.

During the caravan-style ride to the local jail, handcuffed and squished between two odoriferous patrons in the backseat of the police car, I learned that the Dew Drop Inn had been under surveillance for over a year. My arrival had not been a factor in the decision to raid the establishment. I'd chosen a particularly inopportune day to visit, a day when gamblers surfaced like worms after a shower and law enforcement agents could count on copious quantities of money and betting slips to be within the establishment.

It was educational, I suppose, but not the stuff of which warm memories were made. I was subjected to fingerprinting, being photographed (I demanded to be allowed access to a mirror first, but they were less than cooperative), and ultimately placed in a barren cell and informed that they'd get to me sooner or later.

Earlier in the afternoon, after the unpleasantries with Peter, Caron and Inez, and the anonymous caller, I'd assumed things couldn't get much worse. Sitting on a metal bench, acutely aware of the darkness and aroma of urine in the air, idly reading obscene graffiti, facing the possibility that I might be doing the same twelve hours in the future, I had to admit I'd been wrong. And what had I accomplished? I'd met Ed Whitbred, but I had no reason to think he had any involvement in Jean Hall's death or Debbie Anne Wray's disappearance. He was not my man-in-the-moon prowler, unless he'd happened upon an incredibly effective remedy for baldness.

I wasn't at all sure what the appropriate behavior was for my situation. I would be allowed to make a phone call before they interrogated me, but they'd implied it might be some time before my name rose to the top of the list. I had neither a metal cup with which to bang on the bars nor a bent spoon with which to tunnel out. I didn't know any spirituals.

I was considering using my one telephone call to order a pizza when the cell door opened and Jorgeson came in. "Good evening, Ms. Malloy," he said as if we were meeting under the portico of the Book Depot. Had he been wearing a hat, I was certain he would have touched its brim ever so urbanely. "I understand you're in a jam."

"It's actually a cell. How did you know I'd been left here to rot for hours and hours?"

"According to the arresting officer and the desk sergeant, you've been in here for less than half an hour—although I'm sure it felt longer. Time doesn't fly in the Farberville City Jail, or so I've been told."

"What else have you been told?"

He seemed to have a decent idea of the events that had led to my incarceration, and related them in a carefully noncommittal tone, then said, "One of the officers at the scene recognized your name and called Lieutenant Rosen, thinking he'd want to hear about it. He called me."

I'd been irritated earlier, but now I was beginning to get angry. "Why didn't he come down here himself?"

Jorgeson's bulldog face turned red and his ears quivered—a response I'd seen on previous occasions when he was deeply uncomfortable. Looking at something on the wall above my head, he said, "Ah, the lieutenant said something about being busy, being tied up. Once he heard Arnie Riggles had been picked up in the raid, he said he figured you were up to your old—that you were interfering—I mean, involved in an investigation. He said he'd call the desk and tell 'em to release you to my custody until the arraignment."

"The arraignment, Jorgeson? Are you implying that Lieutenant Peter Rosen has no plans to have a quiet word with the head of the operation and make it clear that I am totally innocent of anything more wicked than a tiny lapse in judgment? That I will be brought to court to face a fine or further time in this charming room? Is that what you're implying?"

"I don't think he'll let it go that far, Ms. Malloy. The call caught him in a bad mood, and he was kind of sputtery when he heard about your friend with the motorcycle. I'm sure he'll do something to help in the morning."

"What did you mean when you said he was busy?" I continued relentlessly, my face quite as red as his and my ears tingling, if not quivering. "Just precisely what was he doing when he received the call?"

Jorgeson closed his eyes for a moment, and his gulps were audible. "I think maybe he had company. Let's go back to the desk and arrange your release. You'll be home in no time, sitting on your sofa with a nice hot cup of tea, and all this will seem like a bad dream."

"Company?" I said, although I did leap to my feet and follow him down the corridor.

"I believe he mentioned something about Lieutenant Pipkin. It's none of my business, Ms. Malloy; I'm just following orders."

"That was an inadequate defense at Nuremberg, Jorgeson. Who's this Lieutenant Pipkin? Is he on the CID squad?"

He stopped so abruptly that I narrowly avoided a collision, and he pulled me aside as another of my co-conspirators from the Dew Drop Inn was escorted to a cell. "Like I said, it's none of my business what Lieutenant Rosen does when he's off duty. We sometimes have a beer or go to the college baseball games, but for the most part we go our separate ways. My wife and I were watching a video and I'd like to get home so we can finish it before midnight. If you're curious about Lieutenant Pipkin, call her yourself. She's on the campus security force."

Despite the unruliness of my thoughts, I remained impressively impassive as Jorgeson did the necessary paperwork to gain my release, drove me to the Airport Arms, and waved as he pulled onto the highway. Ed Whitbred's motorcycle was not there, and I felt a little guilty as I realized he wouldn't have been in the Dew Drop den of iniquity had he not escorted me there. Arnie deserved everything that happened to him, and a good deal more, but Ed had been minding his own business—until I'd shown up.

I opened my car door, then glanced at the second story. Ed's apartment was dark, as was the one next to it; I knew where the renters were, and were likely to be until their arraignments in the morning. Would I take advantage of the fortuitous circumstances that had led to my premature release? Would Oral Roberts accept a blank check?

I went upstairs and along the balcony to the penultimate apartment. Back in the Airport Arms' heyday, a renter might have been able to lock the door to protect himself from his feral neighbors, but now the knob felt loose enough to come off in my hand with only a minimal yank. It was just as well; Arnie would have lost a key as easily as he did consciousness. I opened the door a few inches and said into the darkness, "Hello? Is anybody here?" If anyone was there, he or she was not in a congenial mood. I went inside, closed the door, and felt for the light switch, trying not to think about the last time I'd been in a similar situation. Arnie's environment was more likely to host rats.

I flipped on the light and hastily pulled the drapes together. Although the light was visible, I hoped that anyone bothering to notice would assume the tenant was home. The living room was squalid, to be charitable, and decorated primarily with beer cans, plates of petrified food, teetery piles of yellowed magazines and newspapers, and furniture that looked downright dangerous. I knew I was in the right apartment.

The kitchen was filthy, the bathroom more so, and the bedroom surely had been the target of an invasion of the magnitude of Desert Storm. Like the Kappa Theta Etas, Arnie preferred to utilize the floor rather than the closet, although there were no pink cashmere sweaters amid the paint-splattered overalls and dingy gray jockey shorts.

It was hopeless. If there was anything to explain his involvement, I was not going to stumble across it without several hours of intensive search through nasty stuff. I opened the dresser drawers, looked inside the closet, and forced myself to kneel for a quick peek under the bed. If I'd been hunting for dust bunnies and liquor bottles, I would have been incredibly successful, but as it was, I reminded myself of the inanity of my mission and returned to the living room.

On the inside of the doorknob hung a camera on a black plastic strap. I wasn't any more familiar with cameras than I was with male rites of spring, but I examined it and concluded a roll of film remained inside it. Would one shot be of a startled bookseller, her mouth agape, fingers splayed to block the blinding flash? And, more interestingly, of whom or what would the others be? Arnie was not an amateur engaging in his hobby beneath the windows of the Kappa Theta Eta house. Earlier I'd opined that he was not a murderer, but this was in no way to imply that I'd ever doubted his capacities as a voyeur. Or a blackmailer, in which case the film was likely to hold his evidence.

After a series of futile attempts to disengage the roll of film, I decided to borrow the camera long enough to have one of the nice young people at the one-hour photo service assist me. I switched off the light and opened the door.

Ed Whitbred blocked my way, intentionally or otherwise. " 'Sometimes they shut you up in jail—dark, and a filthy cell; I hope the fellows built them jails, find 'em down in hell.' E. F. Piper, of course."

"Of course," I echoed lamely. "I'm delighted that you've been released, Ed. It was my fault that you were at that place, and I want to apologize to you. If they end up pressing charges, I'll certainly testify on your behalf."

"And I won't have to call you at an office in Washington, D.C., will I? I can drop by your upstairs apartment next to the sorority house, or catch you at the Book Depot on Thurber Street."

I was disturbed not only by his faintly sardonic

tone, but also by his undeniable bulk, which seemed to have taken root on the balcony outside Arnie's door. "Any time, Ed. Thanks for the motorcycle ride. It was the first time I'd been on one, and it really is a special sensation of its own, isn't it?" My hands were sweating as I clutched the camera, but it was a little late in the scenario to put it behind my back. "Well, I'd better run along home now. My daughter will be worried, and my brief time in jail has left me ravenous, and of course a cup of tea will be divine. You won't believe this, but I was thinking about using my call to order a pizza when ... they released me. Isn't that silly?"

He was unmoved by my dithering. "What were you doing in Arnie's apartment, Ms. Malloy? The only thing worth stealing is his fancy new camera. It took me more than a week to teach him how to use it, but he finally got the hang of it."

I couldn't force my way past him, and I had no desire to retreat into the apartment behind me. It was something of a stalemate. We stared at each other for what seemed a long time, neither of us commenting on the incriminatory object in my hands. I finally decided it was a checkmate and thrust the camera at him. "I simply wanted to assure myself that no one disturbed Arnie's apartment during his absence. When I saw this, I was concerned that someone might steal it, so I thought I'd keep it for him until his return. However, as long as you're here, you might as well assume responsibility for it."

As he reached for the camera, I shoved it into his belly hard enough to throw him off balance, and darted past him. I clattered down the staircase, fumbling in my purse for my keys, and did not look back until I was inside my car, the doors locked, the windows rolled up tightly, and the key in the ignition switch.

The balcony was deserted. A light shone from behind the curtains in his apartment. While I'd escaped like a gawky heroine, gasping and moaning, imagining his thick fingers encircling my neck or jerking me off my feet, Ed Whitbred had gone inside and most likely opened a beer. If he was to be a villain in the piece, he definitely needed to work on his role.

9

"And he quoted Milton?" gurgled Luanne as she fell back against the bench, laughing so hard that beer sloshed out of her glass. "Why? Did you ask him why?"

I knew what she meant, but I chose to misinterpret it. "I'm sure he felt that the occasion demanded it."

It was noon of the following day, and we'd met at the beer garden to picnic at our preferred table. Nothing had happened after I'd returned from my disastrous outing to the Airport Arms. Caron and Inez were huddled in the bedroom, too concerned with finances to notice my absence, and Peter Rosen must have been too busy with his distaff counterpart from the campus security force to worry about me.

Jorgeson had called earlier in the morning to tell me that my name had been deleted from all reports of the raid and I need not appear at the arraignment. I spurned his offer to send me my mug shot as a souvenir. There'd been no sign of activity at the Kappa Theta Eta house when I'd walked to the Book Depot, and neither Debbie Anne nor my anonymous caller had deigned to interrupt the ensuing hours of idleness.

Luanne wiped tears from her cheeks and attempted a more decorous voice, although little noises that resembled muffled sneezes erupted periodically. "Here's this Hell's Angel with the exterior of—I don't know—the interior of a comic book, but undeniably with the soul of a poet. Having escaped from the local penal colony, the two of you meet on a moonlit balcony. Do you flutter your eyelashes and softly say, 'Good night! Good

night! Parting is such sweet sorrow that I shall say
good night till it be morrow'? No, you knock him into
the railing and run downstairs. You ought to give up
those dreary mystery novels, Claire. Read some romances! Surely Azalea Twilight did one about the raw
and primitive pleasure of the motorcycle between one's
thighs, the wind caressing one's breasts, the taciturn
yet incredibly virile hero. . . . No, the guys usually
have mysterious scars, not elaborate needlework."

I frowned at her. "Ed's no damn easier to character-
ize than anyone else in this mess. I can't decide if he's
a potential party guest or a killer, but why should I
have any more luck with him than with any of the others? None of the character references have come from
what we might consider unbiased sources. The Kappas
adored Jean and loathe Debbie Anne. Mrs. Wray es-
pouses the mundane maternal line. Vouching for Ed
Whitbred is none other than Arnie, who'd profess ad-
oration for a barnyard animal if there were anything in
it for him. Why can't I have a nice group of disinter-
ested parties?"

Luanne finished her sandwich and wadded up the
paper wrapper. "Like some of the professors at the
college?"

"I was about to say that very thing."

When I got back to the bookstore, I called the apartment and let the telephone ring until Caron acknowledged defeat and answered it with a drowsy snarl.

"I need you to watch the store this afternoon, dear,"
I said. "Be here in thirty minutes or kiss your evening
plans goodbye."

"And pass up a Totally Tedious slumber party at
Rhonda's? You mean I can't do the limbo and run
around all night in pink sponge curlers? Dine on ge-
neric chips and onion dip made out of the same chem-
icals as napalm? Make prank calls to the football
team? Please don't throw me in that brier patch, Br'er
Mother."

I was impressed with the quickness with which she
went from somnolence to sarcasm. "Just be here," I

said and hung up before she reached her optimum pitch. I needed Debbie Anne's class schedule. In the past I might have called Peter to see if I could wheedle it out of him with my usual dexterity. Now I would sooner have arranged for an amputation. The registrar's office would refuse in the middle of my first sentence, citing student privacy. Lieutenant Pipkin of the campus security force would be no more forthcoming—and would report my request to her newest boyfriend.

I called Eleanor Vanderson, who did not obligingly answer the phone on the first ring or any of the next fifteen. She was apt to be lunching on chicken salad with the faculty wives, or playing bridge. I suspected she would be very good at the latter—and would never touch the former unless it contained homemade mayonnaise and slivered almonds. No one answered the phone at the Kappa house.

"I Cannot Believe you're doing this to me, Mother," Caron said as she and Inez dragged into the store an hour later. "Although this country was founded on the economic necessity of indentured servants and slaves, I seem to think Mr. Lincoln put a stop to it more than a hundred years ago. I was planning to go through the yearbook and make a list of potential My Beautiful Self clients. Pippa said she did that when she was getting started. Do you know how much money she's made in the last three years?"

"She bought a convertible at the end of her first year," Inez contributed. "Over spring break she went to Cozumel and made enough money while she was there to pay for the entire trip. She did sessions right on the beach."

Caron disappeared behind the self-help rack, but the barrier in no way diminished her voice. "Pippa's mother helped her a whole bunch in the beginning by having parties and persuading her friends to have sessions. Her mother has lots of friends because she's a past member of the Junior League, an active Kappa alumna, something in the hospital auxiliary, and something else at the country club. Decorations chairperson, I think."

"While you're burdened with a mother who has to earn a living," I said as pleasantly as I could. "Perhaps you can drum up some business at Rhonda's tonight."

Caron peered over the top of the romances. "After we limbo?"

Inez blinked with the solemnity of a small brown barn owl. "Rhonda's got this thing about the limbo. It's almost like an obsession, and if you say you don't want to or even lock yourself in the bathroom, she'll literally drag you into the living room and push you under the broomstick."

"How low can you go?" oozed a disembodied voice from the direction of the cookbooks. "No one can go as low as Rhonda, because she carries all that excess weight on her hips and her center of gravity is lower than everyone else's."

"Enough!" I said. "I'll be back in an hour or so. Don't take candy from strangers and don't take one red cent out of the cash register unless you're making change. You can still go through the yearbook to find victims; odds are good that no one will disturb you in my absence. In truth, the odds are excellent."

I put a notebook in my purse and was on my way through the door when Caron said, "That man called again."

"When?" I demanded. "What did he say?"

She'd moved behind the counter and was eyeing the cash register with an enigmatic glint. "It was so dumb. When I answered the phone, all I heard was this heavy breathing. I didn't want to waste my time, so I asked if it was an obscene call, and he—"

"You asked if it was an obscene call?" I said carefully.

"Why should the line be tied up if all he was going to do was breathe, Mother? Someone might have been trying to call to arrange a My Beautiful Self session. Anyway, he kind of harrumphed and said it certainly was not and he didn't appreciate being accused of tacky behavior. I pointed out that he was the one doing the hyperventilation bit, not I. He said he was thinking about what to say. I told him he should have done that *before* he called, and then I hung up."

"But he called back," Inez inserted bravely, then faded behind the science fiction rack. Caron, like any temperamental star, does not care to be prompted by an understudy.

"He called back?" I said.

Caron had taken a compact from her purse and was examining the tip of her nose with the intensity of a microbiologist. When I repeated my question, she snapped it closed and sighed. "About two minutes later, if you can believe it. He did admit that he should have decided what to say before he called, although he was still huffy about my perfectly reasonable question."

Her perfectly reasonable mother was too bemused to do more than murmur, "And . . . ?"

"He said that if you didn't stop butting into his affairs, you'd find yourself on the sidewalk selling burnt offerings. It was So Dumb. I mean, hasn't he ever heard of fire insurance? You do have adequate insurance, don't you?" Her green eyes turned the precise shade of mint ink. "Would there be enough left over to buy a used car?"

"No! There most definitely would not be enough left over to buy anything. I have some insurance, but—" I held in a groan as I looked at the old, dry wood of the rafters, the numerous racks of flammable paper products, the cardboard cartons stacked alongside the wall, the stacks of invoices and order forms, the catalogs. I could have renamed the place Tinder Box Books, had I been in a whimsical mood. I was not. "Did this man say anything else?"

"Not really," Caron said, still appraising the possibilities of a lovely check from the insurance company. "He said something about if you had the negatives, you'd better give them to him."

"What negatives?"

"He didn't say, and frankly, I was getting pretty tired of him. I said I wasn't your private secretary, told him to call you himself if he had any more obtuse messages, and then Inez and I left before he could call a third time. That's why we were late getting here."

"What about his voice?" I said. "Could you tell anything about his age? Did he have an accent?"

"He wasn't a kid, and he didn't have an accent. He was trying to be clever by talking in a whisper, which meant I had to keep asking him to repeat things until I was ready to scream. If you don't have decent manners on the telephone, you shouldn't be allowed to use it." She crossed her arms and gave me a cold look. "Don't you need to go do whatever it is? Inez and I don't have all afternoon, you know. We're supposed to be at Rhonda's at six, and we have to do our hair."

I walked back to my apartment in a daze of confusion and anger. Who was this anonymous jerk? I resented being threatened in such a manner; if nothing else, it wasn't sporting. I could do nothing in retaliation until I knew who he was. I didn't have his damn negatives—of what? It was possible Ed Whitbred had them, or had them until Arnie was turned loose once again on an insufficiently leery society. There were other cameras in Farberville. There were plenty of cameras in the Kappa Theta Eta house, if the number of coy photographs was indicative.

I sat on the edge of my porch. If the prowler was also my caller, he might have been searching the third floor of the sorority house for the mysterious negatives. Was he being blackmailed by one of the girls who'd gone home for the summer? The last thing I needed was another Kappa Theta Eta cluttering up my admittedly tenuous scenario.

Next door, Winkie came out onto the porch, holding an unhappy cat. She looked almost comical in a fussy pink broad-brimmed hat that seemed to have settled on her head of its own accord and refused to leave. After carefully locking the door, she headed for the sidewalk.

"Any word from Debbie Anne?" I called as I approached her. I stopped out of reach of Katie's teeth, although I was in range of her malevolent gaze.

"No, nothing at all. It's been three days now, and I do hope the police will take her disappearance more seriously. Her mother has been calling me at all hours of the day and night, and there's nothing I can tell her. Rebecca and Pippa are quite sure Debbie Anne doesn't have a boyfriend. I called those few girls who were her friends during the year. They could suggest nothing, and none of them has heard from her. This is by far the most inconsiderate stunt she's ever pulled. That girl will never be a Kappa."

"Do you have a copy of her class schedule? I thought I might speak to her professors and see if any of them have any ideas." I held my breath and smiled with the shiny expectancy of a rushee.

"I suppose I do, but it's inside and Katie has an appointment at the vet's office." She hesitated, then said, "I'll go get you a copy. It certainly can't hurt to speak to them, and if we don't find her soon, I'm going to lose my temper and be brusque with Mrs. Wray. You hold Katie while I go back inside."

The cat was thrust into my arms in a manner not unlike that I'd utilized with the camera. "Don't do this! Please!" I said, but Winkie was already on her way to the door, muttering about late-night calls and inconsiderate girls. It took the cat only a few seconds to realize what treachery had befallen her, and she let out a yowl of outrage that emphasized her shared ancestry with jungle cats. Less than a second later, she bit me on the hand so viciously that I instinctively flung her to the ground as I stumbled backward.

I gaped first at the blood welling from the jagged wound, and then at a flash of white as the cat vanished into the shrubbery. Blinking back tears, I fumbled in my purse for a tissue and tried unsuccessfully to stop the blood. The wound throbbed so sharply that I began to feel light-headed. I sank down on the lawn and cradled my hand, oblivious to my surroundings, and therefore was startled when Winkie said, "What happened? Where's Katie? Why are you behaving so oddly?"

I showed her the bite and grimly related the story. "And she ran that way," I said, gesturing with my un-injured hand. I did not continue with a description of what I dearly hoped the animal would encounter on its escape route.

"This is dreadful," Winkie said. "We must take action immediately, Claire."

"The bleeding has stopped, and I don't think I'll need stitches. I have some iodine at my—"

"We must find Katie," she interrupted sternly. "Her appointment at the vet is in less than an hour. I was taking her there so that she can be rendered incapable of reproduction. An irresponsible individual knocked the screen off my window several days ago, and Katie spent the night outside the house. I don't intend to have kittens underfoot in that cramped apartment." She went to the pertinent shrub and called, "Here, kitty kitty kitty. Come on, Katie; that woman won't hurt you again. Come to Winkie."

I stood up, the tissue still pressed to my hand, and tried to stir up a trace of sympathy from her. "She bit me once before. I tried to tell you when you shoved her at me."

"That's ridiculous. Katie doesn't bite." She held out a piece of paper. "Here's Debbie Anne's class schedule. I think I'd better go back inside and have a glass of wine. Being a housemother isn't easy by any means, but this is becoming more than I can bear. Eleanor will have to find someone else for the remainder of the summer term. The pressure's entirely too much for me." She went into the house without so much as a glance at my bloodied tissue. Kappa Theta Eta house-mothers were not, apparently, instructed in the gentle art of first aid.

After I'd doctored the wound as best I could, I set off toward the campus, fantasizing about a rustic cabin somewhere in the woods. No one sat beside me on the deck as the sun sank behind the mountains; I was alone with a glass of scotch and a plate of crackers and cheese. I amended it to freshly baked bread and expensive Brie. No one whined, complained, bit me, badgered me, scolded me, or, most of all, sent me into the arms of a tattooed motorcyclist while reclining with a member of the campus security force.

I went into the yellow brick building that housed the education department. Since it was summer school, Debbie Anne was taking only two classes, and at that moment should have been in a classroom being instructed in Reading Readiness Skills, a.k.a. EE1009.

"Whatever they are," I growled, then accosted a perky young thing in jeans and asked where the room was. The door was ajar, and I hovered in the hall until I determined that Debbie Anne was not among the half-dozen girls numbly gazing at a blackboard as an elderly woman droned at them.

The instructor of Developmental Psychology (EE1147) was not in his or her office, unless he or she was cowering behind a locked door. A second perky young thing informed me that classes would be out in ten minutes, and she didn't know when I might catch Professor Costandaza. She herself had taken the psych course from Professor Simpson because he was "an absolute hunk" and it was all she could do not to "like literally seduce him right there on the desk, you know."

Fearing for the future of civilization, I read the notices on the bulletin board, gleaming tidbits about symposiums on A-V equipment, potluck dinners, and opportunities to study abroad for a zillion dollars. Eventually something buzzed and students drifted out of classrooms. I went to the original room. The woman was packing her briefcase, and was minimally cordial when I introduced myself and told her my proposed topic.

She consulted her watch, sighed, and said, "I have a faculty meeting in fifteen minutes. I heard about the Wray girl on the local news last night, and there was something in the newspaper. Very sad business, that, but faculty meetings come right after death and taxes."

"I was hoping you could tell me about Debbie Anne. Everyone seems to have a strong opinion about her, but also a biased one."

"When I watched the news, I tried to remember what I could of her. I had her last spring in a class, and again this semester. She was shy and quiet, rarely contributing to the discussion, turning in ordinary, uninspired work." She paused to think. "I do recall being surprised when she wore a sorority sweatshirt to class one day. Fewer and fewer of them major in education these days, but I used to have hordes of them in my classes—to my dismay. Now, I understand, they're all majoring in business. She didn't seem the sorority type."

"Did Debbie Anne ever cheat or lose her temper?"

The woman picked up her briefcase. "No one cheats in Reading Readiness Skills; it's much too easy. As for losing her temper, I don't know that she has one to lose, Mrs. Malloy. She's just one of those drab, modestly intelligent, poorly prepared girls from a little town. If this hadn't happened, she'd squeak by, graduate, and go teach in another little town in order to send us more poorly prepared girls."

I went outside and sat on a stone bench. For the first time in nearly three days, I'd made progress, albeit measurable in millimeters rather than leaps and bounds. Debbie Anne Wray was a soggy-nosed ninny, accepted into the sorority by an economic imperative and rejected by a social one. Jean Hall had forced her to do something illegal, and this had sent Debbie Anne into hiding. Someone else had gained access to Debbie Anne's car key and run Jean down in the alley.

There were a few minor unanswered questions, to be sure, along the lines of who and what and when and where and why and how, but I wasn't nearly as confused as I'd been earlier. Contemplating my next target, I stood up, smiled vaguely at a couple of students, and decided to go back to the Book Depot, where I could make lists in the amateur-sleuth tradition. I would be the sole champion of the cause—the innocence of Debbie Anne. The police detectives could sit and wait. I would take action, make brilliant deductions, identify the guilty, and rescue the innocent.

And this time, I told myself, Claire Malloy would not cringe from the limelight and allow the police to take all the credit. I'd grant interviews, appear on the evening news, pose for photographs in front of the Book Depot. If the mayor insisted on giving me some sort of award for my civic-minded behavior, I'd accept it with becoming modesty.

As I came around the corner of the library, I was practicing smiles rather than paying any attention whatsoever to the trickle of pedestrians. I thudded into someone, stumbled back, and looked up to offer an apology (with becoming modesty, of course). And found myself face to face with the man in the moon. I goggled at him; he goggled at me.

"You!" I croaked.

He quit goggling and gave me a shove hard enough to send me across the sidewalk and into a very old, very hard tree trunk. My head hit first and then snapped forward, pain ripped along my shoulder, and all the breath swooshed out of my lungs. I fell to the ground, fighting to fend off swirls of blackness and to regain my breath.

"Are you okay?" asked a voice so close that I nearly screamed.

I opened my eyes. The boy squatting in front of me had dark hair and a lean, nearly cadaverous face. I finally found enough oxygen to say, "The man in the moon—I mean, the man who knocked me down—did you see him?"

"I saw someone go around the corner, but I didn't get a good look at him. Maybe you'd better stay down for a few more minutes until everything stops spinning." He looked over his shoulder at a huddle of students. "Somebody call the campus cops and tell 'em it's an assault."

"No," I said, but as I tried to straighten up, the black blotches flooded my eyes and my ears reverberated as if I'd taken residence in the bell tower . . . or the belfry.

"Just lean back, ma'am," the boy said patronizingly, no doubt certain he knew what was best for an incapacitated octogenarian who'd identified her assailant as the man in the moon.

"Oh wow, it's Mrs. Malloy!" Pippa squealed as she dropped her books and knelt beside me. "What happened? Did you faint? Caron mentioned that you're experiencing menopause, and that can make you dizzy or—"

"Someone pushed me," I muttered. There weren't very many students in summer school, but the sidewalk was so crowded that most of them must have been drawn to the drama.

"That's awful! Who?"

"A man," I said sourly, daring the boy to say a single word. He obligingly stared at the ground. "I crashed into him as I came around the corner, and he overreacted to the lapse in etiquette."

Pippa dimpled indignantly. "Some men are just plain bullies, aren't they? My mother was playing golf last week and these men played through without any concern for safety or common courtesy. They let anyone in the club these days. Oh, good, here come the campus cops. Maybe it's not too late to find this man. He didn't try to molest you, did he?"

"In the middle of the afternoon next to the library? No, Pippa, he merely removed me from his path." I recognized one of the uniformed officers approaching as Officer Terrance. The other was a woman, tall and lithe, moving gracefully. I slumped back against the tree trunk and willed myself to pass out. I scrunched my eyes closed. I held my breath. I told myself that the gender of the officer was a coincidence and that I'd had my quota for the day. For the year. I debated whether to make a deal with the devil. What was the worth of my soul compared to the impending humiliation?

"Mrs. Malloy," I heard Terrance say with what I felt was inadequate surprise. "Do you need medical attention?"

"No, I'll be fine in a minute." I opened one eye to a slit. There on the woman's name tag was the dreaded word: Pipkin. It was preceded by a less specific M, as in Marion or Melinda or Mockery. There had to be a way to force myself into unconsciousness, I thought as I closed the eye and concentrated on the rough bark cutting into my back. My head ached dully, but I knew within the hour it would feel like the beach during a hurricane. My hand still throbbed where the cat had bitten it. I was not enamored of this latest quaint coincidence.

"She muttered something about the man in the moon," my traitorous savior was saying in a low voice. "I caught a glimpse of an older guy heading past the agri building. He was walking briskly, not running."

Pippa squeezed my knee. "Here's your purse, Mrs. Malloy. I gathered up all your things for you. Do you want to try and stand up now? I know more about the psychological aspects of shock than the physical, but your color's come back." She paused, then with what I suspected was a tactful dimple, added, "You really shouldn't wear navy."

That did it. I opened my eyes, and from under a much lowered brow, glowered at her. "I do not need a Beautiful Self analysis to be assaulted in my proper palette!" I brushed off her hand and made it to my feet. "I can describe the man, Officer Terrance. This is the first time I've been this close, and I only had a brief moment before he knocked me down, but I know what I saw."

"I'm Officer Pipkin," the woman said with professional compassion that didn't fool me. "We'd appreciate it if you'd accompany us to the office, and on the way we can swing by the infirmary to let them check you or give you an aspirin."

"Thank you for your solicitousness, Officer Pipkin," I said. I touched the lump on the back of my head and wished I hadn't. "The skin's not broken, and I have ample medication at home. I'd prefer to get this over as quickly as possible."

Officer Terrance cleared his throat. "You said this is the first time you'd been so close. Does this mean you've seen this man before—say, on the third floor of the Kappa Theta Eta house?"

"We can discuss it at your office," I said firmly.

Pippa patted my arm. "Oh, Winkie told us how you freaked out when you saw a reflection in the window. She said you called the police to report we had a prowler, when it was nothing more than the man in the moon! Don't you think that's too priceless?"

10

The campus police department was housed in a relatively new metal building on the far side of the football stadium. Students grumbled as they stood in line to pay traffic tickets at a counter, and others sat dispiritedly on a bench in the hallway. Uniformed officers moved inside a glass-walled room filled with electronic equipment. Unlike the local jail, there was nothing in the air here more sinister than the staleness of a modern office building with sealed windows.

Officer Terrance escorted me to a conference room decorated with maps of the campus and posters that admonished us not to overindulge. Officer Pipkin joined us with a tray holding mugs of coffee, packets of sugar, and a jar of powdered pseudo-cream.

While she busied herself playing hostess, I took a harder look at her, strictly out of curiosity. She appeared to be no more than thirty years old, with short dark hair, a pleasant face, a trim body, and the implicit strength and agility of a gymnast. She'd spoken only a few words while we drove to the department, but her voice held no trace of a regional accent. I had not yet decided if it had held an edge of amusement.

"Now then, Ms. Malloy," she said as she placed a clipboard on the table, "could you please tell us what happened?"

Officer Terrance glanced at his watch and pushed back his chair. "Dammit, I nearly forgot that I have to pick up my wife's sister at the airport. Can you handle this on your own, Officer Pipkin?"

"I'll muddle through, Officer Terrance." She waited

until he was gone, then gave me a quirky grin. "All by my little lonesome, too. I've been on the force three years longer than he has, and could have been his baby-sitter when he was in disposable diapers. I'm a second-degree black belt in karate, have better scores on the firing range, and am working on a master's degree in personnel management. It's not impossible to understand why some women become cloistered nuns, you know?"

"I know," I said, determined to maintain a civil distance between us. This could have been a ruse. For all I knew, she was wearing a concealed microphone and Lieutenant Rosen of the Farberville CID was in the adjoining room, peering through a peephole and smirking as he eavesdropped. "I'd like to get this over with, if you don't mind. My head's beginning to ache. I came around the corner of the library, and—"

"Why were you on the campus, Ms. Malloy?"

Name, rank, and serial number, I told myself stiffly. "It was such a lovely afternoon that I thought I'd go over to the senior walk and read the names, admire the flowers, toss a few coins in the fountain in front of the student union. I came around the corner, admittedly lost in reverie, and crashed into that man. Perhaps he reacted reflexively, and when he realized what he'd done, panicked and fled."

She held a pen in her hand, but she was not scribbling frantically. "Did you get a good look at him?"

"About five foot seven, maybe shorter, small pale eyes, very thin blond hair that gives him the illusion of baldness, and a distinctively round, white face. Anywhere from fifty to seventy years old, I'm afraid. That type of babyish face is hard to read."

"Wearing . . . ?" she murmured, now at least taking notes.

I winced as I tried to remember. "Sorry, I didn't notice. This encounter lasted only two or three seconds, and then I was slumped against the tree while the fireworks and the sirens went off. I didn't see anything for a while."

She gave me a disturbingly acute look. "And have you ever seen this man before, Ms. Malloy? Please, take your time. If you'd like, I can see if anyone has aspirin."

"I have aspirin in my purse." I wasn't sure how to answer her question, and opted to consider it while I dug through my purse for the little metal box. My fingers finally encountered it, but there was something missing, something I was accustomed to touching, to hear jingling. I put the aspirin box on the table and said, "Could I please have a cup of water?"

As soon as she was gone, I opened my purse and searched again for my key ring. I'd walked to the Book Depot, rather than driving, and when I returned home to tend to my cat bite, I'd assumed that Caron had left our front door unlocked. But I had unlocked the store, which meant I'd had the key ring in my purse. And had not removed it.

Officer Pipkin returned with the water. "You seem a little dazed, Ms. Malloy. Please let me take you to the infirmary, so they can make sure you didn't suffer a mild concussion, and then I'll drive you home. Tomorrow, or whenever you feel up to it, I'd like to ask a few more questions, and let you look at some mug shots at the Farberville Police Department."

I swallowed two aspirin with a sip of water. "I don't want to go to the infirmary, but I would prefer to put this off for a day or two and go home to take a nap. Why don't I call you when I'm ready to continue this? Maybe my memory will have improved."

"Let's hope so," she said mildly.

Once we were in the car, I told her my address and then said, merely to make conversation, "How long have you been a detective?"

"Since the report of your assault came in. I'm usually assigned to public relations, but the grown-ups were all responding to other calls, and poor Officer Terrance was stuck with me." She braked at a crosswalk and waited as the students ambled by. "Actually, I'm on a joint task force with the local police department. We're trying to find ways to cut down on property theft. During the last academic year, over a hundred thousand dollars' worth of property was stolen on the campus. We recovered less than a third of it, but that's close to the national average."

This wasn't precisely the subject I'd introduced, but it was preferable to a discussion of my assailant. "Someone mentioned there'd been thefts in the dorms and Greek houses. I can understand how a kid leaves his door unlocked, thus inviting someone within the residence to sneak inside and grab whatever's on the dresser. But how could someone steal a large, bulky computer from a busy office on the campus?"

"We've had reports on computers, VCRs, speakers that were screwed to the walls, overhead projectors, photocopy machines—you name it. The problem is apathy. Someone strolls into, say, the biology department, announces that Professor Smith said to take the computer to the laboratory on the third floor, and carries it out the door. Professor Smith thinks a colleague must have borrowed it, and merrily goes away on his sabbatical for three months. In the next building, someone says he's from the repair service, flashes a form, and takes the photocopier. Not one grad student or secretary bothers to demand credentials, and the polite student who holds the door for the thief is too worried about his thesis to look at anyone's face. Office and classroom doors are left unlocked at night. The storage building for the landscaping crew is in a lonely corner of the campus."

"How can you stop it?" I asked.

She parked in front of my duplex. "We can't, and it costs the taxpayers a lot of money to replace all these electronic toys. While we're on the topic, I saw a report that might interest you, Ms. Malloy. A clerk at a boutique at the mall recognized Debbie Anne Wray's face on the news and called us. Several months ago Debbie Anne went into the store and requested a refund on an expensive wool jacket. Although she didn't have a sales receipt, the tags were still on the coat and it hadn't been worn. Because the store makes every effort to court business from the coeds, it has a liberal return policy. The clerk was counting out the money when the manager returned from lunch and noticed it was a brand not carried there. When he said as much, Debbie Anne burst into tears and ran out of the store, leaving the coat behind. It was so odd that he and the clerk remembered her face."

"Why would you think this would interest me, Officer Pipkin?"

"Just a hunch," she said as she shifted gears. "I'd better get back for a meeting, Ms. Malloy. Please call me when you feel better."

Debbie Anne's peculiar behavior would have to wait. I sat down on the porch steps and made sure my key ring was not hidden somewhere in the murkiest corner of my purse. My purse had been in my presence since I'd left my duplex in the morning. When Katie bit me, I'd dropped it, but it hadn't burst open. Therefore, I thought with a sigh worthy of my daughter at her pinnacle of martyrdom, the key ring must have fallen out of my purse when I was attacked by my man in the moon. Pippa had gathered up the contents and replaced them, but had overlooked the key ring under a leaf or in a clump of grass.

Well-organized people not only have spare keys, they also put tags on them and know exactly where they keep them. Others of us hazily recall the existence of spare keys, likely to be in a kitchen drawer crammed with junk ... or in a little box along with foreign coins and insufficient postage stamps ... or in a shoebox with expired coupons and postcards from unfamiliar people who'd wished we were there. I knew about well-organized people, having once been married to a man who sent in warranty cards, filed receipts, won arguments with the bank, and watched, in precise chronological order, every episode of *Upstairs, Downstairs*. He empathized with the latter group who made the household run smoothly and efficiently, while scorning those dithery sorts who were forever misplacing their parasols and white kid gloves.

I went across the street and trudged toward the library, promising to abandon my slothful ways if I found my keys. Classes seemed to be over for the day; only a few students were sitting on benches outside the library or waiting for the stoplight to change across from the student union. It was not a dark and stormy night, however, and I was more concerned about my keys than about potential muggers in the bushes.

They were nowhere in the grass around the tree. I searched methodically in a fifteen-foot radius, then leaned against the trunk and considered every action I'd taken since unlocking the front door of the Book Depot at nine o'clock. I had not removed my keys from my purse, and it had been in my possession— with the exception of the few minutes when it had been propelled out of my hands. Along with sweet dimples, indignant dimples, and enthusiastic dimples, it seemed possible that Pippa had among her repertoire a few larcenous ones. I glumly contemplated the ramifications of not having a car key, a house key, a bookstore key, or any of the other odd keys that I kept religiously, year after year, in case I ever remembered what they fit.

Clearly, I needed to have a word with Pippa, and a round of fisticuffs if necessary. My reluctant relationship with the Kappa Theta Etas had caused nothing but a series of headaches, of both the literal and figurative variety. I'd been bitten twice, thrown in jail, hurled into a tree, and exposed to several bizarre subcultures that had thus far existed quite successfully without any intervention—or interest—on my part. My resolution to defend Debbie Anne to the bitter end was melting away like a scoop of ice cream.

I continued to allow it to melt for about three steps, faltered, and veered toward the sidewalk that went past the agri building. My assailant was not likely to be dallying behind the shrubs, but I hadn't done noticeably well in predicting his behavior to date. I circled the building, staunchly ignored a pair of coeds who giggled at me, and headed in the direction he'd purportedly taken.

The journalism building appeared deserted, as did a squatty structure that I thought housed philosophy and other cerebral, and therefore nonmarketable, majors. Secretaries were now leaving for the day, replaced by the custodial staff, a few humorless students, and a rare faculty member with a bulgy briefcase and the obligatory leather patches on his or her elbows.

It was approaching five o'clock, which meant Caron was likely to be working herself up to a fine figure of a snit. My meandering had deposited me at the door of Guzman Hall, home of the law school; unlike the other buildings, it was lighted, and students were visible inside a lounge and a library. I decided to hunt up a pay telephone to tell Caron that she could close the store—if she could find a key in the drawer below the cash register ... or in any of my desk drawers, or in the box of junk on the filing cabinet, or in a similar container in the cramped bathroom. If she had no luck on this jolly little treasure hunt, she'd have to call a locksmith and wait until he arrived. My head began to throb steadily as I imagined her response to the final option.

I entered the building with the due caution of a civilian entering a lion's den. The students brushing past me appeared normal, even nondescript, but I was keenly aware of their chosen careers and kept my face averted as I prowled for a telephone. The main office, an adjoining room apparently used for moot trials, and the dean's office beyond it were all dark. No one was home to offer aid at the legal clinic. I heard distant laughter from around the corner of the hallway, and surmised it came from the lounge I'd glimpsed through the window. Surely there was nothing in the *corpus juris* of the library worthy of a laugh, or even a tiny chuckle.

A lounge was the logical place for vending machines, uncomfortable furniture, merriment, and telephones. I turned—and gasped as I found myself once again confronting the eerie white face of the man in the moon. My eyes wide and my mouth flapping mutely, I recoiled into a water fountain before I realized it was only a portrait attached to the wall, the last in a string that decorated the hallway like pretentious ancestors.

Once I'd regained my composure, I went to the portrait and managed to make out the words on the brass plaque beneath it: John W. Vanderson, Dean of the Guzman Center for Law, 1983– . I frowned at this, and then at his depiction, trying to convince myself that I was muddled, addled, mistaken, in the throes of a concussion, just plain crazy. But I wasn't. His face was distinctive and easily recognizable, although in this case he was beaming genially at me from behind a broad, uncluttered walnut desk, with bookcases, framed diplomas, and an American flag in the background.

I made sure I was alone, then sat down on the opposite side of the hall and gazed up at John W. Vanderson, dean of the law school, husband of the Kappa Theta Eta house corps president (whatever that was), parlous pedestrian, and skilled prowler. Despite my efforts to the contrary, I could produce not one flicker of doubt that he was the man who'd stopped in front of the Kappa house to rub his jaw, the man who'd looked down at me from the third floor the next night, and the man who'd only a short time earlier knocked me into a tree and fled. He was the leading candidate for the anonymous caller.

I rubbed my jaw much the way he had as I tried to make sense of this, but I might as well have been sharing my secret whistle with him. I understood why Winkie had recognized him from my description; she would have met him when he escorted Eleanor to alumnae functions at the sorority house, or at the Vandersons' house. Her reticence was more difficult to understand, but for all I knew, it was based on a dictum from National or arose from an anagogic rite of sisterhood.

Clanks, clatters, and bits of conversation from the direction I'd come caught my attention. I stood up, and after a parting frown at Dean Vanderson, retraced my path to the main hall. Offices that had been dark were now lit, and within the nearest I saw a man emptying a wastebasket into a large plastic container, and a second wheeling a bucket into an inner sanctum.

The door of the dean's office was ajar. If he could prowl, so could I, although I chose to do so with a great deal less impunity. I waited until the custodians were both out of sight, then darted into the office. I froze behind the door, and only when my heart stopped bouncing did I smugly conclude I had accomplished this minor intrusion unnoticed and unchallenged. What I now intended to do was a good question, but I saw no reason to pester myself with such paltry details.

The reception room contained a desk, a computer covered with a plastic hood, filing cabinets, and two straight-backed chairs on either side of a small table with journals and a bowl of mints. The door on the far side was closed, but not necessarily locked, I told myself cheerfully as I glanced at the still-deserted hallway and hurried across the room.

Seconds later I was inside Dean Vanderson's private office, gripped by a sensation of déjà vu until I realized his portrait portrayed the room right down to the leather accessories on his desk and the diplomas on the wall. Beyond the windows was an expanse of lawn, and in the distance Farber Hall rose imposingly above the treetops.

I willed myself not to compare it to the tiny, crowded, dusty office at the back of the Book Depot, where I'd always wondered how the cockroaches fared in battle against the mice in the wee hours of the night. Beside the desk was a table, and on it sat a telephone. As long as I was in the midst of a crime spree, I decided there was no reason not to compound the felony and save myself a dime.

I dialed the number and leaned against the desk to brace myself for a barrage of outrage. "Hi, dear," I began as soon as Caron picked up the receiver. "I'm going to be a little late, so why—"

"A Little Late? We are talking one hundred and fifty-seven minutes late, Mother. I told you we had to do our hair before we went to Rhonda's. I called her earlier to tell her I wasn't going to limbo if she paid me, and she said Louis and some other guys on the football team are coming by after they go to a movie. Do you want me to walk in there as if I'd arrived on a watermelon truck? It's bad enough that ..."

She may have added quite a bit here, but I wasn't listening; I was staring at a sliver of pink paper visible under the computer at the other end of the table. The color was familiar, evoking unpleasant sensations not unlike chilblain.

"Lock the store when you leave," I said, hung up the receiver, and cautiously edged toward the computer. I was not tampering with evidence, I told myself as I tried to coax out the insidious pink cat. Not one of the police officials, campus or local, believed my story that I'd seen John Vanderson on previous occasions. Therefore, there could be no evidence because there'd been no crime, even of the *lex non scripta* variety. Half an hour in Guzman Hall and I'd already prepared my first brief, I realized, increasingly irritated that I couldn't get enough fingernail on its edge to pull it out.

I poked at it with a pencil borrowed from dear John's leather cup, but it was pinned firmly by the weight of the computer. Honest soul that I was, I replaced the pencil, studied the computer for potential handholds, and had hoisted it up a few inches when a cold, unfriendly voice said, "Put that down."

I did.

"Whaddaya think you're doing, lady? If you want a

computer, go buy one at the store instead of stealing it from the college."

I looked back at a middle-aged man who wore a gray uniform and brandished a mop. His expression was as unfriendly as his voice. "I was not stealing this," I began, paused to clear my throat, and with more assurance than I felt, continued. "It does look odd, doesn't it? I feel awfully silly being caught like this, but all I was trying to do was ... well, what may appear to be ..."

"You work on it while I call the campus cops," he said, shaking the mop so hard that drops of water rained on the floor. "Every time one of you steals something from the law building, the cops come sniffing at me. I need this job, lady. I've got a family just like everybody else, and three kids to put through college." He glowered at me as if I'd announced an increase in tuition. "Three kids, all wanting to be something more than a janitor."

"I understand," I said soothingly. "I have a fifteen-year-old daughter who's demanding a car at the end of the summer. And the cost of four years of college is enough to—"

"Just stay there, okay?" He went into the front room and reached for the telephone.

I had all of ten seconds to lift the computer, grab the construction-paper cat, stuff it into my pocket, and rush into the front room before he hit the final button. "Wait!" I said as I grabbed his wrist. "Please don't call the police. The computer's still attached to everything; there's no way I could have moved it more than an inch or so without undoing cables and unplugging it. I swear I wasn't stealing it."

He did not appear any more impressed by my logic than he had been by my previous attempt at parental camaraderie. "That's what they all say, lady. What were you doing? Moving it so you could dust? I don't remember hearing you'd been added to this building's crew."

It hadn't occurred to me that I needed to concoct an

explanation before I made my unauthorized entrance
into the dean's private office. Unlike glib characters
in mystery novels, my mind went as blank as the top
of John Vanderson's head. "I'm not—no, well—it's
obvious that I'm not on the crew," I managed to stam-
mer.

"No shit, Sherlock." He disengaged my hand and
began to redial a number that would result in a veritable morass of complications for me.

He was on the sixth digit when I finally thought of
something. I pushed down the button to disconnect
him, lifted my eyebrows, and said, "I think Dean
Vanderson will be very displeased if you bother the
campus security department. Since I am his wife, I
am more than entitled to be in his office. In fact, he
asked me to come by and pick up a file for him. He
thought it might be under the computer, but he was
mistaken."

"His wife?"

"I am Eleanor Vanderson," I said, articulating carefully and wondering what to do if he'd met her in the
past.

We seemed to clear that hurdle, but we encountered
the next one with dizzying speed. "You got any identification?"

"My dear man," I said with the imperiousness of a
Kappa Theta Eta alumna interviewing a rushee over
tea, "I most certainly do have identification, but I have
no inclination to show it to you. On the other hand, I
will be happy to call the dean and explain that I was
delayed because of your petty suspicions. We are due
at a faculty engagement at six o'clock sharp. It's at
Thurber Farber Manor, home of the president of the
college. I have no quarrel with you, but I can only
hope the dean doesn't file a complaint with your super-
visor. I should hate for you to lose your job with those
three college-bound offspring."

He continued to entertain his petty suspicions for a
long while, but at last he shrugged and said, "I dunno
about this, lady. If you're really the dean's wife, you

would have said so in the beginning, instead of acting like a thief caught in the act. But I got work to do, and I'd like to catch the end of the ball game when I get home." He picked up the mop and went to the door. "I'm gonna lock this office. Next time you come by on an errand for the dean, plan to show proper identification."

"I shall impress the dean with your cooperation," I said, still caught up in my role. I swept past him and sailed out the door of the Guzman Center for Law, and only when I was on the far side of the agri building did I sink down on a bench and allow myself to revel in the absurdity of the scene. I had no qualms about awarding myself an Oscar. Best actress in an *ab libitum* role seemed apt.

I took the folded construction-paper cat out of my pocket, smoothed it, and steeled myself for a sugary message. As expected, the photocopied line read: "Katie the Kappa Kitten Says Thanks!" The handwritten addendum was: "For remembering to pay your dues."

Pay his dues? John Vanderson was not and never would be a Kappa, and his wife was hardly the kind to need cutesy notes to remind her of anything whatsoever. I doubted alumnae paid dues, although they were likely to be dunned by National on a regular basis right up until the opening strains of the funerary procession.

The handwriting was feminine in its swirls. I hadn't saved the two previous cutouts, but as best I remembered, this newest message was not written by the same hand. If I ruled out Jean and Pippa, I was left with Rebecca, Debbie Anne, and the other sixty or so Kappa Theta Etas who had access to what I envisioned as boxes and boxes of pink construction-paper cats. I examined it carefully, but there was no way to determine if it had been sent that day or six months ago.

The cat was in my hand, if not out of the bag, and it proved my theory that Dean Vanderson was in some way involved. Perhaps not to Officers Terrance and Michaels, or even to Officer Pipkin and Lieutenant Rosen, who were having such a grand time on their joint task force that they were willing to work overtime.

I strolled across the lawn, the cat fluttering between my fingers, and paused on the opposite side of the street. Scaffolding had appeared on the front of the Kappa Theta Eta house, indicative of the imminent arrival of painters. If Ed Whitbred and his beetleheaded assistant had won the contract, they might well be there the next day. I had no idea what I needed to ask them, but I was confident questions would spring to my lips as easily as lies had in the law building. I would pin them down with no more mercy than a lepidopterist, wrench answers from their treacherous mouths, and walk away with some semblance of a hypothesis that would lead me to the whereabouts of Debbie Anne Wray, the murderer of Jean Hall, and maybe the definitive solution to global warming.

Much later the latest paper cat was propped against the coffee pot. A rusty key lay on the kitchen counter; I dearly hoped it fit the door of the Book Depot. No one had answered the telephone at the sorority house, so there was nothing I could do about my key ring for the moment. Caron's cosmetics case and sleeping bag were gone, as was she. I'd called Luanne and related the highlights of the afternoon, eliciting gurgles, snickers, sharp intakes, and a few brays of laughter. We'd agreed that my next assignment needed to be an appointment with John Vanderson. A package that had contained a low-fat, low-sodium microwave meal was discarded in the wastebasket, its contents having been made palatable with the addition of salt and butter.

I was soaking in the bathtub, occasionally twisting the hot-water tap with my toes, allowing the heat to nurse away the day's accumulation of bruises, and reading a mystery novel in which the clever amateur sleuth, a woman of moderate years who had the courage to admit she hated cats, was outwitting bumbly, fumbly, grumbly policemen on every page.

I was reaching for my drink when I heard a scream.

11

I gulped down my drink as I dried myself, scrambled into my clothes, and hurried downstairs and across the lawn to the Kappa Theta Eta house. How could these women—and their neighbors—get any sleep, if they insisted on screaming at every opportunity? As much as I loved my duplex with its view of the campus and convenience to the bookstore, it might be time to move farther away.

I was wondering just how cold the winters were in Fairbanks as I pounded on the front door. Winkie jerked it open and gaped at me. "Claire?" she said wonderingly, as if I were dressed in a tutu and clutching a glittery wand. She was the one who warranted a second look, dressed as she was in a naughty scarlet peignoir, with enough makeup on her face to intimidate a seasoned hooker, but very little she or any of the Kappas did these days surprised me.

"Who screamed this time?" I asked.

She pulled me inside and locked the door. "Pippa. She and Rebecca are in my suite, both of them so upset that I felt a glass of wine would serve a medicinal purpose. I even splashed a wee bit in Katie's saucer."

She's splashed more than a wee bit in her own saucer, I decided as I followed her unsteady path across the foyer. The two girls sat on the sofa, both wearing robes. Pippa's face was pale and her hair disheveled, but she managed to convey a glass to her lips with only a minimum of twitches.

If Rebecca had been in need of a medicinal dose, it had worked miracles. She gave me a sharp look over the rim of her glass, then finished off its contents and said, "So we've disturbed you once again, Mrs. Malloy. You must think we're absolutely crazy, but sometimes literally weeks and weeks go by with nothing more exciting than the discovery of a mouse in the pantry."

"Would you like a glass of wine?" Winkie asked me with a bright smile. "It's our little secret weapon to fight off overly active imaginations."

I wasn't sure whose she had in mind, mine or Pippa's. "Thank you, but this is not a social call. In truth, my late-night visits are beginning to irritate me as much as they seem to irritate you. Just tell me why Pippa screamed and I'll run along home."

In the ensuing silence, Katie stalked into the room and sprang into Rebecca's lap, evidently no more pleased to see me than I was to see her. She seemed fascinated by the bandage on my hand, and no doubt proud of her handiwork. Winkie wandered into her kitchen, returned with a bottle of wine, and settled cozily in the rocking chair. Pippa sniffled. Rebecca gathered her long black hair and curled it around her neck like a scarf.

"Why did you scream?" I snapped at the offender. "Did our mysterious prowler reappear, or was it a mouse in the pantry?"

"It was weird, Mrs. Malloy. I was so startled that I didn't even realize I'd screamed until afterward. I think I must have been repressing my anxiety to the point of psychoneurosis, understandably precipitated by depression over Jean's death. Had I made more of an effort to explore my innermost—"

"Someone was outside her window," Rebecca said, stroking Katie with a gesture as languid as her voice. "He stepped on a dry twig and the sound frightened her."

Pippa giggled nervously, if not psychoneurotically. "I'd taken off my bra and was examining my tan lines, so he must have gotten an eyeful." She looked down with a modest dimple or two. "I've been sunbathing in a really cute little bikini. Then tonight, when we were at the mall, I found this absolutely adorable one-piece, my very best shade of pearl gray, but I don't see how I can wear it with a white stripe across my back."

I ordered myself to stop grinding my teeth. "I'm sure you'll find a way. So you were in your bedroom, and someone was outside your window. Did you see his face?" She shook her head. "Has anyone called campus security?"

"Oh, Claire, I don't think it's necessary," Winkie said reproachfully. "What must they think of us? A sorority is only as strong as its reputation, as you well know, and each chapter must endeavor to—"

I was not in the mood for an in-depth analysis of the perils of a dubious reputation. "You need to call Eleanor Vanderson and ask her about notifying the campus security force. If she agrees with you, at the least she can have her husband come over and ascertain that the peeping tom has fled and the screens and doors are secured."

Winkie frowned at me. "I wouldn't want to disturb her, and Dean Vanderson is a very busy man with numerous responsibilities. It's much too late for me to call them."

"Then I will." I reached for the telephone. "Tell me the number and we can all go back to bed shortly." I was surprised when she complied. Seconds later, I was surprised and disappointed when a male answered.

"Is this Dean Vanderson?" I said crisply.

"Yes, it is." He spoke in an even voice, as opposed to a voice indicative of frantic activity within the last ten minutes. "Who's this?"

"I'm calling on behalf of the Kappa housemother. She needs to speak to Mrs. Vanderson about a situation at the house." I thrust the receiver into Winkie's hand and started for the door, then returned and sat down next to Pippa. Speaking softly in order not to interfere with Winkie's sputtery apologies, I said, "There's something we need to discuss. This afternoon when you picked up what had fallen out of my purse, you failed to replace my key ring. If you kept it as a souvenir, I'd like you to return it. You're causing me a great deal of inconvenience."

"I wouldn't take your key ring, Mrs. Malloy," she said, sounding shocked. "That's stealing. Kappa Theta Eta pledges take a solemn oath to uphold this really involved code of honor so they won't ever disgrace the organization. We have to promise not to be seen drunk in public, not to cheat, not to get caught in sleazy bars and nightclubs—"

"Or motels," Rebecca inserted neatly.

Pippa flushed. "Or motels, or anyplace that might make us look like tramps. We always dress for dinner on Monday nights as if it were a dinner party, and—"

"Then you don't have my key ring?" I said. "Did you see anyone else who might have picked it up?"

She reiterated her ignorance with such earnestness that I was considering believing her when Winkie replaced the receiver and said, "Eleanor agreed that we have no reason to call the campus security department. She and her husband were in bed when you called, and she isn't willing to ask him to get dressed and come here. She'll send someone tomorrow to make sure all the screens are set properly and hooked from the inside."

"What about yours?" I said as I went into her kitchen and pushed back the pink gingham curtains. "It's barely propped in place, and one tiny nudge will send it to the ground." I proceeded to prove my hypothesis to be correct. "Oops, sorry, but it was begging for it," I called. "You really ought to keep the ground-floor windows locked until this prowler is caught."

Pippa gasped. "My window's wide open. What if this voyeur is in my room?"

I closed and locked the window before I returned to the living room. "I think we'd better check all the windows on this floor, especially those in unoccupied rooms."

"Mrs. Malloy has a point, Winkie." Rebecca held out her hand. "Give me the keys and I'll go with her.

You and Pippa can wait here until the drawbridge is raised and the alligators are circling in the moat."

Winkie seemed a little confused, but she took the keys from her purse and handed them to Rebecca. We went first to the kitchen and made sure the door and windows were locked. We did the same in the lounge, then went to the hallway with the bedrooms.

"My room is a pit," Rebecca said, although with a noticeable lack of distress. She went inside, stepping over clothes and clutter, locked her window, and returned with an indecipherable smile. "No nocturnal visitors for me, anyway," she said as she unlocked Pippa's door and gestured for me to precede her.

I'd taken a quick look at all the paper cats taped to her walls. They had messages along the lines of "You're a great big sister!" and "I got an A on my paper!" The handwriting varied; apparently they served as in-house memos as well as official stationery.

Pippa hadn't done any housekeeping since I'd last visited. The pearl-gray bathing suit hung from a knob on the dresser, books had been added to the mess on the floor, and an open desk drawer filled with oddments reminded me of my own. The blinds were pulled up and the window was open as far as it could go. The screen was hooked, however, and showed no signs of tampering.

We went into Debbie Anne's room, still neat and clean and sadly impersonal. The only addition was a thin patina of fingerprint powder. I picked up the photograph of her parents. "I'm really worried about Debbie Anne. She didn't sound particularly terrified when she called me, but she may have—"

"She called you?" Rebecca swept her hair back to stare at me. "Why would she call you?"

"She seemed to have found me sympathetic, and she asked me to get in touch with her mother. I did, hoping the woman might have some suggestions as to where Debbie Anne is."

"Did she?"

"Her mother was under the illusion that Debbie

Anne was a treasured member of the sorority and spent all her free time with her sisters," I said with a hint of acerbity.

"She would say something like that, wouldn't she?" As she made sure the window was locked, she added, "She stole things from us, ran down Jean in the alley, and now is hiding as if she fancies herself to be a maligned victim. I'm not at all surprised to hear she lied to her mother. Let's finish this up, if you don't mind. I have an audition in the morning, and I need to study my lines."

I went to Jean's door and waited while she unlocked it. The dead girl's clothes and personal effects had been placed in suitcases and cardboard boxes stacked in the middle of the room. The bed had been stripped, and the pink cats were gone.

"Debbie Anne Wray tried to destroy Kappa Theta Eta," Rebecca said from the doorway. "We did our best to mold her into one of us, but she couldn't cut it. I don't care if they never find her. I hope she's hiding in the woods, and the bears get to her first." She backed across the hall and leaned against the wall, her face mottled with anger and her hands curled so tightly that her fingernails might have drawn blood. Turning away, she began to cry.

I decided to ignore her outburst and get out of the place before I lost my temper. Even the mildest of mild-mannered booksellers can turn militant if provoked. I went around the cartons, made sure the window was locked, and was on my way out of the room when I noticed a scattering of items that had been left on the dresser, presumably unworthy of being packed. There were bobby pins dusted with powder, an empty pack of menthol cigarettes, plastic pens, paper clips in a chain, and a white cap from a shampoo bottle. And a matchbook from a motel called Hideaway Haven. I slipped it into my pocket. "Who packed up Jean's things?" I asked Rebecca.

"I offered to do it, but looking at her things was too painful and I just couldn't go through with it," she

said, trying to stanch the tears that slinked down her
cheeks. Unlike most of us, she cried delicately, with no
puffiness of her eyelids or redness of her nose. "I think
Winkie told the cleaning woman to finish, or maybe
she did it herself."

"Did you find a packet of negatives?" I asked ever
so artfully.

My question dried up her tears. "Negatives of what,
Mrs. Malloy?" she said. Her hair hid her expression,
but the coolness of her tone was unmissable.

"I have no idea," I said, although the matchbook in
my pocket was glowing like an ember and I was beginning to see some possibilities. They were downright
nasty ones, too. "Everything's secure, so you can go
study for your audition and I'll stop by Winkie's on my
way out."

I'd hoped she might leave me in Jean's room, but
she waited while I turned out the light, closed the door,
and joined her in the hall. She went into her room, and
rather than snooping through Jean's possessions, I was
reduced to doing as I'd promised. Winkie was asleep in
the rocking chair, and Pippa was dangling a pink rib-
bon for Katie's amusement. She assured me that she
would help Winkie to bed and thanked me for being so
concerned.

I wasn't, but I nodded wearily and went back to my
apartment. Earlier, the steamy hot water had been so
intoxicating that I was relaxed and anticipating bed.
Now, thanks to the Kappa Theta Etas, my mind was
sizzling with chaotic thoughts, most of which had to do
with blackmail. I wished I could talk to someone, but
the someone who came to mind was not an option.
This was going to be a solo effort, and not until my solution was tied up with a pretty pink bow would it be
presented to the appropriate authorities.

I sat down and looked at the advertising on the
matchbook. The Hideaway Haven, a dumpy place west
of town that I'd noticed but failed to visit, offered its
clientele "adult" movies and king-size waterbeds. I
suspected it also offered not only weekly and monthly

rates, but an hourly one for those who availed themselves of certain services indigenous to truck stops.
What could I do with this concrete bit of evidence—
other than light candles and sit around in their glow?
Peter kept candles in his dining room, living room, and
bedroom, and was forever muttering about my pragma-
tism when I flipped on a light to avoid stubbing my
toes. Officer Pipkin was likely to be able to see more
keenly in the dark than a cat.

Admittedly, I was brooding, a useless and deleteri-
ous pastime that was beginning to stir up a goodly
amount of self-pity. I realized I was in real danger of
putting on a Johnny Mathis record and sniveling
throughout the night. Physical action, if not exertion,
was called for, I decided as I stuck the matchbook in
my purse and started through the kitchen to the back
staircase that led to my garage. Considering how to
pose questions to the night manager about his college
clients, I had my hand on the doorknob when it occurred to me that I wasn't driving anywhere unless I
hot-wired my car.

I dropped my purse on the table and began to paw
through drawers in search of a spare car key. By the
time I found a key that might qualify, it was well after
midnight. With a chortle of triumph, I went to bed.

Early the next morning, Caron and Inez dragged in
while I was drinking coffee. They both had bloated
faces, red-rimmed eyes, and surly expressions, all
symptomatic of a sleepless night. Things thudded to
the floor in Caron's room, and I was hastily finishing
my coffee as they came into the kitchen.

"I am never leaving this place as long as I live,"
Caron announced. "I will stay in my room until my
hair turns gray, my teeth fall out, and my skin is overcome with liver spots and hairy, disgusting warts. Little children will creep cautiously into the yard,
whispering and pointing at my window, but at the
slightest twitch of my curtain, they'll scream and run.
I shall become a legend in Farberville, but one day ev-

eryone will cease speculating and forget about the pathetic old hag who resides in the attic."

"You said your room," Inez began, then stopped out of consideration for her continued well-being.

"There is an attic," I said. "I've never been up there, but a couple of summers ago the landlord had someone spray for wasps. There's a trapdoor in the ceiling of the hall closet."

"You are not amusing." Caron lay down on the floor and closed her eyes, her arms crossed in the classic pose of the dearly departed. "Rhonda Maguire is nothing more than a garden tool," she said in a doomed voice. "I don't care if I never see her again for fifty years, but she'd better watch out after I'm dead. I'm coming back as a carnivorous zombie."

I frowned at Inez. "A garden tool?"

She nodded soberly at me, looked at the body attempting to decompose on the kitchen floor, and tiptoed to the nearest chair. She mouthed something at me, but it could have been almost anything, from a malediction to a sonnet.

"A hoe, Mother," Caron said impatiently. "Are these hot flashes impairing your ability to relate to your current culture?"

"Most definitely." I swallowed the last of the coffee and stood up. A benign parent would have slipped away soundlessly, or perhaps inquired with such sympathy that she would be regaled with the entirety of the tragedy. "So, how'd the limbo go? Win any prizes, or did Rhonda's center of gravity prevail?"

"The minute Louis Wilderberry walks onto the patio, Rhonda grabs him and starts telling these really incredible lies about how I claim to be the ultimate fashion dictator of the century, even the millennium. Everybody—Present Company Included—giggles and snickers, and then Rhonda goes, 'Why don't we all chip in so Miss Perfect Palette can do a My Beautiful Self analysis of Louis?' He was so embarrassed that he literally ran back to his car. This was deemed Too

Funny for Words, and I heard about it right up until the rooster crowed three times at dawn."

Inez slid down in her chair until her eyes were on the plane of the table top. "I didn't say one word, Caron. I thought Rhonda was being really stupid about it, but I still say you went too far when you locked yourself in her room for over an hour."

"And did what?" I asked as calmly as I could.

Caron squeezed her eyes shut more tightly. "Nothing at all, Mother. I am not a vengeful person. If Rhonda calls, tell her I moved to France to live in a chateau."

I looked at Inez, who shrugged and continued her slithery trip toward the floor. "Whatever you say, dear. I may need you to help out at the store this afternoon. I'll let you know—"

"You seem to have forgotten that I am never leaving this apartment. Furthermore, I am not answering the telephone, so your anonymous pervert's going to have to bother someone else. Inez, see if there's any orange juice in the refrigerator. I already feel my bones turning brittle."

I left before I could learn what Caron had done in Rhonda's bedroom, although I knew I'd find out sooner or later. The key from the drawer fit the car, and the key from the kitchen counter fit the front door of the Book Depot. If only, I thought as I sat down on my stool, the clues I'd chanced upon fit as well. Arnie and Ed Whitbred had something to do with whatever was taking place, and I had proof of sorts that Dean Vanderson was involved. The active Kappa Theta Etas, the alumnae, the missing one, and even the deceased one qualified for some role in the muddlesome puzzle.

The most expedient plan would be to line up every last one of them and ask the manager of the Hideaway Haven if he'd seen any of them. However, that was a course available only to the authorities, who were not likely to cooperate with me. Neither was John Vanderson, but I called the college switchboard and asked for his office number, then dialed it.

"Dean Vanderson is in a meeting," a secretary informed me. "Then he has appointments all afternoon, and a reception at five for a federal judge. After that, he's hosting a dinner party for the judge and some of the faculty. Tomorrow he leaves for a week-long legal symposium in Las Vegas. If you can catch him, say hello for me."

I waited a moment to see if she'd finished reciting the litany. "This can't wait for a week," I said.

"Neither can final approval of the grant proposal that's due on Friday, nor can the editor of the *Law Review*, nor can the coed with a sexual harassment charge, nor can the faculty adviser of the judicial committee." She hung up.

Humph, I thought as I went to the door and gazed at the traffic rattling over the train tracks. It didn't sound as though I would be able to regain access to Dean Vanderson's office as easily as I had the night before, not with a Medusa in the front room turning students and visitors alike to stone. Even if I were to risk such a fate, I was leery about running into the unfriendly custodian.

The mock Mrs. Vanderson decided to see what she could wheedle of the legitimate one. I resumed my seat, looked up her number, and called it, hoping it was too early for the luncheon circuit to have begun.

"Vanderson residence."

I was shocked into silence, wildly wondering if my brain had been turned to stone. I gulped, blinked, and finally said, "Debbie Anne? Is that you?"

"No, it isn't!"

My entire body must have been turned to stone. I was unable to do anything except listen to the dial tone until a series of beeps nudged me into a semblance of consciousness. I numbly redialed the number. After a dozen plaintive rings, I replaced the receiver and considered the five words that she'd said. The twangy nasality of the voice was distinctive, and she had identified the residence. Had I made a mistake that offended the responder so deeply that she'd stalked out of earshot of the telephone? Or out the front door? If it had indeed been Debbie Anne, why had she reacted with abruptness? And what on earth was she doing at the Vandersons' house?

I jotted down the address, locked the store, and ran to my car, congratulating myself on having driven to the bookstore on the off chance I might need to meet Dean Vanderson in a remote spot. "Just stay there," I muttered as I pulled onto Thurber Street and headed for Farberville's historic district.

I'd repeated the plea a hundred times as I crept down Washington Avenue, looking for the house number. Enough of the historically correct occupants had numbers affixed to their porches to allow me to home in like a Scud missile and park in front of a well-preserved yellow Victorian house with a turret topped by a brass eagle. It and the lawn surrounding it were immaculate. There were no cars in the driveway.

No more than fifteen minutes had elapsed since the call, I tried to reassure myself as I hurried to the porch and knocked. No skinny girls had been walking on the sidewalks, and I knew she hadn't driven away in her car. I knocked again, then spotted an old-fashioned doorbell and twisted it vigorously. I could hear it grinding within, pleading for someone to heed its call and answer the door. No one did, however, and I finally let my hand drop.

"Are you looking for Eleanor?"

I looked back at a blue-haired woman wearing a raincoat and holding a leash with a gloved hand. At the end of the leash was a cocker spaniel dancing with excitement. "Yes, I am." I struggled not to look as if I'd been considering breaking into the house with the brick at the edge of the porch. "Do you know when she'll be back?"

"She's at her garden club, and then I believe it's her afternoon at the gift shop at the hospital." The woman glanced at the brick. "I live next door, and I'll be happy to let her know you dropped by for a visit."

"That's so very kind of you. Actually, I'm looking

for one of the Kappa Theta Eta pledges who's staying here."

"Eleanor didn't mention that she and John have a houseguest. Last summer her niece came for two weeks, but she's an alumna rather than a pledge. A lovely girl, I must say, and very clever. She has a degree in business administration, but what with the twins and her fund-raising efforts on behalf of the sorority, she's put her career on hold. Her husband is an orthodontist."

"Isn't that interesting," I murmured mendaciously. I waited, but the woman clearly intended to remain rooted to the sidewalk. Her dog had collapsed at her feet and was licking her shoe, out of either affection or starvation. "So you haven't noticed a tall, thin girl with brown hair?"

"They're all tall and thin these days, aren't they? When I was a gal, we were encouraged to have a few curves, but now they all strive to look like matchsticks." She yanked on the leash. "Stop that, Brandy. Are you a Kappa Theta Eta, dear? I myself was a Chi Omega; I had so many legacies that I was almost carried through the door and bestowed on a throne on the first day of rush. My granddaughter's pledging this fall at my very own alma mater."

She was a formidable opponent. I conceded her the win, smiled vaguely at the dog, and said I'd try to catch Eleanor at another time. She was still standing on the sidewalk as I drove away, more because of the entanglement with the leash than out of suspicion—or so I hoped. I drove past the library and up the hill, gnawing on my fingernail and considering what to do. I knew what I *should* do, of course. There was no question that I was teetering at the fringe of propriety, of what I could justify even to myself. Peter would listen to me (in between his ever so tedious remarks about my propensity for meddling), and he would be able to question the Vandersons, search the house, and eventually determine if they were harboring a fugitive. I, in contrast, had been stymied by a woman with a dog. A boot-licking cocker spaniel.

Short of storming the garden club to take Eleanor hostage, I was at a loss for ideas. I finally parked in a site popular with moonsick lovers, cut off the engine, and let my head fall back against the seat. Jean Hall had coerced Debbie Anne into doing something— something that related to the boutique at the mall? Why dash away instead of acknowledging the mistake and heading for the proper store? Had Dean Vanderson stashed Debbie Anne in the attic and gone to the sorority house to get the negatives? Negatives of what? It was frightfully irksome that the anonymous caller preferred to deal with Caron, I thought with a sigh.

My next move was obvious, if not pretty.

12

Shortly before seven o'clock, I parked in a strategically chosen spot on a street perpendicular to Washington Avenue, and slouched in the seat in the tradition of a jaded private eye resigned to a boring and bitterly cold night of surveillance (it was a balmy evening, and we had two hours of daylight to go, but I was, as Caron would say, In A Mood). The Vandersons' Mercedes was parked in the driveway under the protection of an ancient magnolia tree, and as I watched, the car I'd seen in front of the Kappa Theta Eta house pulled in behind it. My quarry hurried into the house.

I was dressed not in a trenchcoat and fedora, but in a becoming green dress. I'd gone so far as to don pantyhose, heels, and faux pearls for the occasion. Having never hosted a federal judge, I wasn't sure when the festivities would begin, but I was praying I had a few minutes to speak in private to the dean.

My prayers went unnoticed. Before I reached the house, a black Cadillac stopped at the curb, followed by an entourage of imported vehicles. Those who emerged were dressed to kill, in the figurative sense, and were chattering amiably as they started for the house. Adopting my contingency plan, I slipped through the group and tucked my hand under the arm of a man with the white hair of a televangelist, the deceptively trustworthy eyes of same, and a hawkish red nose—and therefore the man most likely to be the revered judge.

"Isn't this lovely of John and Eleanor?" I said as I propelled him to the porch.

He squeezed my hand. "And of you, my dear. I don't believe we met at the reception. Are you on the faculty?"

"I waved at you from across the room, but it was so crowded, wasn't it? Let's do make an effort to have a nice little talk tonight, Your Honor."

The front door was open and we streamed into the house like starlings to their roost. Eleanor greeted her guests with professional aplomb, transferring coats and wraps to a waiting maid, welcoming us with warm smiles and gracious words. Most of us, anyway. "Judge Frankley, I'm so honored and delighted you were able to come tonight, you and . . ." She dribbled to a halt. A tiny wrinkle appeared between her eyes, and a few more at the corners of her mouth.

"Claire," I prompted her politely. "I think I see the bar, Judge Frankley. How about a martini?"

He rumbled happily as we continued into a living room right out of a glossy magazine spread. High ceilings, polished wood, antiques, doilies protecting table tops, a basket of pine cones next to the fireplace, an afghan draped over the arm of the sofa—the whole Americana bit.

"How long are you staying in Farberville?" I asked my abductee while we jostled for position in front of a table lined with bottles, a silver ice bucket with silver tongs, and crystal bowls of olives and citrus slices.

I missed his answer. John Vanderson was frozen in the doorway to the dining room, regarding me with such panic that he appeared on the verge of an apoplectic attack. I smiled and wiggled my eyebrows at him. He stumbled out of sight. Was this any way for a proper host to act?

". . . little party at my hotel later," the judge was saying. "A very select group, of course. I'll be absolutely heartbroken if you refuse, my dear." He squeezed my hand more firmly. "I might have to hold you in contempt of court."

"I wouldn't dream of missing it," I said. After a brief struggle, I disengaged my hand. "Excuse me, but

I must have a word with Dean Vanderson. Why don't you sit right there on that cozy loveseat, and when I come back, you can tell me all about your clever decisions."

I slithered through the crowd and into the dining room, where the glare from silverwear and crystal was enough to blind me momentarily. Dean Vanderson apparently had escaped through the door on the far side of the room, so I headed that way. The kitchen was a crowded, bustling place, and none of the staff responded to my question. I moved on, hoping I wouldn't find myself at the top of the basement stairs—or the bottom of the attic stairs. The room beyond the kitchen proved to be nothing more horrifying than a sunroom with windows that looked out on a landscaped yard and a swimming pool.

I was about to try the next door when I saw Dean Vanderson in a corner, his head bowed and his shoulders drooping. I approached him as I would a wounded animal (although, of course, I value my extremities far too much to do such a thing), reasonably sure the kitchen staff would come to my aid if he flung himself on my admittedly alluring carotid artery. "We need to talk," I said gently. "We can do it in private, or we can do it in front of your wife and your guests."

"Shall we take a stroll by the pool, Mrs. Malloy?"

"I'm a competent swimmer," I warned him as we went down stone steps to the yard. Azaleas and rhododendrons bloomed in studiously casual confusion, and honeysuckle vines swarmed over the crumbling brick walls of an old well. I'd read too many mysteries not to take a quick look into the shaft. It was less than ten feet deep, the ground appeared undisturbed, and Debbie Anne was not cowering at the bottom.

"Were you on the guest list?" Dean Vanderson asked, having observed my detour with mild perplexity.

"No, and I'll fade away unfed as soon as you answer my questions. I'm not sure exactly how you're involved with the Kappa Theta Etas, but I have some fairly plausible guesses that I will share with the police, if necessary. I don't know if they'll stand up in court, but they will cause you a great deal of trouble." I halted at the edge of the pool and made sure no bodies were adrift near the drain. All I saw was a magnolia leaf curled into the shape of a devilfish.

He pulled together two aluminum chairs and gestured for me to sit. "Indiscretion may have occurred, but it was in the past and has nothing to do with the girl's death. I will admit I pushed you down this afternoon. Coming upon you so abruptly, I was startled and reacted without thinking. For that, I apologize most sincerely. I trust there was no serious damage?"

"I don't want to talk about this afternoon, Dean Vanderson. I want to talk about Jean Hall."

He shivered despite the sunshine, and pulled out a handkerchief to wipe his forehead. "Ah, yes, I hired her to run errands and do office chores. Her salary was in line with our tight budget, so as an added inducement, I arranged for her to sit in on some of the lectures in order to help her prepare for law school in the fall. Eleanor informed me of her accidental death. A terrible tragedy for her, for the driver, and for the sorority in general."

"She was murdered," I said bluntly.

"Do the police concur?" His pale eyelashes were almost invisible as he blinked at me. "Eleanor said they'd concluded it was an accident, caused by one of the pledges."

"Who came here to hide."

"Here? That's impossible. If she came here after the accident, Eleanor would have counseled her to turn herself in, even have driven her to the police station, and surely would have mentioned it to me. I have a position to maintain in the academic community, Mrs. Malloy, and the sorority means everything to my wife. Neither of us would jeopardize our achievements by harboring a fugitive."

"John!" Eleanor called from the door. "What are you and Claire doing out there? In case you failed to notice, we have guests. Judge Frankley is asking for you."

I smiled at her, and in a low voice said, "Where shall we discuss the negatives—here or on the loveseat with Judge Frankley?"

He regarded me for a moment, as if assessing my alleged swimming ability should I find myself in the proximity of the drain. "Here, I should think," he said resignedly, then called to his wife, "I shall be there shortly, dear. Just tell everybody there's been a small crisis at the law school that must be resolved before I leave in the morning."

Eleanor didn't look convinced; I could think of no reason why she should. However, after a minute she nodded and disappeared into the house to appease her guests with cocktails, canapés, and little white lies.

Dean Vanderson was struggling to radiate judicial dignity, but he looked more like a small boy on the verge of tears, his mouth puckered, his eyes downcast, his porcelain forehead beaded with sweat. Patting him on the shoulder, I said, "Come on, you can tell me. If you cooperate, I promise not to go to the police."

"Jean approached me last fall. I'd seen her at sorority affairs"—he cringed at his ill-chosen word—"such as luncheons and teas, but we'd only made small talk. However, on this particular occasion, a football brunch at the house, Jean asked me if she might make an appointment to elicit my advice about law school. She came to my office several times, always with catalogs and questions, and I was more than happy to offer her what assistance I could."

"And also at the Hideaway Haven?"

He gaped at me, then managed to swallow what must have been a most unpleasant taste. "You appear to be well informed, Mrs. Malloy."

"Thank you," I murmured, accepting his compliment with a modest nod—and wishing it were deserved.

"I will not deny that I am aware of an establishment known as the Hideaway Haven. Whatever may have taken place there can be best described as a series of perfectly harmless dalliances. My wife has become more and more involved with her volunteer work, her various clubs, and, of course, her Kappa Theta Eta responsibilities. Often she is exhausted by the time she arrives home. Eleanor is an attractive woman and an exemplary hostess, but when we manage to . . . retire together, she responds so distractedly that I suspect she's mentally making out guest lists or contemplating menus. I find this frustrating."

I tried to keep the disgust out of my voice, but I may not have given it my personal best. "You have a beautiful wife, a lovely home, a respected position at the college and in the community. Federal judges drink martinis in your living room. Uniformed cooks crowd your kitchen. Students scribble down your opinions, and faculty members beg you for pennies to buy legal pads and paper clips. Why would you risk the culmination of a lifetime of hard work and ambition to have an affair with a student in a sleazy motel?"

"It's difficult to explain," he said, wiping his neck. "It was flattering, you see. I've never been attractive. Eleanor married me for my family connections and my potential for success; I married her for similar reasons. When I was in law school, I became obsessed by the handsome young studs with their wavy hair, smoldering eyes, some as bright and disciplined as I, others less so but destined to succeed in their future endeavors simply on the strength of their physical attributes. I retreated into academia, where I could wage war on an intellectual level, but even now, when I address a class or interview applicants, I find myself . . ." He made a gesture with a taut white hand. "This is not the time to present the defendant's closing statement, is it?"

"I'm not the one with a houseful of guests, but I'm willing to acknowledge these psychological ravages of your past and move right along. You and Jean met at the Hideaway Haven. Someone took a photograph of you in the midst of this indiscretion and has been blackmailing you since then. How am I doing?"

He gave me an odd look, no doubt impressed by my acuity and acumen. "To some extent, you are correct in your suppositions, Mrs. Malloy. Approximately three weeks ago, a distressing depiction of activities that need not be detailed was sent to me, accompanied by a peculiar construction-paper cutout and a handwritten request that I make a private endowment. I was able to do so without undue problems. A second followed, and a third only yesterday. It became clear that I am to be hounded in perpetuity by a member of Kappa Theta Eta with the alias Katie. I've begun to dream of strangling that cat, of burning down the house, of penning a suicide note and disappearing into the wilds of Canada."

I remembered Officer Pipkin's remark about cloistered nuns as I leaned back in the squeaky chair and crossed my arms. "But hasn't it occurred to you to confess and accept whatever punishment is meted out by your wife and the administration? Blackmail is a particularly nasty crime. Are you willing to allow the perpetrator to continue on her merry way? Aren't you committed to justice and all that stuff?"

"John!" Eleanor called sharply from the doorway. "Judge Frankley is still asking for you, and dinner is ready to be served. What can you and Claire be discussing that must be resolved while the quail toughen?"

"I'll be there in a moment," he called back, waited until she was gone, and then gave me the look of a harshly chastised puppy who'd savaged a slipper. "I must see to my guests. I made a mistake, and it seems I am to pay for it. There's your justice, Mrs. Malloy."

"But you do admit you searched the sorority house for the negatives of the photographs of you and Jean?" I demanded as he rose to his feet. "Did you search her purse, too?"

"After I ran her down in the alley?"

I stopped congratulating myself on the guile of my leading question. "Something like that," I admitted with a shrug.

"Allow me to correct some of your hazy, unsubstantiated, and fallacious ideas. I did have an appointment with Jean Hall the night she was killed, and we met in the enclosed patio of a fraternity house that borders the alley. At that time, she acknowledged that she was the blackmailer and informed me that larger endowments would be required, although none so outrageous that I could not comply without arousing suspicion. Negatives were to serve as my receipts. She took one out of her purse and an exchange was made."

"You're positive she had her purse with her?"

"Do try to listen, Mrs. Malloy. She took the negative out of her purse and showed it to me. Less than a minute later she put an envelope full of twenty-dollar bills into her purse."

I attempted to envision the scene, but what flashed across my mind was not this icy entrepreneur in the patio but the bloodied body in the alley. And something was missing. "Was she wearing her sorority pin?"

"I was not concerned with her accessories, but I seem to remember thinking how ostentatious it was. Please do not quote me on that. In any case, I left her sitting on a bench, licking her lips in a disturbingly contented fashion. I never saw her again."

"You drove by the house later. I saw you from my bedroom window."

"After I'd had time to consider the situation, I decided to suggest to Jean that we terminate our contractual relationship with a single payment in exchange for all the negatives. I went by the house to propose it, saw the police cars in the alley, and went home. Only when Eleanor returned did I learn what had happened."

"But now someone else is blackmailing you," I said encouragingly (if one can use the term in that context). "You were searching the third floor, presumably with no success. How did you get in?"

"Eleanor has a full set of keys, in case an emergency arises that requires the immediate presence of a plumber or an electrician. I borrowed them from her desk, and replaced them as soon as I was home." He gave me a reproachful smile. "I'd intended to work my way from the top floor to the basement, but you had the pinched look of a police informant. I haven't found sufficient nerve to go back and continue my search."

"Jean's room is on the ground floor."

"I wasn't aware of that, but she wasn't the sort to put her damning evidence in her dresser drawer or leave it lying on her desk. She implied the negatives were hidden somewhere in the house. I am by nature a methodical man, Mrs. Malloy."

"Who do you suspect has the photographs of you and Jean in the Hideaway Haven?"

"They're not of Jean and me, Mrs. Malloy." Dean Vanderson replaced his handkerchief in his back pocket and looked down at me as if I were a sluggish student. "Earlier in the week I wondered if you had them, but now I see that you don't. I never said I'd had an affair with her. She merely arranged introductions to some of her nubile young friends who enjoyed the companionship of . . . shall we say, experienced older men."

"She what?" I leaped to my feet so suddenly that I was in danger of an unscheduled swan dive. "She was pimping for you?"

"She merely arranged introductions," he repeated patiently.

I battled to regain my balance in all senses of the phrase. "She arranged introductions to girls with whom you subsequently had sex? Her nubile young friends? At the Hideaway Haven with its porn movies and waterbeds? Why don't you tell me your definition of a pimp, Dean Vanderson?"

My words had been spewing out rather raggedly, but he seemed to get the gist of them. "Jean was providing a service, and until I conceded to the first blackmail demand, I'd given her nothing but avuncular advice and a part-time job. Actually, Eleanor suggested that. As for the girls, I often insisted on showing my appreciation for their youthful enthusiasm and lack of inhibitions. One particular girl was so delightfully inexperienced and reticent in her attempts to be introduced into the sweet mysteries of love that I rewarded her most handsomely. I'm an educator and aware of the importance of positive reinforcement in learning situations."

I clutched my hands behind my back to restrain myself. "Were all these girls Kappa Theta Etas?"

"They did not wear their sorority pins, Mrs. Malloy." He brushed back the pale peach fuzz on his head and nodded at me. "I really must attend to my guests. I have met the conditions you stipulated, and I hope you intend to adhere to our arrangement."

"Take one more step and I'll go sit in Judge Frankley's lap and tell him the entire story," I said, still so appalled that I was trembling. "Do you admit you called my house and made threats to my daughter?"

"She has a very disconcerting manner on the telephone. If I may ask, what precisely constitutes a color analysis? Is there truly a reason why I should pay ten dollars when I wear dark suits and white shirts every day? The only item that ever varies is my tie."

It was sheer lunacy, I thought, as well it should be. I was standing beside a pool conversing with the man in the moon, who was worried about his palette. Romping with coeds thirty years younger was not a problem, and blackmail was pesky—but the color of his tie? Was dark red too adventurous? Dare he try green and navy stripes?

"I'll check and get back to you," I said numbly, then went past him and through a gate to the driveway. I made it to my car, rolled up the windows and locked the doors, and rested my forehead on the steering wheel. I waited to see if I was going to laugh or cry, but at last decided I was much too confused to do anything at all.

I'd been told Jean Hall kept the pledge class busy with picnics, parties, and community activities. No one had mentioned less innocuous but more profitable endeavors. Was Dean Vanderson the only self-righteous satyr on the campus? And, most important, did National know about this? Was it right there in the pledge handbook, along with the rules, regulations, and secret whistle? Was it a sanctioned fund-raising activity for the spring semester?

A fist knocked on the window. Before I could scream, which I fully intended to do, a concerned male voice said, "Are you all right, ma'am?"

I exhaled and determined the voice belonged to a policeman barely out of his teens. "I'm fine, thank you. I was just thinking for a moment before I drove home."

He drew circles with his finger until I reluctantly rolled down the window. "Would you step out of the vehicle, ma'am?"

"Under no circumstance will I step out of the vehicle, sir. That would make it impossible to drive home, and as soon as you move back, that's exactly what I'm going to do."

"I'm asking you again to step out of the vehicle," he said with a good deal less cordiality in his voice. "If you refuse to comply, I'll be forced to take action against you."

"You're going to drag me out of my car and sling me on the pavement? Is this because you don't think I parked close enough to the curb, or because ordinary, law-abiding citizens are not allowed to sit and think, but must instead cater to whatever idiotic whim overtakes an officer of the law?" It was good, but based on his deepening scowl, not good enough. I continued, "And why are you here, anyway? This is a residential neighborhood, not a housing project with crack dealers and fences and gang members on every corner. Look right there, Officer. Is there a vicious killer on that deserted corner? I think not."

"I'm on a security assignment because of a prominent public figure visiting in this area. I'm going to say this one last time. Step out of the vehicle, ma'am, and keep your hands in sight at all times."

I did as requested, but I expressed my vexation in

colorful detail throughout the time it took him to find that I could indeed walk a straight line, touch my nose with my eyes closed, and watch his fingertip flitter in and out of view. My driver's license and registration were examined carefully, and verified via his radio. All the while, I wanted to tell him there was a philandering potential killer inside the yellow house not a hundred yards away, dining on quail and conversing with a prominent public figure on genteel subjects such as torts (but not, I should think, tarts).

"This never happened to Miss Marple," I snarled as I took back my license and registration. "She didn't have to deal with overly zealous policemen who ought to be home with a baby-sitter rather than out harassing the citizenry."

"Do us both a favor and move to St. Mary Mead," he said as he went to his car.

Grumbling like the boiler at the Book Depot, I drove home and parked in the garage. There were no traces of successful decomposition on the kitchen floor, nor in the child's bedroom. A note on the coffee table informed me that her resolution to never set foot outside had been cruelly undermined by an invitation to accompany Inez and her parents to a triple-header at the drive-in movie theater. I made a drink and flopped across the sofa, the evening's events swirling in my head like brown water gurgling down the drain.

The Kappa Theta Etas with their expansive gums, even teeth, bright eyes, pink cashmere sweaters, expensive athletic shoes, and twenty-four-karat gold pins were not quite as nice as their reputation purported. Some of them were earning their dues and tuition at the Hideaway Haven, while at least one of them was immortalizing the climactic moments with a camera. Dean Vanderson had mentioned the blackmail cutouts; did one "Katie the Kappa Kitten Says Thanks!" include a handwritten "For being such a generous old goat"?

Had Jean Hall been too greedy? Vanderson claimed to have met Jean shortly before her death and given her whatever sum she demanded. He'd left her in a patio, supposedly alive and well and significantly richer. She'd tucked her ill-gotten gains in her purse and walked down the alley toward the Kappa Theta Eta house. Someone driving Debbie Anne's car had run over her, either accidentally or with purposeful malice. A second blackmail victim? As far as I knew, Jean's purse was still missing, and more strangely, her sorority pin. This implied an extraordinarily composed hit-and-run driver had gotten out of the car, grabbed the purse, and then dallied long enough to take the pin off the chest of the corpse. It seemed more likely that either Dean Vanderson was wrong or I'd failed to notice it. There had been a lot of blood, I reminded myself with a shudder. It certainly could have been as blinding as the cluster of jewels and chains.

Also missing was Debbie Anne Wray. Had she answered the telephone at the Vandersons' house—or had I suffered a mild concussion? Dean Vanderson had sounded truthful in his denial that she'd ever been there. Eleanor was at her garden club at the time. Could Debbie Anne have broken into the house? Those in the midst of committing burglaries rarely pause to serve as social secretaries, but no one, including myself, had accused Debbie Anne of being Mensa material.

I needed to talk to Eleanor, but I doubted I could sidle into the dining room and ask my questions while I nibbled tough quail and sipped champagne.

And there was the minor predicament of what to do with this new information. Dean Vanderson seemed to feel we had a contract, and he was the lawyer, not I. I hadn't precisely sworn not to divulge his story, but perhaps I'd implied as much. If he was telling the truth, his crimes were indictable only by the guardians of morality and good taste. I finally decided to wait until I'd talked to Eleanor before I called Lieutenant Peter Rosen and related what I knew . . . or at least what I felt he deserved to know.

"Those damn Kappa Theta Etas," I muttered as I

went to my bedroom and looked at their house. Lights shone from the ground-floor windows, and the faint sound of music wafted from one. Surely it was time for someone to scream. It had been nearly twenty-four hours since the last blast, after all, and they knew the agenda. Where was our reliable prowler?

Inexplicably irritated by the lack of an uproar next door, I changed into more comfortable clothes, snatched up a paperback, and returned to the living room to swill scotch and read something that made a semblance of sense.

It ended with a tidy denouement in the drawing room of the country house, seconds before the constable came through the door, delayed as usual by the impenetrable snowdrifts. The villain, overwhelmed by the relentless logic of the wily amateur sleuth, had crumbled like a chunk of feta cheese and confessed all. Maybe I ought to move to St. Mary Mead and take up knitting, I thought as I put down the book and went to fetch another from my bedroom. I could knit Caron a Camaro.

I was contemplating my next foray into felonious fantasy when I heard what sounded like an airplane landing in the alley. Smiling at the absurdity of the idea, I selected a book and reached for the light switch. As the noise sputtered to a stop, I recognized it. The alley was not too narrow for a motorcycle, not even one the size of Ed Whitbred's behemoth.

I peered out the window, but what little patch of pavement I could see was as deserted as the corner of Washington and Sutton streets. The motorcycle had not stopped behind my house, and it sounded as though it had gone past the sorority house. But it had not gone all the way down the alley and dwindled into the distance as its driver turned onto Thurber Street.

I switched off the light, returned to the sofa, and tried to reimmerse myself in a charmingly ordinary pastime. After I'd read the same page three times, I acknowledged that I was listening for the motorcycle—or, more ominously, for footsteps on my stairs.

Blaming my nervousness on my reading matter, I put aside the book and made sure my doors were locked. All the fraternity and sorority houses were closed for the summer, with one notable anomaly. The Baptist student center, incongruously set between two of the rowdiest fraternity houses, was also closed.

I'd characterized Dean Vanderson as a wounded animal, but I was pacing like a caged one. Why had the motorcycle stopped in the alley—now more than an hour ago? Was someone breaking into one of the unoccupied houses?

There had to be a thoroughly innocent reason why the motorcyclist was parked somewhere in the alley. However, if he didn't start his engine and drive away soon, I was in peril of pacing to death. I wasn't going to relax until that second proverbial shoe hit the asphalt.

Twenty minutes later, berating myself with a goodly amount of acrimony, I went out the back door and down the stairs to the alley.

13

It really wasn't very late, I assured myself as I peered in both directions, then walked past the Kappa Theta Eta dumpster. I'd been home by eight o'clock, and Caron and the Thorntons would be watching only the second of the mutant insect thrillers. It was a good half hour shy of qualifying as a midnight prowl.

I arrived at the far end of the alley without spotting the motorcycle. Disappointed, but a little bit relieved, I retraced my steps, glancing at the dark windows of unoccupied houses. The parking lots were empty, and the backyards already were sprouting stubble.

I stopped by a high wooden fence behind one of the houses. It was likely to be the enclosed patio where Dean Vanderson met Jean Hall the night of her death, I thought as I eased open the squeaky gate. There were a few battered lawn chairs, a picnic table, a great scattering of crushed beer cans and cardboard pizza boxes—and one large, chrome-infested motorcycle. Admittedly an amateur in such matters, I had no idea whether it was Ed Whitbred's.

I determined that the back door of the fraternity house was secured by a heavy padlock. The interior was unlit, and as far as I could tell, vacant. I sat down on the picnic table and looked more carefully at the motorcycle, but I was unable to convince myself of its familiarity or lack thereof (I have a similar problem with other people's pets and offspring).

And where was its driver? Not inside the fraternity house, not ambling in the alley, and not likely to be in one of the bars on Thurber Street, where parking was plentiful in the summer.

I wasn't wearing my watch, so I had no idea how long I'd been sitting and thinking when I heard footsteps beyond the fence. Crunch, crunch, crunch went the gravel; squeak, squeak, squeak went the gate. Rather than scream, scream, scream, I waited in a mantle of dignified silence until the black-clad motorcyclist was inside the patio, then said, "Hey, Ed, how's it going?"

He located me on my shadowy perch, sighed, and said, "It's been better. What are you doing here, if I may ask?"

"Trying to figure out what's going on at the Kappa Theta Eta house. I wish I could say I'd worked it out, but I'm still confused. However, I am making progress, and I'm confident it will all tumble into place at some point. That's what I'm doing here. What are you doing here?"

His small eyes were almost invisible in the less than intrusive light from a lone utility pole on the far side of the alley. "I left my bike here, and I came back to get it," he finally offered.

"Now, Ed," I said, mimicking his sigh, "I've walked the length of the alley, and my duplex and the Kappa Theta Eta house are the only two currently occupied dwellings. The woman in the apartment below mine is a lovely soul, but she's not the type to invite veteran Hell's Angels into her living room. You didn't come by to see me. That leaves only one destination, doesn't it?"

"So it would seem." He sat on the opposite end of the picnic table, nervously toying with the zipper of his leather jacket while, I presumed, trying to concoct a remotely plausible lie.

Taking pity on him (and tiring of the incessant prickling of mosquitoes), I said, "Eleanor Vanderson said something several days ago that now has some significance. She mentioned that Winkie all but awarded you the contract for the remodeling. Now why would

Winkie risk the wrath of National by such blatant disregard of its regulations for the bidding process?"

"Winkie?" he said with a puzzled frown.

"You know, the petite housemother who can't keep her screens in place." I slapped at a mosquito, trying not to acknowledge any metaphorical parallels. "She keeps stressing the importance of the sorority's reputation, but I think she's equally concerned with her own. Housemothers are not allowed to drink, smoke, carouse—or entertain gentlemen in their private rooms. I'm just guessing, but I think housemothers would be especially pressured not to entertain aging bearded motorcyclists who are adorned with a significant number of tattoos."

He chuckled, but I sensed his heart wasn't in it. "I wouldn't know about that, although they sure do have rules for everything else. 'Any fool can make a rule, and every fool will mind it.' Bear in mind Mr. Thoreau had never dealt with the likes of the Kappa Theta Etas. When Ms. Vanderson officially awarded me the contract, I had to plow through dozens of pages of small print about workman's comp, bonding, liability insurance, penalties, and assessments. You'd have thought I was adding a wing to the Pentagon rather than painting one shabby house."

"And now you're trying to convince me that you went to the house after dark to shake the scaffold? I wasn't born yesterday, Ed. I was born . . . earlier than that, and I've learned to recognize taurian excrement when I hear it. You and Winkie have something going, don't you?" I said all this with the confidence of a teenage entrepreneur. In that it was sheer speculation, I felt I'd presented it well, and I waited expectantly for him to collapse on the table top and blubber out an admission of guilt.

"I went by there tonight to drop off some paint chips. She's supposed to show 'em to Ms. Vanderson tomorrow and get back to me."

I barely stopped short of shaking a finger at him. "This is not the time for fairy tales, Ed. I've been sitting here for hours, working on a very good theory to explain Winkie's problem with the screens and all these sporadic manifestations of an unidentified prowler. In the interim, my foot has gone to sleep and I've donated several pints of blood to an endless stream of mosquitoes. You didn't park in front of the house; you chose to come through the alley and hide your motorcycle behind a fence. The last thing I need is this nonsense about paint chips!"

"They want white, but they can't seem to decide if they want bone white, antique white, shell white—"

"I'll find proof," I interrupted with an edge of petulance caused, no doubt, by anemia. I started to stand up, but sank back down as an idea struck. Had Jean Hall found proof? She had already been blackmailing one person, and with her light summer course load, surely she'd had enough free time for additional victims. I frowned at the fence, trying to imagine her in an avaricious confrontation with Winkie. Jean Hall, seated and gloating as Dean Vanderson leaves. The gate creaks open, and in comes Winkie. Money is tendered, then Winkie tells Jean to wait for a few minutes while she trots back to the house and positions herself in Debbie Anne's car. Several problematic issues came to mind, the most obvious being why conduct business in the patio rather than the suite. Winkie was hardly wealthy. Debbie Anne might object to handing over her keys and taking the rap by default. There were more holes in this than in the fence, I concluded.

I opted to disarm him with a new topic. "So, Ed, why was your best friend Arnie in the bushes the night Jean was killed?"

"Arnie in the bushes? What are you talking about?" He came over to my end of the table, braced himself with his knuckles, and loomed over me like a leather monument. "What was he doing?"

"That's what I asked you," I said, resolving not to shrink. "I was walking home, contemplating nothing more complex than dinner, when Arnie hissed at me. He emerged from the bushes, begged me not to tell anyone, flashed his camera in my face, and drove away before I could demand an explanation."

Ed turned away and sat down on the steps that led to the back door, muttering unpleasantly under his breath. What little I could hear consisted of such phrases as "low-down sumbitch" and "filthy little rodent" and other less decorous descriptions of good ol' Arnie Riggles. I could offer no rebuttal, since I was in full agreement.

When Ed finally calmed down, I said, "If he suspected that you and Winkie were . . . behaving indiscreetly, he could have been trying to get evidence to blackmail her. Something like that would be enough to ruin her career with the Kappa Theta Eta organization, and she's within one year of retirement and the pension fund. Is there any way he might know?"

"He made a snide remark regarding her size, and I felt the need to discourage any further ones," Ed said reluctantly. "A couple of times I saw a green truck in the alley near the Kappa house, and asked him about it. The first time, he cackled and said he'd been at a female mud-wrestling match out in the country somewhere. The other, he just said it wasn't his truck. I decided to forget about it rather than try to figure out what he'd be doing in the alley so late."

"So you do admit that you and Winkie are having a relationship?"

"I seem to have admitted it. We met in line at a movie theater during spring break, had coffee, started talking about this and that, decided to catch another movie later in the week. We're both misfits in our own ways"—he held up a hand to repudiate any arguments I might proffer—"and we have a lot in common. Then one of the girls who lives in town told Winkie she'd seen us, and made some snippy remarks concerning my personal habits and mode of transportation. Winkie freaked and decided we couldn't be seen together in public anymore. We met a couple of times at motels, but then she became paranoid about that and suggested we confine ourselves to late-night trysts in her suite.

Randolph was right when he said, 'Stolen sweets are always sweeter: stolen kisses much completer.' "

"Were you climbing out Winkie's kitchen window when Debbie Anne came up the path alongside the house?"

Abashed, he cleared his throat before saying, "I was so preoccupied with what had just happened that I didn't even see her until we collided. She has a good set of lungs, doesn't she?"

"She certainly does," I said absently, trying to keep straight the sequence of events in the sorority yard. "But you couldn't have knocked down Eleanor Vanderson the following night. It was no later than nine o'clock, and therefore much too early for an illicit liaison. Could that have been Arnie?"

"It might have been, but I don't think he's blackmailing Winkie. Someone else may be, though. A month ago I spotted one of those idiotic pink paper cats in the wastebasket and fished it out. Whoever sent it had taken a felt pen and drawn semicircles over the eyes so it looked as if it were asleep. The written message was a reminder that she had only a year until her retirement. I asked her about it, but she said it was a little joke and clammed up. She's been skitterish ever since then, drinking too much, taking by the handful what she says are mild tranquilizers, and continually fretting that the curtains aren't drawn tightly."

I had known her for no more than a week, but I had noticed how nervous she was when she prattled on about the sorority's reputation. Unlike Dean Vanderson, she was not taking blackmail with composure and a vague aura of contempt. "Arnie can't be behind it," I said, mostly to myself. "He's only been around recently, and he has no access to the paper cats. And he's the last person I'd accuse of being aware of the sorority's rules—and being devious enough to take advantage of them."

"Or sober enough, anyway," Ed said wryly. "But you caught him snooping in the bushes with a camera, so he must be up to something. I'd like to wrap my

hands around his scrawny neck and choke it out of
him."

"What a great idea, Ed. Why don't you do it, and
call me afterward?"

"He never came back to his apartment after the gambling raid, so I called the jail. The desk sergeant said
he'd been released on bail. I don't care if he drowned
in a creek, but I've got to go down to the unemploy-
ment office tomorrow and hire another assistant." He
rose and put on his helmet. "I hope you don't feel obligated to speak to Ms. Vanderson about all this.
Winkie's under so much pressure now that she's liable
to flip out if she loses her job."

"I see no reason to tell anyone," I said, adding yet
another tidbit to my growing list of things I ought to
pass along to the authorities. "But wait! You have
Arnie's camera. Why don't you have the film developed? Then we'll know if Arnie's into blackmail, or
was merely astray on his way to the nearest bar."

He agreed to do so, wheeled his motorcycle out to
the alley, and rocketed away in an explosion of gravel.
I walked back toward my apartment, having some difficulty imagining Winkie and Ed in passionate aban-
donment, the dragon and mermaid on his back rippling
convulsively. National would surely frown on an alli-
ance between a housemother and a biker, no matter
whom he quoted.

What a busy girl Jean had been, what with pledge-
class picnics, lectures at the law school, pimping for
her sisters, and blackmailing the dean, her housemother, and quite possibly other people. Of the two re-
maining Kappa Theta Etas, Rebecca was the logical
successor to that particularly heinous throne. She'd
even needled Pippa about motel rooms, as if challenging me to decipher her innuendo. Little did she know
she was dealing with a woman renowned for both her
deductive prowess and her dedication to meddling to
the bitter end.

When I arrived home, I gazed at the telephone for a
long while, debating whether I should call Lieutenant

Peter Rosen and tell him what I'd learned. Scowling, I finally continued into the kitchen and put on the tea kettle. It was much too late; the bleary-eyed patrons at the drive-in theater were well into the third movie by now. None of my revelations were particularly urgent. Dean Vanderson had a motive to kill Jean, as did Winkie ... and Ed. Rebecca might have decided to take control of a lucrative business. Pippa was a less plausible suspect, but possible. And I couldn't completely rule out Debbie Anne Wray, owner and presumed operator of the lethal vehicle.

"Where can she be?" I demanded of the whistling tea kettle. "She doesn't know anyone outside the sorority. She has no other friends and she's not with her family. The two campus police officers searched the house thoroughly, and—" I stopped conversing with the kettle as I realized they hadn't, not by a long shot.

I turned off the burner, locked the front door, and went down the stairs to the front porch. Only one bedroom light was still on in the sorority house, and after a moment of calculation, I decided that Pippa was awake. Tapping on her window would result in yet another bout of screaming. The Kappas were rather edgy these days.

My knuckles were sore by the time Pippa opened the front door. "Mrs. Malloy?" she said as she gestured for me to come inside. Her hair was wrapped around sponge rollers hidden, for the most part, by a lacy pink cap; a phrenologist would have had a stroke at the possibilities. "Is something wrong? Did you see another prowler?"

"Get the key to the chapter room."

She dimpled uneasily at me. "Winkie has the only one, and she's asleep. Besides, I'd be in really awful trouble if I let you go in there. Only Kappas are allowed to go into the chapter room. There's stuff that's incredibly secret."

"Get the key, Pippa."

Rebecca came into the foyer. She wore a pink nightshirt and her face was glistening with cream, but she was by no means drowsy. "Get the key to what?" she asked.

Winkie emerged from her suite, dressed in the gaudy peignoir I'd seen before. "What's going on, girls? It's much too late to have—Claire?"

My hope that I could take a quick, discreet look around the chapter room was not to be realized. "I think it's possible that Debbie Anne may be hiding in the chapter room," I said. "Everybody agrees she has no friends outside the sorority and no place else to go. The campus police searched the upstairs, but not down there."

"She couldn't have a key," Rebecca said with a trace of scorn. "There's only the one, and it's in Winkie's possession at all times. Unless you're accusing her of collusion with our errant pledge, you're wrong, Mrs. Malloy."

I wasn't in the mood to deal with minor details like keys. "I'm not sure whom I'm accusing, or of what. Why don't we check the chapter room and whatever other rooms are in the basement, and then I'll go home and you can go back to bed?"

Rebecca shook her head. "No one except members and pledges is allowed in the chapter room. If you and Winkie want to wait here, Pippa and I can go down-stairs and make sure Debbie Anne's not huddled be-hind the furnace. I'm the ranking house officer, and I must insist the rules not be violated."

I crossed my arms and glowered at all three of them. Just once, I thought, it would be nice if my suspects behaved according to the traditions of crime fiction. They should have been so overwhelmed with my re-lentless logic that we already would be halfway down the stairs, a dog howling mournfully in the distance, the key clutched in someone's sweaty hand, the stairs creaking, our path illuminated by a flickering candle—or at least a single dim bulb swinging crazily from a frayed cord. I wanted melodrama, not obduracy.

"Do the rules also cover what goes on at the Hide-away Haven?" I said abruptly.

Pippa and Rebecca exchanged startled looks. Winkie, in contrast, gurgled and staggered backward until she hit the edge of the desk hard enough to topple the vase of plastic flowers.

"How did you . . . ?" she gasped.

Ignoring her, I said to Rebecca, "Either you get the key or I call Eleanor Vanderson right now. It would be a pity to disturb her." I paused to slather on emphasis lest they miss the point. "Not to mention her husband."

"So it would," said Winkie, her voice tinny and her white fingers entwined in the collar of her peignoir. "My keys are in my handbag on the coffee table, Pippa. Please fetch them and allow Claire to satisfy herself and leave. I'm sure she won't mention what she sees in the chapter room, and National need never hear about it. It will be our little secret, won't it?"

"Go ahead," Rebecca ordered Pippa. "You and Winkie can wait in her suite until we're finished with this idiotic mission."

Shortly thereafter she and I went to the basement, although there was ample light and the stairs failed to produce any sounds whatsoever.

"This is the door to the chapter room," muttered Rebecca. She continued down a hallway, opened an unlocked door, and explained without enthusiasm, "This is where we store props for the rush skits." A second door opened into the furnace room, a third into a cavernous room containing a single trunk and a few pieces of lumber. Costumes hung from metal racks in yet another, and the final room was devoid of anything except mouse droppings and a fuse box.

We returned to the door of the chapter room. Feeling as if I were about to be ushered into the innermost sanctum of a shrine, I was almost reluctant to follow Rebecca into the room. I don't know what I expected, but the haphazard rows of metal chairs, a couple of tables, and a droopy banner riddled with Greek letters and stylized pink roses failed to impress me.

"This is it?" I said.

"She's obviously not here." Rebecca stepped backward to force me out of the room. "You saw for yourself that there's no place to hide. There's no way she could survive down here unless she brought food and water and only availed herself of a bathroom in the middle of the night."

I remembered something Debbie Anne had told me. "What about the ritual closet?"

"How do you know about that?"

"I just assumed all sororities have them," I lied smoothly. "I'm not going to count the candles or divulge the color of the high priestesses' gowns, but I think we ought to take a quick look. If Debbie Anne heard us coming, she might be hiding in there now."

"Don't be absurd! It's already been explained to you that she couldn't have a key in the first place. Winkie has the only key. At noon the day of meetings, she gives it to the president so the room can be prepared, and it's returned to her right after the meeting. Pledges never touch the key."

"But Jean Hall had it for several hours every week," I pointed out. "If she had a copy made, she might have kept it in her purse. The purse disappeared the night she was killed. You're convinced Debbie Anne is the culprit, so why couldn't she have taken Jean's purse and now have her key?"

Rebecca stewed on it for a moment, then shrugged and allowed me to reenter the room. "Let's get this over with, okay?" she said as she headed for a door along the back wall. As we wound through the chairs, she slowed down and eventually stopped, her nose twitching like that of an amorous rabbit. "What's that nasty smell?"

I could smell it, too, and it brought back memories of my torturous tenure in the Farberville lockup. "It seems to be coming from the closet," I said, measurably less eager to explore the sacred room. "Maybe we ought to call the authorities."

"National would have a fit if they found out the police were in the chapter room, let alone if they were allowed to look inside the ritual closet." She wound her hair around her neck and stared at the door, her mouth flattened unattractively as she seemingly considered the available options.

I held out my hand. "Give me the key, Rebecca. It's likely that an ammonia-based cleaning solution spilled inside the closet. Tomorrow you and Pippa can mop it up without any illicit tourists to unsettle you."

She complied, then edged away as I fit the key into the lock and opened the door. The stench roiled out like tear gas, causing my eyes to flood. I made myself stay long enough to see the body on the floor, then shut the door and retreated as far as I could within the room.

Rebecca coughed and said, "What is it?"

"Arnie Riggles is in there," I said, gulping for air. "He's unconscious but not necessarily dead. We've got to pull him out and do what we can until an ambulance can get here." I wiped my eyes and cheeks and ordered my stomach to stop convulsing. "We'll both stand by the door. When I say so, you open it and I'll grab him. As soon as I have him out, shut the door and go call for an ambulance."

It was not something I want to remember, this extrication, but it was accomplished and Rebecca ran out of the room, alternately gagging and whimpering. The worst of the stench was contained within the closet, but Arnie's jeans were soaked with urine and a veritable plethora of new smells made me feel as if I'd been whisked to the Dismal Swamp.

As I studied Arnie's inert form, saliva bubbled out of his slack lips. He wiggled into a more comfortable position and began to snore. I came to the cold-hearted conclusion he was drunk. How he'd managed to end up in the Kappa Theta Eta ritual closet was a bit of a poser, but Arnie was a man of amazing slyness, and I wouldn't have checked myself into the butterfly farm if I'd found him in a baptismal font—or in Eleanor Vanderson's bed.

I retreated to the hallway to wait for the paramedics and campus officers to come storming down the stairs to collect a despicable drunk. Ed Whitbred had said Arnie had not come to his apartment since his arrest. How had he gotten from a locked cell to a locked closet?

A low, throaty growl interrupted my futile thoughts. I looked over my shoulder. At the top of the stairs sat Katie the Kappa Kitten, her fuzziness silhouetted by the foyer lights, her amber eyes unblinking as she considered how best to rid the Kappa Theta Eta house of this latest intrusion of vermin.

14

I was sitting in Winkie's suite when the paramedics and campus cops arrived. Rebecca had dressed and taken charge of the proceedings, which was fine with me. I could hear her cool, decisive voice from the foyer, but I made no effort to follow any of the conversations. A wine bottle and mismatched glasses were on the coffee table, and Katie was clutched in Pippa's arms.

"I might as well pack my bags," Winkie said morosely, but with a lack of sincerity that made me wonder if she was less than horrified by the idea—or secretly confident that it would not happen. "This is inexcusable. Men in the chapter room, and that besotted fool in the ritual closet. Eleanor will be on the phone to National in the morning, and I'll be out on the street by noon."

Pippa nuzzled the captive cat. "I just don't understand how that man got in there, unless he . . ."

"Took the key from Jean's purse," I said.

Winkie hiccuped, and with a giggle touched her lips with fluttery fingertips. "Which means he and Debbie Anne are in this together, doesn't it? One or the other, perhaps both of them, ran Jean down, stole her purse, and used her key to get into the chapter room and the closet. What an odd place for him to choose to hide, if that's what he was doing." She hiccuped and giggled once again. "Are you certain Debbie Anne wasn't in there with him? The two might have found it exciting to come up with a few rituals of their own."

"I think we'd have heard about it," I said dryly. My wits were dulled by now, but I battled back a yawn and replayed her remarks—hers and Rebecca's and someone else's. "It's possible there are several keys to the chapter room. You have the original. Jean Hall had a duplicate made. But doesn't Eleanor Vanderson have a complete set of keys?"

"Of course not," Winkie chided me. "She has keys to all the exterior doors, the bedrooms, and the main-floor storage rooms, but National allows only one key for the basement. Security is vital, quite vital."

Pippa's dimples were mere shadows on her pale cheeks, and she spoke with the solemnity of an IRS auditor. "And you've got to promise not to ever tell anyone what you saw in there, Mrs. Malloy."

As if the world's citizens were panting to know how many folding chairs were in the Kappa Theta Eta chapter room, I thought sourly. I was about to expound on this when a campus cop stepped into the doorway. To my delight, he was middle-aged, paunchy—and unfamiliar.

"We've sent the trespasser to the detox unit at the city hospital," he said. "According to his driver's license, which was revoked eight years ago, his name's Arnold Riggles and he's itinerant. He'll be interrogated whenever he's sobered up, and if he remembers anything, he can tell us what he was doing here. Miss Faulkner took a quick look around and said nothing had been disturbed. She claims she doesn't know how he got there or why. Do any of you ladies have anything to say that can't wait until the morning?"

We shook our heads, and Katie sneezed her denial. He said the investigation would continue in the morning, stressed the need to make sure the house was secured, and promised frequent passes by patrol cars. After a bit more thumping and muttered comments in the foyer, the front door was slammed and Rebecca joined us.

"Have you put a curse on the Kappa Theta Etas?" she asked me as she poured a glass of wine and curled up at the end of the couch, regarding me with the same meditative glint I'd seen in Katie's eyes. "Up until last week, nothing much happened. Now, every time I leave the house for an audition or to shop, I find myself wondering if I'll return to a pile of ashes."

"Rebecca!" Winkie said. "You of all people—"

"I was joking, Winkie," Rebecca cut in.

Pippa dumped the cat and stood up. "I'm going to bed. I have a really tough exam in Abnormal Psych in the morning. Good night, all."

"Would you wait a minute?" Rebecca said to me, then followed Pippa out of the room. After a hushed conversation, she returned to the doorway and crossed her arms. "It was awfully clever of you to figure out there was someone in the closet, Mrs. Malloy. Thanks so much for warning us."

"I'm sure Arnie will be equally grateful if and when he sobers up," I said.

Pippa reentered and handed me my key ring. With a dutifully apologetic smile, she said, "It was my fault, and I'm really sorry for not finding it the first time. I went back and crawled around and around and around the tree until I found it in a hole. I do hope you'll forgive me."

"I do," I said hastily, and then left before I found myself in possession of a pink paper cat and yet another invitation to dinner. I hadn't put a curse on the Kappa Theta Etas. Quite the contrary. Vowing to forget the entire matter and dedicate myself to more important concerns, such as bankruptcy and involuntary celibacy, I returned home.

The door was unlocked and all the lights were blazing away. Caron sat cross-legged on the floor, a calendar spread in front of her. She poised a pencil above it, saying, "Okay, I'll put Merissa down for Thursday morning, but Ashley can't do it that afternoon." She glanced up at Inez, who sat on the couch amid a great flutter of pages torn from a notepad.

"If Tara switches to Saturday," Inez said with a

frown, "then Ashley can have Friday afternoon. But that means we'll have to juggle the schedule for the rest of the weekend."

"Hi, girls," I said cautiously. "Are you planning an invasion? If so, you ought to call CNN and give them some warning. And remember, I don't want to see any nuclear weapons on my credit-card bill."

Caron crossed out an entry before scowling at me. "We are arranging the schedule for about a dozen My Beautiful Self analyses, Mother. It's very complex, and would be a whole lot easier without interruptions. Look, Inez, some of them may have to change their plans. I Cannot Accommodate every last person who has a dentist appointment or wants to go to the mall."

Inez peered at one slip, then another, her face wrinkling with dismay until she resembled a distressed Pekinese. "But if Charlene has to baby-sit all afternoon Friday . . . ?"

"She can find a substitute!" Caron banged down the pencil and stalked into the kitchen. "You want a soda?"

I considered asking Inez about the sudden demand for Caron's expertise, but I was afraid I'd hear an answer that would result in indigestion and insomnia. It was well past three o'clock. I went to bed, a pillow over my head to drown out the sporadic outbursts from the boardroom of Caron Malloy, Inc.

The following morning I dallied over the morning paper and several cups of tea, hoping to hear the sound of Ed Whitbred's motorcycle so that we could discuss Arnie's unseemly appearance. It was remotely possible that I was hoping—but with less sanguinity—that Lieutenant Rosen might have seen a report of the most current nonsense at the Kappa Theta Eta house and feel motivated to call for details.

When the telephone finally rang, I carefully put down my cup and blotted my lip with a napkin before I picked up the receiver. "Yes?" I responded melodiously.

"Is Caron there?" said an unmelodious and much younger female voice.

"She's asleep, and I have no idea when she'll rouse herself. If you like, I can take a message."

There was a distinct sniffle, then the voice said, "You tell her that my dad's a lawyer, and he says what she's doing is blackmail or extortion or something like that, and she'll be in really big trouble if she keeps this up."

"Who is this? What are you talking about?"

"Just give her the message."

I couldn't persuade my hand to record a single word of the alarming conversation with the latest anonymous caller. My telephone was becoming a veritable pipeline that spewed out threats and dire warnings. I went to Caron's room and shook her shoulder, but all I received in response to my questions was a grumpy, mumbled admonishment to leave her alone. Her co-conspirator kept her eyes squeezed tightly shut, and although I suspected she was emulating an arboreal American marsupial (more specifically, a *Didelphis virginiana*), I returned to the kitchen, gulped down an aspirin with a mouthful of tepid tea, and left them to be dragged away to a juvenile detention facility by someone with more persistence than I.

Once at the Book Depot, I took out a piece of paper and amused myself making yet more notes of noticeably little help. I made one list of potential blackmailers, grimly adding Caron Malloy, and a second of potential blackmailees. Everyone who qualified for neither list went into a jumble at the bottom of the page, and I was trying to devise categories for them when the door opened.

For her morning outing, Eleanor Vanderson had chosen a robin's-egg-blue seersucker suit with a crisp white blouse. Her accessories included a white belt and pumps, a swirly blue-and-purple scarf draped artfully around her neck, a slender silver watch, and a white straw purse. Clearly, she was in harmony with her palette and destined for chicken salad and bridge. Others of us, having chosen frayed denim shorts and one of Caron's old gym-class T-shirts, accessorized with a cheap watch and a tarnished wedding ring, also cheap, felt destined for nothing more dainty than a hamburger and a diet soda. However, burdened as I was with the knowledge of her husband's dirty little secrets, I deserved no better.

"Oh, Claire," she said as she came to the counter and squeezed my hand, "you must be ready to bulldoze down the sorority house—and I wouldn't blame you one bit if you'd already arranged it. It's been one nightmare after another for you, hasn't it? The screams, the purported prowlers, that dreadful accident in the alley, that pledge pestering you with her calls, and now this incident last night!"

I eased my hand out of reach and folded my arms to cover my incriminating lists (which, regrettably, incriminated only me). "It's not been an auspicious beginning for the summer," I said, aware that I was mirroring her superficial smile and speaking with an identical undertone of sisterly sympathy. They were finally getting to me, I thought with an edge of hysteria as we continued to twinkle at each other. I'd seen the chapter room. I'd seen the ritual closet. I'd toured the house and eaten their spaghetti. I was becoming Kappa Theta Eta–ized, and before long I would crave pink cashmere. The bookstore would be home to a fluffy white cat. I would become increasingly distraught that Caron had not selected a silver pattern shortly after her birth. Had Eleanor clutched my hand with the secret handshake? Were her lips puckered just a bit? Would I need gum augmentation?

She must have sensed that I was not a sane woman, in that she retreated a few steps and gazed thoughtfully at the store. "This is so charming, Claire. I can't think why I've never been here before, but I certainly will make a point of coming by in the future. I love the way you've arranged all this to create a warm, cozy feeling."

"Thank you."

"There's something I'd like to discuss with you," she continued, "but it's very painful for me and I'm hoping we might find a place with complete privacy, a place where we won't be disturbed."

"This may be it. No one has set foot in here all morning, and I have no reason to believe anyone will in the foreseeable future."

"I'm so sorry to hear business is slow, but surely things will pick up before too long. Would it be inconvenient if we sat in your office?" She gave me the look of a poster child from a Third World country.

I led her to the office, took a dozen books off the chair and dumped them in a corner, squinted unhappily at the blackened crust in the coffee pot, and finally settled behind the desk to regard her over a stack of invoices, a cup filled with stubby pencils, several self-help books on the gentle art of organization, and a scattering of dried roaches.

"This is so difficult." Eleanor took a handkerchief from her purse and dabbed the corner of her eye. "After the party ended last night, I asked John what you two had been discussing out by the pool. Initially, he refused to tell me, but I persisted, and this morning, while I was driving him to the airport, he finally related the gist of it. Oh, Claire, I can imagine how you must have felt as he told you those . . . repulsive stories, but surely you realize what they were."

"Surely," I said obediently, if also blankly.

"I suggested he cancel his trip to Las Vegas, but he became so upset that I reluctantly kissed him goodbye and let him go. I've already spoken to his physician, and the very first thing we'll do when John returns is schedule a complete evaluation of his medication." She dabbed the other eye, then gave me a brave, quivery smile. "I'm so glad you understand, Claire. These last few years have been a living hell for me, and sometimes I wonder if that's why I've immersed myself in the sorority. My grandmother never tired of reminding me that the best cure for personal troubles is a worthwhile charity in need of a chairperson."

"You're saying that what he told me . . . ?"

"Is nothing more than a pathetic fantasy. John is a brilliant scholar and has published hundreds of articles in the most prestigious journals across the country. He successfully argued in front of the United States Supreme Court on two occasions. There's a rumor afoot that the new wing of the law building will be named after him." She paused to allow me the opportunity to gasp in awe, but I managed to restrain myself. "Five years ago he began to develop a few mild eccentricities—nothing too bizarre at first, but later they became more obvious. I eventually took him to the medical complex in Houston, which diagnosed a degenerative neurological disease that impairs him both physically and mentally. He functions well most of the time, but every now and then he does or says something that has absolutely no basis in reality."

I considered this for a moment. "He sounded perfectly normal when he told me about his assignations at a motel. I didn't demand details, naturally, but he seemed to have a vivid memory of . . . what took place and with whom."

"He sounded perfectly normal when he explained to our daughter that he'd joined a convent and henceforth was to be called Sister Beatrice." She shook her head and sighed. "Thus far, we've been lucky that these episodes have been isolated and have occurred outside the university community. But to tell a virtual stranger that he . . . Well, it's clear he'll have to submit his resignation as soon as he returns home."

Trying not to envision Dean Vanderson in a fetching black habit, I said, "Then he had no assignations with sorority girls at the Hideaway Haven and Jean Hall was not blackmailing him?"

"Oh, Claire, I knew you'd understand!" Eleanor replaced the handkerchief in her purse and once again rewarded me with a dose of sisterly sympathy. "You'll be relieved to learn that I've decided to close the Kappa house for the remainder of the summer. Winkie,

Rebecca, and Pippa have been told that they must be out by six o'clock today, and they were looking at the classified ads and calling various apartment complexes when I left. It will be inconvenient for me to drop by every day to supervise the remodeling, but I'll just have to do it."

Although I was cheered by her news, I wasn't ready to dismiss Dean Vanderson's revelations as the ravings of a neurological degenerate. "If your husband wasn't being blackmailed, why was there a pink paper cat in his office?"

"You were in his office?" she said, politely incredulous.

Since I hadn't exactly arrived at the law school with a search warrant, I bypassed her question and said, "Yes, and I found a cat hidden under a computer. It looked like your basic blackmail note to me: terse, ominous, slightly obtuse. I came to your house last night to ask him about it."

"How odd," she murmured as she found a gold compact and made sure her mascara had not dribbled down her cheeks during her less than histrionic confession of her husband's disability. After she'd flicked off an invisible speck, she snapped the compact closed. "Unless, of course, he wrote it as additional proof to himself that he's not only virile and sexually insatiable, but also an actor in some dark soap opera unfolding around him. He's become childlike these last few years, and this is the sort of thing that would appeal to his need to see himself as anything other than a pale, plump, middle-aged law professor."

I did not leap to my feet, point an accusatory finger at her, and utter words to the effect that John had no access to pink construction-paper cats. "And you have a drawerful of the things at home?" I asked in a resigned voice.

"I keep them in a carton in my study, along with the correspondence with National, confidential reports from alumnae, and the endless files. You and I seem to wage the same battle not to drown in all the paperwork, don't we?" I nodded as she stood up. "There is one thing more I must beg of you, Claire. It's terribly important that what I told you not become a topic of gossip. John is not well, and were his reputation to be tainted by lurid and unfounded accusations, it might kill him. I can trust you, can't I?"

I assured her that she could, escorted her out to the street, and resumed my seat at the counter. I now was withholding from the authorities enough information to alphabetize it and publish a set of encyclopedias. On the other hand, the fact that John Vanderson had not carried on with sorority girls and therefore had not been blackmailed was not likely to overwhelm anybody.

The afternoon dwindled along, as did my attempts to put a lot of seemingly unrelated tidbits into tidy little compartments. No one called to threaten me or my child, and no one called to inquire if I was meddling in an official investigation—if there was one. The police were satisfied with an accidental death and a fugitive who would appear sooner or later. Although I could vindicate myself with the revelation that Ed Whitbred and Arnie Riggles had indeed prowled in the bushes outside the sorority house, I could find no other reason to tell anyone. With the house closing, Winkie would have to find an apartment for the summer, and she and her hairy Don Juan could dally in a more routine fashion. John Vanderson would resign from his position at the law school and perhaps occupy his time writing fiction. No doubt the New York publishing house that purchased *Nebrasqué* would be enthralled by juris-imprudent porn. Caron would throw her sixteenth birthday party for the benefit of her fellow inmates; I would celebrate my fortieth birthday alone, toasting myself in the mirror while monitoring the ravages of menopause.

It was a splendid foray into self-pity, and I was enjoying myself enormously as I walked home late in the afternoon. As I went past the soon-to-be-vacant sorority house, however, I realized there was a minor glitch in Eleanor's explanation of her husband's peculiar behavior. He had been on the third floor several nights ago. I tried to tell myself he was engaged in a fantasy, playing detective rather than cowboy or astronaut, but my arguments failed to convince me. He had been there, just as he had stopped at the curb the night of Jean's death. Eleanor might wish desperately to believe her husband was delusional, that what he'd told me was nonsense—but she could be wrong.

Miss Marple-Malloy was back in business. I hurried home, found the directory, and called Ed Whitbred. "I presume you heard about Arnie," I said without wasting a precious second of sleuthing.

"Winkie told me," he said. "She's upset about the house closing, but I think she's better off getting away from those leeches. This morning she and Eleanor had a major row over the chapter-room key. Winkie swears her key has been in her possession since the last meeting of the semester, back in May, and Eleanor finally conceded that saintly Jean Hall must have made a duplicate."

"Will Winkie keep her job?"

"She thinks so. I told her I'd help her look for an apartment, so I'd better—"

"Did you have the film from Arnie's camera developed?"

"I dropped it off at the drugstore on Thurber Street, but I forgot to pick it up after work. How about I bring it over tomorrow when I—"

"That'll be fine, Ed. Happy hunting." I hung up, then went to Caron's bedroom to see if there were any messages concerning bail or impending court appearances. All I found were dirty glasses, a crumpled potato-chip bag, fuzzy dishes under the bed that might lead to a Nobel Prize in biochemistry, and her calendar. The last item indicated that Gretchen was slated to have her palette adjusted within the hour.

Idly speculating why Caron's friends had relented, I made a drink and wandered to my bedroom to stare at the Kappa Theta Eta house. The shadows from the scaffold resembled long diagonal bars across the weathered surface. The effect was fittingly sinister.

When it began to grow dark, I drove to the drugstore. After a spirited debate with a genderless dullard regarding my lack of a receipt versus my willingness to stand there all night and argue, I proffered money for a packet of prints. Once I was in the car, I took a deep breath and pulled out the product of Arnie's arcane activities.

He'd been thorough, capturing not only Pippa in gleeful admiration of her breasts, Jean halfway out of a shirt, Rebecca brushing her hair in a diaphanous gown, and Debbie Anne in a struggle with a pair of overly tight shorts, but also a dozen more of unknown girls in varied degrees of undress. The backgrounds contained enough pink to identify them as Kappa Theta Etas. Apparently our aspiring *Penthouse* photographer had lurked in the bushes prior to the end of the spring semester.

Arnie had occupied a position on my list of potential blackmailers, but I mentally drew a line through his name and relegated it to a newly established list of voyeurs. It was odd that he'd selected this particular sorority, I thought as I pulled out of the parking lot and headed for the highway. It was the only house open this summer, but during the previous semester he could have chosen any of the sorority houses on campus, some of which would provide stimulating photo opportunities from less prickly sites. Was it just another damn coincidence?

I drove by the Hideaway Haven twice before persuading myself to bounce across the pockmarked lot and park at what was optimistically designated as the office. Through the dusty window I could see a stumpy orange-haired man in a stained T-shirt and plaid shorts. A cigarette smoldered between his lips, and ashes trickled down his belly. He appeared to be reading a tabloid, although it was as likely that he was unable to meet the literacy challenge and was merely looking at the pictures.

There was no delicate way to handle it, I told myself as I cowered in the car and perspired like a woman eighteen hours into labor. Not even one of my role models from a cozy novel could find a way to transact this distasteful business without some tiny slip of her composure. I slunk down further as a car pulled in beside me. Its driver seemed familiar with the process and was in possession of a key within minutes. His buxom companion sauntered after him as he hurried to a nearby room. The lack of luggage suggested professional services rendered at an hourly rate.

I, on the other hand, had all the time I wanted to explore my motives for sitting in my car outside the office of the Hideaway Haven. Was I in the throes of a quest for truth and justice? Was this indicative of my dedication to law and order? Was I genuinely concerned about Debbie Anne Wray—or any of the blasted Kappa Theta Etas, their lovers, or even their painters? Or could it be that I was going to show Lieutenant Peter Rosen that I was not the least bit interested in his extracurricular activities and was perfectly content to meddle in someone else's official investigation?

I snatched up the packet and went into the office. "Excuse me," I said coldly, "but I'd like you to see if you recognize any of these girls."

"What are you—a high school principal?"

I spread out the photographs. "I do not care to discuss my personal life. Have any of these girls ever rented rooms here?"

Clearly daunted by my steely demeanor, he studied each photograph with great care, occasionally whistling softly or holding one so closely his breath clouded it. He licked his lips so often that soon his chin was glistening, but no more so than his beady little eyes. I was finally getting somewhere, I told myself smugly as I waited for his response.

"No, never seen any of them." He picked up the tabloid and flipped it open. "Can you believe this about Elvis? I for one think he's deader'n a doornail, but people keep seeing him all the time. I don't see how he can keep popping up like this if he's dead." He scratched his head with enough enthusiasm to send flakes of dandruff adrift.

"Elvis is dead, and you have seen these girls before," I retorted, a shade less smugly but determined to hear the truth if I had to shake it out of him. "If you refuse to admit it, I will call the police and report indications of prostitution and drug transactions on these very premises."

He wrenched one eye off the "actual artist's depiction" of Elvis entering the White House. "You got no proof."

"No, but I'll tell them I do, and once they start poking around, I'm sure they'll find plenty of evidence. If nothing else, there must be enough violations of the health and fire codes to close you down."

He plucked the cigarette butt from his mouth and gaped at me as if I'd arisen from the page in front of him and, like the Peoria housewife, claimed to be capable of spontaneous combustion. "But that's lying, lady."

"It most certainly is, and I must warn you that I've had a great deal of practice at it and will be quite convincing. Would you like to take another look at the photographs?"

"Maybe I ought to ask Doobie," the man said as he dropped the butt and ground it out on the floor. "He's usually on the night desk, but he wanted to switch so's he could watch some fool basketball game. Won't take more than a minute." He gathered up the photographs and disappeared through a doorway, the door closing behind him before I could protest.

As I waited, I became aware that I might as well have been on the screen of the drive-in movie theater. The darkness outside emphasized the lights of the office, and I knew I was visible from the far reaches of the parking lot, if not the highway. Unlike the Kappa Theta Etas, I was not haunted by the specter of a tainted reputation, but the thought of having to explain my presence at the Hideaway Haven was so chilling that goose bumps dotted my arms and whatever hackles I possessed rose on my neck. I was tempted to hide behind the lurid pages of the tabloid, then considered the additional hardship of explaining both my presence and my reading material to anyone who drove by. Such as a cop.

Nearly fifteen minutes had passed by the time the manager returned, the photographs in his hand and a deeply distrustful look on his face. I closed the tabloid, thus doomed never to find out the facts about Big Foot's amorous attack on a Canadian farmwife, and smiled expectantly.

"Doobie ain't seen any of them," he reported, avoiding my eyes and speaking with all the animation of a dead Elvis. "He sez they're welcome anytime, dressed or otherwise, and in particular that piece of angel food cake with the black hair, but he ain't seen any of them. But"—he held up a grimy hand to stop me from retorting—"Doobie sez Hank might have been on duty some of the time, so you can come back next week and ask him. Hank took his wife to a bowling tournament over in Sallisaw, on account of it being her birthday."

"It took all this time for Doobie to say that?" I said.

Once again dandruff rained softly on his shoulders as his fingernails dug into his scalp. "Doobie studied the pictures real carefully before he decided he hadn't seen them girls. We get all kinds of college kids out here, especially on the weekends, and they all look the same, a bunch of Kens and Barbies in designer clothes and fancy athletic shoes."

As I put the photographs back in the packet, I decided to take one last shot. "There's someone else who might have been here frequently," I began, then proceeded to describe John Vanderson.

The manager flinched, his eyebrows furrowing for a

second, his lips suddenly in need of a lick. "No, nobody like that."

I'd seen the recognition in his eyes, the same flicker
I'd seen in Winkie's when I'd rattled off the description in her suite. I said as much, but he steadfastly de-
nied having seen John Vanderson, and at last took his
tabloid and went into the back room. This time the
door slammed a sullen goodbye, although I suspected
in his mind it was a more colorful idiom involving
areas of his anatomy—or mine.

Lacking the courage to storm after him, I went
back to my car. As I reached for the handle, I heard a
faint groan, and swung around to stare at the impenetrable darkness of the parking lot alongside the building. "Hello?" I called tentatively. "Is someone hurt?"

A second groan was as slight and insubstantial as
the breeze that carried it. It was not the whimper of a
sick animal, I decided as I moved toward the corner,
crushing the packet in my damp hand, keenly con-
scious of my vulnerability and my inexperience in
dealing with mishaps at brothels.

A few cars were parked in front of motel units, but
heavy curtains kept any light from spilling onto the
pavement. Across the narrow lot stretched a vast field
that undulated like a serene expanse of ocean, dotted
only by stubby, skeletal trees and the rotted remains of
a car.

I stopped in the oblong of light from the office,
shielded my eyes, and peered for some indication of
the location of the groaner. "Is someone there?" I
called.

Headlights came to life, blinded me, startled me as
if I were a deer on the highway, left me rooted and
unable to so much as blink. An engine roared. Tires
dug into the gravel, spinning and shrieking. The headlights charged me. What flashed before me was not an
encapsulated version of my thirty-nine years of life,
but a much more vivid image of what I'd resemble if
I didn't move pretty darn soon. Pancake batter came
to mind.

I flung myself into the side of the building. The headlights veered at me, then swept past while gravel pelted me like hail. I peeled myself off the wall in time to see swirling taillights as the car squealed onto the highway and sped away.

15

The manager and his unseen pal Doobie did not rush out to ask me if I was all right, and in fact did not so much as poke their noses out of the back room to ascertain if the window was shattered and the floor splattered with blood from my mangled corpse.

Massaging my shoulder with one hand while picking gravel from my elbow with the other, I made it to my car and eased awkwardly into the driver's seat. Once the doors were locked, I inventoried the innumerable throbs, and concluded nothing was broken or even seriously damaged, with the exception of my amiable nature and sense of humor. What a lovely target I'd made, I thought angrily as I removed a chunk of gravel from my raw knee. Had I been invisible to a pie-eyed drunk or had someone tried to frighten me—or kill me in the same fashion he or she had killed Jean Hall?

A station wagon pulled in next to me. Two teenage girls, both dressed in skimpy shorts and skimpier halters, tramped into the office, banged on the silver bell, and exercised their magenta-lined lips until the manager emerged from the back room. After some discussion and a great deal of hilarity, a second man came out the same door, his arms laden with beers and his porcine face contorted with a leer.

If he was Doobie, then neither of the men had exited through a back door and attempted to run me down. Then again, it had taken Doobie a suspiciously long time to determine that he didn't recognize any of the Kappas. It had certainly been long enough to call someone. But who? I hadn't caught so much as a

glimpse of the driver, and I was fairly sure no witnesses would come out of the motel rooms to offer a
description of the car or its driver. Calling the police
might lead to momentary amusement when they demanded the names and addresses of the Hideaway Haven clientele, but it ran the real threat of obliging me
to explain all sorts of complicated things ... to Lieutenant Rosen.

The little party in the office was well on its way to
an orgy by the time I went inside, politely ignoring
Doobie's hand inside a halter and the semi-seduction in
progress on a noxious red plastic couch, and announced, "Someone tried to run me down in the parking lot. I insist that you call the police right this
minute."

"Oh, honey," said one of the girls, her fake eyelashes fluttering like moribund spiders, "look at your
poor knee. Doobie, why doncha take your hand off my
tit and get the first-aid box for the lady? Can't you see
she's bleeding like a stuck pig?" She gave me a solic-
itous smile as she guided me to a chair and settled me
down as if I were an errant patient from the nursing
home. "I'm taking a course in home nursing this summer. If Doobie'll get his lazy butt in gear, I'll fix you
up in no time flat."

Perching on the counter, the other girl popped her
gum as if she were chomping down on a firecracker.
"Why'd somebody try to run over you? Did you like
have a fight with your boyfriend or something? Me
and my boyfriend had a fight last week, and he showed
up drunk at my house and tried to rip out all my hair.
I learned him a lesson or two."

Doobie and the manager were conferring nervously
behind her. My would-be nurse repeated her demand
for medical supplies while her friend described in
gruesome detail how she'd dealt with someone named
Billy Bob or Bobby Bill or whatever, who reputedly
was limping. I simply sat and waited for the two men
to figure it out, and after a final exchange of bellicose
whispers, they did.

The manager came across the room and thrust out his hand. "Lemme see those pictures again."

The girls attached themselves to his arms and oohed and giggled as he flipped through the photographs. Shrugging them off, he said, "Yeah, a few of them have been here, but I dint ask for names or anything. This is the sort of place where everybody's name is Smith, and the only thing I care about is the color of the cash."

"Which girls?" I asked with commendable composure.

He handed me half a dozen shots. "Some of the others may have been here, too, and stayed in the car while their friend paid for the room. Sometimes I happen to see 'em when they come out to get sodas from the machine, if I'm looking."

Four of the girls were unknown to me. I was less than astonished to find Pippa among the crowd, but my jaw dropped as I gaped at Debbie Anne Wray wiggling into pink shorts. "Are you sure about this one?"

He looked over his shoulder at Doobie, who nodded sullenly. "That one," he said, sucking on his lower lip, "was staying here up until yesterday. I dunno what she was doing, but she paid for a full week and dint bother anybody."

I rose slowly out of deference to both my knee and a bout of dehabilitating bewilderment. "How did she get here? Did she have any visitors? When she left, did she say anything about where she was going? Who picked her up?"

"This ain't a Girl Scout camp," he said, beginning to retreat as I closed in on him. "She showed up middle of the afternoon on maybe Friday, no suitcase or anything—but that's nothing new. Once I saw her going across the highway to a convenience store, another time at the soda machine. The only reason I know she split is that the door was open in the morning and I went over to see if she'd dropped dead. There wasn't nothing in the room but cups and hamburger wrappers."

"I saw her getting in a truck," volunteered the girl who'd popped her gum so bombastically. "Darlene and me were hanging out here while Doobie went to buy us some beer, and the only reason I noticed was that the truck was green like Doobie's and I was gonna be pissed if he'd forgotten to get our beer on account of some simpery whore."

"That's right," Doobie said from the doorway. "She left with some clown and never came back. Look, lady, the girls came by to have a little fun, and unless you'd like to join us in the back room, why don't you run along?"

I was moderately confident that I would not be assaulted in view of the highway, but his tone held enough menace to suggest distasteful possibilities. I wished them a pleasant evening, darted to my car, and drove away from the Hideaway Haven as briskly as the law allowed.

Once I'd parked in my garage, I sat in the dark and examined this most peculiar story. Debbie Anne had appeared at the motel on Friday, the afternoon of Jean's death, and remained there until the previous morning, when she'd gotten in what had to be Arnie's truck and found a new burrow. Based on what little I'd heard, she'd done so with no visible coercion or intimidation. And where had the photographer who would be chauffeur taken her? Not to the sorority house. Ed Whitbred had mentioned that Arnie had not been home since the raid, and presumably he would have noticed if Debbie Anne had been hiding next door.

If she'd moved to another motel, I'd never find her—and I was beginning to feel it was imperative that I did. I preferred to think someone had tried to frighten me; whoever it was had succeeded. Suddenly, the dark recesses of the garage seemed more a hiding place for aspiring killers than a storage area for broken tennis rackets, brittle newspapers, and furniture that would never be refinished.

I made sure the bolt on the kitchen door was firmly in place before I snapped on a light and called for

Caron. Her failure to answer did not prove she wasn't there, but a quick search did. I was by no means surrounded by silence, however. The bottle clinked against the rim of the glass as I poured myself a stiff drink, and the ice cubes rattled as I went into the living room and settled on the sofa. Nocturnal birds chirruped in the trees, as did tree frogs and crickets. The woman who lived below me was watching television. An occasional car drove past the house, its headlights flashing on the ceiling.

No motorcycles thundered in the alley, nor could I hear music and/or screams from the Kappa Theta Eta house. Eleanor must have supervised its orderly evacuation by now, I thought as I sipped scotch and studied the ceiling for celestial inspiration.

Eleanor might be a nonpareil of efficiency, but she had been wrong about her husband. The manager of the Hideaway Haven had recognized him, and it was impossible to imagine it as a site for seminars and faculty banquets. Had she also been wrong about his itinerary? Instead of being in the midst of a legal convention (or a hand of blackjack), could he be in the midst of searching the now vacant sorority house for the damning photographs?

I went to my bedroom and peered hopefully for a pinprick of light from a bobbling flashlight. No light appeared, nor did a disembodied white face drift across a window pane like a reflection of the man in the moon. Only one side of the house was visible, and there was no reason to think he'd be accommodating enough to show himself on command.

All I'd do was circle the house from a prudent distance, I told myself as I went downstairs and paused in my yard to dredge up an ounce of courage. Foolhardy heroines might creep around attics and dungeons, but I'd had a minor problem with that in the past—and only the arrival of the police had allowed me to remain in any condition to relate the highlights to future grandchildren.

Impressed by my singular display of common sense,

I strolled along the sidewalk, my eyes darting furtively at the windows on the upper stories. Once past the house, I cut through the yard of a fraternity house and emerged in the alley, ascertained no cars were lurking in the shadows, and moved cautiously along the side of the sorority house.

At the edge of the porch, I stopped and retraced my path back to the alley, scanned the windows on the back facade, and then went into the area of the yard that adjoined my duplex.

Five minutes later I'd completed the circle and seen absolutely nothing worthy of my stealth. I leaned against the porch and acknowledged the possibility that John Vanderson was in Las Vegas, Debbie Anne and Arnie were at the Dew Drop Inn, Winkie and Ed were cruising down a moonlit country road, Rebecca and Pippa were entertaining men at the Hideaway Haven, Eleanor Vanderson was on the telephone with a neurologist, and I was a failure as an amateur sleuth. A bruised and battered failure, approaching forty, accused of being menopausal, with a daughter already embroiled in a life of crime. And able to alienate a man in a single bound.

A small white form streaked past me and disappeared into the shrubbery. Gulping back a shriek, I stared as it clawed its way up the side of the house to the windowsill, and, with a yowl, squirmed beneath the screen and vanished. Katie had chosen to ignore Eleanor's eviction orders, or some inkling of instinct had compelled her to return home.

If the cat wanted to prowl through the house all night, it was not my concern. Winkie would know where to look and come back for it in the morning. My charitable impulses were confined to my own species, and I had teeth marks on my hand and ankle to reinforce my absolute lack of interest in the cat's well-being. Right.

Loathing myself, I pushed my way through the hostile shrub, lifted the edge of the screen, and gracelessly slithered over the windowsill and onto the table in Winkie's kitchen.

"Katie!" I whispered, lacking the sibilance to hiss.

No amber eyes appeared in the dark. Repeating her name softly, I squirmed across the table and managed to get my feet on the floor without banging my head in the process. There was enough light from outside for me to see that Katie was not in the immediate vicinity. The doors to the bedroom and bathroom were closed, precluding her escape into those rooms. I went into the living room. The furniture remained, but personal effects had been removed.

I glumly noted that the front door of the suite was ajar, thus allowing the cat access to the entire house. And I, too, had access to the entire house, I realized as I spotted Winkie's key ring on the coffee table. Beside it was a pink paper cat with the standard saccharine message and a handwritten note explaining how sorry Winkie was that in her haste to move she'd not had the opportunity to deliver the keys to Eleanor's house. What a shame, I thought as I picked up the key ring and went to the foyer, reminded myself of my mission, and dutifully called the cat as I roamed through the kitchen, living room, lounge, dining room, and hallway of the wing where the girls had lived.

I stopped outside what had been Jean's room. The last time I'd been in there, all of her possessions had been packed in boxes and suitcases and piled in the middle of the room. Eleanor could have arranged for them to be sent to California, but she might have overlooked this chore in her haste to empty the house.

I tried more than half the keys before I happened upon the right one. Inside the room was adequate light to determine that the boxes and suitcases were still there. Jean wouldn't have hidden the packet somewhere else in the sorority house, I thought as I sat down on the edge of the stripped bed and propped my chin with my hand. Even the ritual closet would be risky, since the sorority sisters went in and out of it on meeting nights. I recalled what I could of Jean's possessions, trying to envision each as a receptacle for photographs featuring the dean of the law school in ignominious disarray. When enlightenment failed to strike, I turned on the light, sat down on the floor, and opened the first box.

More than an hour later, I knew that none of the books had been mutilated to provide a hiding place. Nothing had been tucked in a shoe, a pocket, a cosmetics case, a briefcase, or anything else with tuckability. She'd accumulated a daunting number of pink paper cats with coy handwritten messages, but they seemed to be her only concession to college memorabilia.

Except for the incriminating photographs, which she'd been selling. It occurred to me that Rebecca might have found them when she packed Jean's possessions, and was settled in a new apartment busily modifying a payment plan for John Vanderson—one that precluded dark alleys.

I'd searched in a neat and efficient fashion, conscientiously replacing items once I'd examined them. I gathered up the stuffed cats and lobbed them one by one into a box, wishing I could gather up Katie as easily and return her to her mistress. The cats made quite an armful . . . as did the beers Doobie'd served to the girls . . . and the used textbooks that Debbie Anne Wray had brought to the Book Depot on what Caron would describe as a Fateful Day.

New textbooks cost a fortune, and used ones were worth a decent amount of money. Selling them wouldn't generate as much as the return of a coat that had been shoplifted from a mall store, nor would their resale be as lucrative as that of a personal computer or a portable television.

The stuffed cats tumbled from my arms as I returned to the bed and lay down. Were the Kappa Theta Etas, under the leadership of Jean Hall, raising money not only from prostitution and blackmail, but also from theft? I remembered what Peter had said about Arnie's patronage of a known fencing operation. With the owner of the pawnshop in prison, had Arnie taken over the business? It would explain his newfound ability to pay rent and buy beer at the Dew Drop Inn, and it would explain why he and Rebecca were acquainted, why he'd parked in the alley at midnight, and why he'd been outside the house and able to avail himself of occasional photo opportunities. Like any ambitious businessman, he'd provided curbside pickup and delivery service.

Finally I had something that I had to tell the police, even if it meant facing Peter. Surely he and Officer Pipkin would be so grateful for the tip that they could restrain themselves from physical intimacy long enough to congratulate me on my brilliance. The serial numbers on the computers stashed in the upper-story rooms would prove my hypothesis, and Arnie could be surprisingly compliant when invited to confess to various crimes. The police would question the entire membership of the sorority, and the girls would break down eventually and incriminate each other with the enthusiasm they evinced for the Kappa hymn, as would Winkie if she was aware of what her young thoroughbreds had been doing. Debbie Anne was apt to turn up along the way, especially when the manager of the Hideaway Haven and his buddy found it expedient to adopt a more cooperative and loquacious attitude.

And then, I told myself as I arose from the bed and again gathered up the cats, I would take the Herodian approach and wash my hands of the entire business.

As I tossed the last stuffed cat into the box, I decided to make a quick search for the animate one, then exit in a more dignified fashion and call Peter from my apartment. If I interrupted anything, I would offer not a single word of apology, but would simply relate everything I'd learned over the last few days, efface his name from my mind, and inquire about real estate prices in St. Mary Mead. Caron could join me when she was paroled.

I noticed a stray cat under the desk and picked it up, and had started back to the box when I realized that it might serve a more important purpose than interior decor. I examined the cat's seams for indications that it had undergone surgery on at least one occasion. It had not, but I dragged the box next to the desk and methodically examined all the cats. A particularly pink one with a dumbstruck expression proved to be a pajama bag with a pouch that contained a nightgown, a pair of lacy underpants, and a thin packet of photographs.

Feeling as dumbstruck as the cat feigned to be, I dropped it in the box and opened the flap of the packet. There were four prints and strips of film encased in cellophane sheaths. I swallowed several times, trying to convince myself that I was in no way behaving pruriently, but I finally slipped the packet into my pocket and decided to wait until I was home before I discovered just how depraved Dean Vanderson and the Kappas could be.

I flipped off the light and went into the hallway. Before I could take a step, I heard the front door close with a faint yet discernible click. It was not a welcome sound. I'd allowed Jean's door to lock behind me, and I knew how long it would take to find the right key and stay inside the room until whoever was in the foyer was gone. Too long.

Trying to convince myself that a campus officer had dropped by to check the house, I waited for him to turn on a light in the foyer. Instead, I saw the sweep of a flashlight at the end of the hallway. "Oh, dear," I mouthed silently as I crept across the hall and into the bathroom, where no exterior light glinted on the pink tile surfaces.

Earlier I'd scorned the addle-brained gothic heroines who forever put themselves in peril. I'd assured myself I was much too clever to be stalked in a brooding manor house. What a pity I hadn't listened a little harder, I thought as I strained to hear footsteps in the hallway—or the sound of someone leaving through the front door.

Something brushed against my leg. Terrified that I was in the company of a rat or someone's pet boa constrictor that had escaped in the house, I clamped my hand over my mouth and looked down. The very same cat that had bitten me twice and eluded me all over the house now had decided that my left ankle was its best friend. It slinked and slithered around me, caressing my leg with its tail, then abruptly began to purr like a vacuum cleaner.

"Ssh!" I hissed. If anything, it purred more loudly as it circled my leg. Feline psychology was not my field, and all I could do was stare helplessly at it.

The overhead light came on. No longer in the mood for affection, Katie scampered out the doorway. I was too startled to do anything more than gape at Eleanor Vanderson, who appeared equally unnerved.

"Claire?" she said in a shaky voice. "Oh, thank goodness it's you. I was afraid I was about to encounter—I don't know. I'm so relieved it's you." She came into the bathroom and leaned against a sink, her carefully applied makeup doing little to counteract her paleness. My reflection in the mirror behind her indicated I fared no better; the whiteness of my face above the black shirt gave me the appearance of a character in a freeze-frame from an old movie.

"What are you doing here?" I asked.

She turned around, twisted the tap, and splashed a scant handful of water on her face. Glancing at me in the mirror, she said, "I came by to make sure the house was locked, and noticed a light in one of the windows in this wing. I assumed one of the girls had been negligent, but there've been so many prowlers and trespassers of late that I thought I'd better check."

I told her how I'd seen Katie enter the house and gone to the rescue, omitting to elaborate on my subsequent actions. The words echoed off the ceramic surfaces, sounding hollow and even less probable as they faded. "I panicked when I heard the door, and came in here to hide," I concluded.

"It's very kind of you to worry about Katie, Claire, but it may have been foolhardy on your part. I'm certain that I saw a light. Someone else may be in the house at this moment." Shivering, she glanced at the hallway, then tried to give me the standard Kappa smile. "There's no need to be melodramatic, is there? It's probably Rebecca or Pippa coming by for something overlooked during her packing, or even Winkie. In fact, she may have come to search for our runaway kitty, had no luck, and left through the back door by the time I came in the front."

"I didn't see anyone, but there are a lot of rooms and hallways," I said truthfully. "I don't know why I thought I could find the cat in this labyrinth."

Eleanor had recovered enough to glance at her watch, shake her head, and say, "Well, let's make sure the light is out, then we can both go home. John promised to call me from his hotel room at eleven, and he'll be frantic if I'm not there." She took a key ring from her purse and sailed out of the bathroom, confident that I would accede to her plan.

She hesitated only a second, then zeroed in on the door of Jean Hall's room and utilized her flashlight to pick out the correct key. "How peculiar," she said as she turned on the light and frowned at the pyramid of suitcases and boxes. "I thought Winkie had sent the poor girl's things to her parents. It was only a matter of telephoning one of the moving-van firms and arranging for them to include all this in their next shipment to California. I wonder why she never did."

I was about to point out that Winkie had been busy when the front door in the foyer opened and the floor creaked as someone crossed the threshold. Eleanor grabbed my arm and yanked me inside the room, closed the door, and switched off the light. Her ear pressed against the door, she whispered, "Someone else is here."

I sat down on the edge of the bed. "Are you certain that your husband is in Las Vegas?"

"Why wouldn't he be?"

"I'm afraid his fantasies have some element of reality," I said carefully. "I spoke to the manager of a motel that's known to be a place where . . . adults consent, and he reacted as though he recognized your husband from my description. He also identified some of the Kappa Theta Etas as regular patrons."

She stopped listening at the door and stood up. Her face was indecipherable in the shadows, but her voice was skeptical and unfriendly. "What exactly are you saying, Claire? I explained about John's condition, and I thought you understood me. He is not well. To be candid, he's physically incapable of doing what you've implied, even if there was the slightest reason to consider the possibility. As for the girls, we have strict rules about where they can be seen in public, and they're aware of the severity of their punishment should they disobey. The only one of them that would set foot in a place like that is Debbie Anne Wray."

"Who set foot in it last week, and stayed there for several nights," I said. "A second witness saw her get into a green truck and leave yesterday morning."

"A green truck?" Eleanor sat down beside me, her purse crinkling in protest as she squeezed it. "That dreadful man found in the ritual closet drives a green truck, doesn't he? I don't understand any of this. Debbie Anne has been hiding at a motel, and that man picked her up and took her someplace else? He's just a painter. There's no reason she would know him, much less trust him enough to go away with him."

Hoping she didn't subscribe to the kill-the-messenger school of retribution, I said, "There may be a reason that she and some of the other girls know Arnie. I suspect they've been transacting business with him since the spring, using him to fence stolen property."

"Stolen property?" she echoed in a stunned voice. "But these are Kappa Theta Etas, not common girls who struggle through high school and marry factory workers and stay pregnant for fifteen years. We can't be as choosy as we'd like, but we do examine their backgrounds and scholastic records before we accept them, and once they become pledges, we do everything we can to train them in appropriate behavior. First you slander my husband, and now you accuse us of theft and promiscuity!"

"I'm sorry, but I must tell the police what I've discovered. When Arnie sobers up, he can tell us where Debbie Anne is. She seemed a reluctant participant in all this, and I won't be surprised if she's willing to spill the whole sordid story. The motel manager might want to bargain, too."

"The police are going to believe those three? A known drunk, a farmgirl, and an employee of the Hideaway Haven? I'd give more credence to the butcher, the baker, and the candlestick maker."

"None of whose daughters could ever be Kappa Theta Etas," I said in defense of the working stiffs of the world. "In any case, it's going to be out of our hands, and we'll have to see what happens. I don't know who's prowling in the house, but I really don't care if it's your husband searching for the photographs or Winkie for the cat. I'm going home."

She followed me to the hallway, talking faster than I was remotely capable of walking. "I wish you'd reconsider before you call the police with your wild accusations, Claire. You've no evidence of any of this, nothing but your own convoluted ideas and less than credible witnesses, but rumors will leak out and have a disastrous effect on rush. This will be our first time to have someone from the National Board with us. It's vital to make a good impression on her so we can be sure of continued financial support until we can get our budget straightened out."

I slowed down. "Winkie mentioned that someone was coming to audit the books at the end of the summer. I wonder if the reports of theft and shoplifting shot up the day after the girls learned an accountant would be looking at their ledgers? Jean Hall would have been the most alarmed. Yale might retract its invitation if it learned she'd been embezzling from her sorority, and National sounds like a group that would press charges."

"Embezzling?" Eleanor said, apparently content to repeat my more startling words and phrases.

"I doubt it would be overly taxing to a business major. Float some bills, dip into one account to cover deficits in another, exaggerate an assessment for party favors, tamper with invoices—all so very simple until a trained auditor appears. Jean had to scrounge up enough money to cover what she, Rebecca, and maybe Pippa had been using to update their wardrobes and pay their house dues." I went to the foyer, where there was no sign of the newest arrival. I was vaguely aware that Eleanor was continuing to plead with the oiliness of a lawyer, but a couple of insights had occurred that led me to think I needed to leave immediately.

"She took my keys," said a chilly voice.

I kept heading for the door as Winkie stepped out of her suite and gave me a disapproving look. There was nothing charmingly childlike about her now; she was as malevolent as a gnome from one of the more gruesome fairy tales.

"And she searched Jean's things," said a downright icy voice from within the unlit living room.

I may have faltered just a bit as Rebecca came into the foyer. She swept her hair back and continued, "You'd better hope she didn't find anything, either."

"Not me," I said as I reached for the doorknob. And heard the sound of a gun being cocked. And froze.

16

"I'll shoot you if I must, Claire," Eleanor said in a conversational tone more suitable for cocktail parties at the country club. "I don't know exactly what I'll tell the police, but I'm sure I can concoct some perfectly adequate excuse about mistaking you for a burglar. Thanks to you, there are numerous reports on file at the campus security office."

I reluctantly lowered my hand and turned around to look at the gun in her hand. Although it wasn't pink, it was small and stylish, the perfect size to be slipped into a beaded bag for an evening at the opera. "For pity's sake, Eleanor, you aren't going to shoot me in front of two witnesses."

She showed me all her teeth and a fair quantity of moist pink gums. "We're Kappa Theta Etas. We'd never testify against our own sisters. Loyalty is the very basis of our initiation ritual; once we've attached our pins, we're intimately linked, and even in death, we're steadfast members of Chapter Eternal."

Winkie and Rebecca nodded grimly, and the latter said, "Besides, I'm going to New York at the end of the summer, not some women's prison. It would be too dreary."

"Is John Vanderson sponsoring you?" I asked evenly.

She flinched as Eleanor's gun wobbled in her direction. "I don't know what you're talking about. I mean, Jean had some deal with him, but I didn't have anything to do with it."

"Oh, come now," I said with a chuckle. "You found

the photographs in Jean's room and sent Dean
Vanderson a blackmail note just the other day. On
Monday, I believe he said. I saw it in his office."

"She did?" said Eleanor. The question was aimed at
me, but the gun, at least for the moment, was still
aimed at Rebecca.

Rebecca spoke quickly. "I did not! Jean must have
put the photographs in her purse when she met your
husband in the alley. If anybody is in a position to use
them, it's Debbie Anne. She has Jean's key to the
chapter room. Why wouldn't she have the photographs,
too?"

"I don't think she does," Eleanor said. After a moment, she pointed the gun at Winkie. "Did you happen
to look through Jean's things?"

Winkie jerked her head back and forth. "No, and I
know nothing about this matter. I was aware that Jean
and some of the girls were . . . behaving badly, but she
made it clear that I was to mind my own business. If
National were to hear of some of the things that have
happened right here in the house, they'd revoke our
charter. You know how desperately I need the pension,
Eleanor."

I decided to aid and abet the erosion of Kappa loyalty. "But why did you return to the house tonight? Did
you want to enhance your job security with something
to dangle over Eleanor?"

"I was worried that I hadn't locked all the doors. I
may have heard something from one of the girls about
Dean Vanderson, but I would never stoop to blackmail.
Well, I did think it was important to make sure that no
evidence of misconduct be sent to Jean's parents."

"That's right," Rebecca contributed, still speaking
rapidly and in danger of flubbing her lines. "Jean's
parents might have gone crazy and called National.
Her father's a state senator, and he's got enough clout
to force the local police to reopen the investigation. A
thorough search of the house would be a disaster for
all of us."

"Stop!" Eleanor leaned against the wall and rubbed

her face with her free hand, a frown deepening on her face as she studied each of us in turn. "This is terribly confusing, all these accusations and lies. I think we need to sit down and talk this over, and reach an agreement about what will be said to National and what need not be mentioned. We're Kappa Theta Etas, after all."

It was not the moment to correct her. I nodded and said, "Why don't you put down the gun and we'll do just that?"

"What about her?" said Rebecca, not bothering to gesture in my direction.

Eleanor hesitated, then pointed the gun at me. "I'll have to ask you to wait in the chapter room while we deal with this, Claire. Earlier you made rash and injudicious remarks concerning our chapter, and I cannot allow you to leave just now. Winkie, would you be so kind as to retrieve your keys from Claire's pocket and unlock the door at the top of the stairs? Rebecca, why don't you make tea in the suite for us? I'll be back in a jiffy."

She kept the barrel jammed into my back as we went down to the basement. I was hoping she would have a problem unlocking the chapter-room door, but rather than using Winkie's unwieldy key ring, she took a single key from her pocket and used it with no lessening of pressure in the middle of my back.

"I'd welcome you to the chapter room," she said as she shoved me into the room, "but you've already seen it, haven't you? Some sororities have open chapter rooms, but it's a bother to have to put away the banners and scatter the chairs after the meetings. It's really quite a lot easier to keep it locked."

I was not in the proper frame of mind for a lesson in sororal protocol, being more concerned with the current situation. "Let's get this over with," I said. "Decide who gets to blackmail whom, and then let me out of here so I can go home and go to bed."

"I'm afraid it may be a long wait. Did you get a good look inside the ritual closet when you discovered

Arnie?" I shrugged. "The Kappa Theta Etas have a very special initiation ceremony, filled with mystery and symbolism. What's said and done here can never leave this room; the very first vow taken is to honor the sanctity and confidentiality of the ceremony. Then guess what happens?"

I warily noted the brightness of her eyes. "I have no idea whatsoever, Eleanor. Why don't you go upstairs and—"

"Each pledge steps into a real coffin, and when she senses that she's ready, she comes out to be welcomed by her new sisters. It's symbolic of her rebirth as a Kappa Theta Eta!" She giggled at my expression. "Oh, we have more symbols than you can imagine. Periodically during the year, the pledges are lined up in the backyard and sprinkled with a hose to make them grow. When the moon is full, the members wake the pledges and sing to them while they pretend to be roses in the flowerbed."

"You shouldn't be telling me your sorority secrets," I said with heartfelt sincerity, mindful of her remark about certain subjects never leaving the room.

"Then why don't you tell me what secrets you know? No, let me see if I can guess! You seem to know about John's sordid little sessions at the motel, don't you? It took me quite some time to figure it out, but he actually kept the photographs Jean took from inside a closet. I found the little souvenirs in his dresser drawer, along with the pink notes."

"Including the one that ordered him to meet Jean at the fraternity-house patio on Saturday night?"

She beamed at me. "I am so impressed with your cleverness! Tell me more, please."

I decided to participate in her maniacal game in hopes that someone might intervene. The odds were slightly more in favor of mummified alumnae staggering out of the ritual closet than of police thundering down the stairs, but there was little else to do. "Don't be so modest, Eleanor. You acted quickly and cleverly when Debbie Anne came to you to confess about the thefts and shoplifting. Did you pretend to be horrified and tell her to stay at the Hideaway Haven until you took action?"

"I did, I did! I told her she was in great danger from Jean and Rebecca, and that she had to hide until I called National on Monday morning. I even offered to move her car to a different location in case someone might see it at the motel." She clucked her tongue disapprovingly. "Debbie Anne should never have been encouraged to pledge. She lacks initiative."

I sat down on a folding chair and crossed my legs. "But she called me, didn't she? That must have annoyed you enough to take her to your house for a lecture."

Eleanor sat down, but at a distance that precluded any reckless heroics on my part. If we'd constituted a quorum, we could have held a meeting about gun control. Still beaming like a spotlight, she said, "I was annoyed, yes, but the reason I told Arnie to bring her to my house was so that she could clean for me. My housekeeper quit on the very day we were entertaining Judge Frankley. Debbie Anne did a competent job, but she found a newspaper with an article about Jean's death, and became so agitated that I had to slip her a sedative before I took her to the guestroom on the third floor. It seemed most expedient to leave her there until John was on his way to Las Vegas."

"Why did Arnie agree to this?"

"I paid him, of course. He called me from jail. His accusations were preposterous, but I needed someone to keep an eye on the girl until I decided what to do. I posted his bail and told him to take the room next to hers at the motel. Once Debbie Anne became my houseguest, there was no reason for me to continue to pay for his room—or for his silence. After he delivered her, I asked him to park on Thurber Street and meet me in the alley, hurried him down the back steps, and told him to take a television set out of the closet." She giggled again at my expression. "If I'd had any idea that you would insist on searching it for Debbie Anne, I would have selected a different place. There was no reason to think anyone would open the door until the middle of August, and I did intend to deal with his remains long before then."

I looked at the door and tried not to imagine what she would have encountered after two hot months. An even less palatable idea came to mind. "May I assume that's where Debbie Anne is now?"

"And where you're going to be, too," she said, her ebullience fading as she stood up, the gun aimed at my cold, cold heart. "I had to give Debbie Anne a stronger dose of the sedative, but she'll awaken before too long and you can keep each other company. Eventually you'll grow too weak to visit, and you might even decide the coffin looks cozy. Now that I think about it, one of the pink robes might make a splendid shroud. There's no point in pounding on the door or shouting; such activity will deplete the oxygen, and the closet door is very sturdy. No one will be in the house for two months."

"Forget it, Eleanor," I said, refusing to rise. "Winkie and Rebecca will figure out what you've done, and you cannot count on their continued loyalty in the face of three murders, including that of a Kappa Theta Eta."

"I do believe I can. Neither is aware that I, in my capacity as an alumna and a chapter sponsor, had to stop Jean Hall from threatening everything dear to Kappa Theta Eta. Using Katie the Kappa Kitten like that is an inexcusable violation of our creed!"

"Is that why you took the time to remove her sorority pin?"

"She was no longer worthy of it, but the process through which a girl is expelled is long and painful for everyone from the local chapter level to the judicial branch of National. It was so much more expedient to do it myself. Jean was in no condition to protest, was she? In any case, I shall encourage Winkie and Rebecca to think Debbie Anne committed the crime and fled the state, and I suspect they won't question it too seriously. Winkie is very keen to keep her job for one final year, and Rebecca's a lovely girl, so wonderfully ambitious and talented, and hardly apt to confess her involvement to the police." She tapped her foot impatiently, but her voice remained cool and courteous as she said, "Please cooperate with me on this, Claire. We both know how difficult it is to get bloodstains out of a carpet. I'd like to be home in time for John's call, and I'm sure Winkie and Rebecca have their own plans for the evening."

She might have been inviting me to contribute to my favorite charity (presumably the Red Cross Bloodmobile), and she'd clearly chaired one too many committees in her day. If she'd been angry or frothing at the mouth, I might have been less terrified; as it was, locking me in the closet was merely the next item on the agenda after the treasurer's report. The heavy metal door to the chapter room was closed, and I doubted Winkie and Rebecca could hear a shot. After a nice cup of tea, Eleanor would assure them she intended to release me, wave a warm farewell from the door, and go home to await a long-distance call from her husband.

"Claire," she said with a flicker of irritation, "let's not make this any more awkward than necessary."

"It is rather awkward for me."

Her finger tightened on the trigger. "I do wish you'd take this in the proper spirit."

I could think of only one thing that might distract her. I rose unsteadily and took a step, stopped, and with my eyes widened to their roundest and my eyebrows arched, pointed at the corner behind her. "Oh, look!" I trilled. "It's dear little Katie!"

She turned involuntarily, and I grabbed a metal chair and swung it at her. At the last critical moment before it slammed into her face, I knew from her look of deep disapproval that Caron Malloy would never be invited to become a Kappa Theta Eta.

I was beginning to wonder if Peter intended to remain in front of his office window in perpetuity. His back had rippled for a while, and the muscles in his neck had been visible for the first hour or so after dawn. Every so often his hands had curled into bloodless white fists. Now he was motionless.

"Why didn't you tell me what was going on?" he said.

This particular question had been posed numerous times during the lengthy interview. I took a sip of cold, scummy coffee and said, "Nothing was going on until I went to the Hideaway Haven. Even then, I didn't have absolute proof that Jean was blackmailing John Vanderson, thus giving Eleanor a motive to intervene on his behalf—if it was on his behalf. She's spooky about the sorority. Then again, the sorority's pretty darn spooky."

"But you knew a lot of things that might have helped us," he said, still staring out the window as if wishing to see workmen erecting a gallows. "You knew Arnie was skulking in the bushes, as was this biker who was having an affair with the housemother. John Vanderson admitted he met Jean the night she was killed, and also admitted he'd been in the house."

"But Eleanor told me he was—"

"Delusional," Peter continued smoothly. As I mentioned, we'd repeated this particular conversation for several hours, and we were confident of our lines. "Rather than allow us to investigate the allegations, you chose to do so on your own. And broke into the house to save a cat, no less."

"To save a cat, no less." It was my turn to sputter, but before I could begin, Jorgeson came into the office.

"I interviewed the third girl, Pippa Edmondson," he said, his ears quivering in response to the tension, which had to be as thick as fog. He put a paperback book on the corner of the desk. "She asked me to return this to Ms. Malloy, and said Caron could keep some case of color strips. According to the Faulkner girl, who's spilling everything she can think of like Niagara Falls, Pippa's a kleptomaniac. Whenever anything disappeared in the house, the girls would wait until she went to class and then just retrieve their things from her room. Jean threatened to have her kicked out of the sorority unless she agreed to utilize her talents around town and focus on items of value."

"Rebecca made her return my keys," I said as I stashed the book in my purse. "I suppose she thought it might keep me from suspecting them of their other activities. Did she admit she sent the blackmail cat to Dean Vanderson?"

Jorgeson nodded. "Yeah, she said over the last two years she and Jean Hall had redirected upward of thirty thousand dollars from house accounts to their personal accounts. This spring Jean realized they'd better replace the missing funds before the books were audited, so she supervised some nasty fund-raisers. Vanderson wasn't the only libidinous professor to be caught with ... his pants down and required to pay for it. Did you look at the photographs, Ms. Malloy?"

"I never did," I admitted with a shrug.

"Just as well. They might have diminished your respect for the sorority. The Faulkner girl had taken over the operation. She said she went back to the house to search once more for that particular set of photographs, but she figured she could bluff the dean without them."

"Has Debbie Anne Wray recovered consciousness?" Peter said without turning.

"Not yet, but the doctor said she'll come around okay. They got Arnold Riggles sobered up and transferred him to our jail, but he claims he doesn't remember anything since"—Jorgeson cleared his throat—"he made a bet with a certain senator. We'll see if his memory improves when he starts aching for a drink." He nodded at Peter's back and edged out of the room.

I was getting bored with the scene. "Listen, Peter, I've already said that I was on my way to call you when Eleanor pulled a gun on me. That was partly my fault. I didn't realize she was guilty until she mentioned the name of the motel. Only then did it occur to me that the manager must have called her, and after she missed me in the parking lot, she followed me home and waited to see what I'd do."

"Which was to keep sticking your nose into the case until it was in peril of being shot off." His shoulders rose and fell as he sighed. "I suppose we've been over this before, haven't we? You don't give a damn what I say to you—as a cop or as a person; I'd have more luck with a pink construction-paper cat. Schedule a time with Jorgeson to give an official statement, and then you can go out in search of your next corpse."

"All right," I said and stalked out of the room. I didn't bother to speak to Jorgeson; he would call me when he had time to take a statement. I flew out the door, and blindly started for the Book Depot, making no effort to temper my anger or analyze its cause. Despite my lack of sleep, I was going to open the store and snatch customers off the sidewalk.

I was not too distraught to detour past the doughnut shop for a sweet roll and a large cup of coffee, and I was devouring same when the bell jangled.

"Mother," Caron said as she pounded across the room, "I have this incredible way to make money this summer! This time I won't have to beg a bunch of bitches to make appointments, then listen while they cancel with Really Stupid reasons about—"

"Why did they change their minds?"

Caron ducked behind the science fiction rack. "How should I know? I mean, they change their minds like other people change channels."

"What do you know about this?" I asked Inez, who'd sidled in more decorously and looked as though she wanted to sidle right back out. "Did something happen while you and Caron were at the drive-in with your parents?"

"Like what?" Caron said with a scornful laugh.

I spotted the top of her head as it wafted in the direction of the gardening section. "Like something that provoked one of your clients to call yesterday and suggest that you were engaged in extortion."

"It wasn't like that," Inez said, blinking somberly

and keeping a judicious eye on Caron's head. "The junior varsity football team went on a retreat, so their girlfriends were kinda bored and some of them went to the drive-in with—"

"One lousy night without a date, and they're fooling around with the basketball players!" Caron chortled, now approaching the true-crime novels. "All I did was wander around the cars to see who might want to have a My Beautiful Self session. I didn't say one word about ratting on them to their boyfriends."

"Not exactly," Inez said thoughtfully, "but they seemed to be a little bit worried about it. And it's a good thing you saw Rhonda Maguire coming and hid in the playground until she gave up. My parents would have been upset if you'd gotten in a fight with her."

Surely the Mad Hatter had come in with them, I told myself, and would offer me a refill while the Dormouse gazed dreamily at me from inside the cup. "And why is Rhonda so enraged?"

Inez seemed more concerned about a more substantial life form somewhere in the store. In a voice almost inaudible, she said, "Caron found a tube of Super Glue the night she locked herself in Rhonda's room."

"Caron!" I said coldly. "Stop acting as if you were in a maze and get out here this very minute. This is too much." I waited for a moment, but heard no response. I came out from behind the counter to stalk her, and was plotting the most advantageous path when a motorcycle roared under the portico and backfired once before dying.

Caron's face appeared over the classics rack. "What was that, Mother?"

"You may consider it a temporary reprieve from the governor," I said, "but nothing more."

"Good morning," Ed said as he came through the door, dressed as I'd last seen him in a black leather jacket, the helmet in his hand. He looked older, however, and his mouth sagged dispiritedly as he tried to smile at Inez, who promptly scuttled into the racks. To me, he said, "I heard what happened at the sorority house, and I just came from visiting Winkie at the jail. Jeez, what a mess!"

"Indeed," I said. "Have you talked to Arnie?"

"Why would I talk to him? 'And from the extremest upward of their head to the descent and dust below thy foot, a most toad-spotted traitor.' If Shakespeare wasn't talking about Arnie, I don't know why not."

"Rhonda Maguire is a toad-spotted traitor," Caron intoned from an invisible locale.

"Pay no attention to that girl behind the curtain," I said, aware that I was mixing cinematic metaphors but too tired to control myself. "What does Winkie think will happen to her?"

"Her lawyer says not much. She was suspicious, but she didn't participate in anything illegal, and she swears she thought Eleanor Vanderson eventually would allow you to leave."

"Did she?" I said dryly as I remembered her eagerness to unlock the door and her complaisant expression as she watched Eleanor escort me downstairs. Perhaps conspiracy to commit murder was in her job description. Would she have helped Eleanor plant us under the roses shortly before rush? Did Katie the Kappa Kitten say thanks?

Ed grimaced faintly as if he were reading my admittedly twisted mind. "Oh, yeah, and she said several times how kind it was of you to go after the cat. Unnecessary, but kind. Anyway, she won't be arraigned until early next week, and I was wondering if"—his cheeks reddened and he glanced nervously at the racks, from which fierce whispering emanated—"you might want to ride out in the country sometime. I promise we won't so much as go past the Dew Drop Inn."

"I don't think so, Ed. I suppose I'm not quite ready to be a free spirit on the back of your bike. But come by the store and sling quotes at me whenever you want."

Caron and Inez emerged only after Ed was gone, and I couldn't recall when I'd seen either of them so awed. I was hoping they were also speechless, but Caron finally gave me a piercing look and said, "He Asked You for a Date."

"He asked me to go for a ride," I said mildly.

"On a motorcycle," breathed Inez.

I considered pointing out that the encroachment of my fifth decade did not require me to take up an eremetic life of crocheting and counting liver spots. Self-sufficiency did not demand solitude any more than a few new gray hairs precluded companionship. It might have evolved into one of my finer lectures, but instead I said, "You're grounded until you clean your room and the garage."

"I was going to clean out the garage anyway," Caron said with typical—and insufferable—smugness. "I have to do it so I can start earning money for a car. Come on, Inez, a few spiders won't hurt you."

"Brown recluse spider bites can cause your skin to rot," Inez countered as they started for the door. "It's called necrosis, and if it's really bad, they—"

"Wait a minute!" I snapped.

"Oh, Mother," Caron said as her lip shot out and her eyes rolled upward, "is this another hot flash? The plan's foolproof, and it won't depend on some toad-spotted traitor to make it work. It's one hundred percent guaranteed or your money back, and now that Pippa's dropped out of school and left town, I don't have to give her what I earned as a My Beautiful Self consultant. If you don't mind, I'd like to go home and start on the garage."

My fingers may have tightened around the plastic cup, but I kept my voice steady. "What are we talking about, Caron?"

"Night crawlers. They're these icky worm things that people buy to use as bait. I've already sent in a coupon for a starter set, and all I have to do is find some wooden boxes and a lot of dirt. You dump coffee grounds and rotten vegetables on them, and then you sell them for a lot of money." She frowned at Inez. "This palette stuff is nonsense. I don't see why I can't have a red sports car if I want."

"If the palette stuff is nonsense, then I want my yellow blouse back," Inez said.

"So you'll look as though you're terminally sallow?"

The bell jangled as they sailed away to entertain pedestrians with their latest topic of debate. I was in my office, scraping the bottom of the coffee pot and vowing to make some abiding changes in my life, when it jangled less violently.

I came to the doorway and stopped. Peter Rosen stood by the counter, doing his best to appear relaxed despite the thrust of his jaw and the intensity in his brown eyes.

"Do you want to talk, Claire?" he said.

It took me most of a minute to consider. "Yes," I said at last. "I suppose I do. What happened to the cat?"

"Officer Pipkin took it into temporary custody, despite her husband's objections. He's allergic to cat hair. Is there anything else you'd like to discuss?"

I nodded.

"No," Luanne said after a goodly amount of thought, "I don't suppose he's the perfect potential mate. There's a possibility he murdered his wife."

"I suppose that could be considered a flaw," I said as I stared across the picnic table at a woman who heretofore had seemed a singular beacon of sanity in a world beset with neon. We were sitting in the beer garden on a balmy June evening for the first time in several weeks. We usually met every Wednesday, but I'd been badgered night and day by my spotty old accountant, who reputedly glows in the dark during tax season, and for most of a month I'd been hiding out in either the back of my bookstore or my bathtub (sessions in the former dictate sessions in the latter). I finally found my voice and said, "Exactly how strong is this possibility?"

"The whole thing's absurd, but the investigator from the sheriff's department continues to pester Dick several times a week. The poor baby—and I don't mean this captain, who's an anal-retentive jerk—is getting an ulcer, and his performance in the sack is indicative of his stress. Were I a saint, I wouldn't even notice, but it's become a factor."

I was perplexed by Luanne's attitude. She'd survived a divorce and a migration from a wealthy Connecticut suburb to distinctly middle-class Farberville, an amiable town of several thousand college students and twenty-odd thousand civilians. She presumably made enough money from her funky used clothing store, Second Hand Rose, to keep herself in beer and pretzels. Her hair was dramatic—black with streaks of silver. Her Yankee boarding school accent was rarely discernible. And she was in the midst of an affair with a man who might have murdered his wife.

I replenished my cup from the pitcher, then said, "You're quite sure he didn't?"

"Dick wouldn't step on a spider. He's a pedodontist, and he spends his days putting braces on little teeth for great big fees. He donates time to a community clinic, attends the Episcopal church on major holidays, and calls his mother every Sunday night. He's a decent golfer and an avid racquetball player. He makes his own pesto. He can sew a button on a shirt. Does this sound like the résumé of a murderer?"

"Then why does the investigator keep implying that he is?" I asked with impressive reasonableness. "Surely there must be some sort of case."

"Becca died in a boating accident, but Captain Gannet is determined to prove Dick masterminded it."

"A boating accident?"

Luanne automatically reached for a pack of cigarettes that was not there, sighed, and began to shred a napkin. "Dick has a gorgeous house at Turnstone Lake that he and Becca used every weekend. There's a private bird sanctuary in the area. It consists of a few thousand acres of abandoned pastures, forests, and swampy creeks, and it supports a large population of bald-headed eagles in the winter. Eagles are an endangered species, you know, as are hawks, owls, and even turkey buzzards. It's a federal offense to so much as muss their feathered heads."

"This is all terribly interesting," I said, yawning. "Shall we move on to the accident?"

"Becca received a phone call late one afternoon that an eagle was flapping about on one of the islands, so she went down to the marina to take their boat out to investigate. Halfway to the island, there was an explosion, probably caused by a propane leak in the cabin."

I gave her a Miss Marplish smile. "How do we know she received a call?"

"She left a message on Agatha Anne Gallinago's answering machine. Agatha Anne's the president of the foundation that owns the sanctuary. As soon as she arrived home and found the message, she drove to the marina to try to catch Becca before she took the boat. She and the manager at the marina both saw the explosion."

"And this purported leak?" I continued delicately. "Why not sabotage of some sort?"

"Agatha Anne smelled gas earlier that day and reported it to the manager, who admitted he hadn't done anything about it. It didn't occur to either of them that anyone would use the boat."

"If it's all so straightforward, replete with witnesses and odiferous leakage, why is this captain suspicious of your pesto-making prince? Law enforcement agencies don't have the manpower to hound innocent citizens to any great extent. There must be some reason that you haven't mentioned."

Luanne shrugged. "Well, the night before the accident Dick and Becca had a argument at one of the bird group's parties. She threw a piece of quiche at him, so he stormed out of the house and walked home." She was trying to sound nonchalant, but her eyes flickered nervously and the pile of white shreds was growing steadily. If she'd not quit smoking, I was quite sure she would have had a cigarette in each hand and another smoldering in an ashtray. "He was so angry that he drove back to town and didn't return until the next night. A deputy arrived shortly afterward to tell him the news."

"When did all this take place?"

"About three months ago," she said in a low mumble, no doubt hoping the chatter from the adjoining tables would drown out her words.

As the mother of a teenager, I was accustomed to such evasive tactics and adept at exposing them. "Did you meet him at the funeral, Luanne, or were you lurking behind a headstone in the cemetery?"

"I met him two weeks ago at the bank. We chatted,

then ended up having coffee. One thing led to another. I really thought I'd found the perfect man. Dick's good-looking, rich, sensitive, virile ... and available. He took me to his lake house last weekend. It's not especially large, but it's equipped with every appliance in the western world, and has an enormous redwood deck. I can already imagine myself in a lacy little something, gazing at the sunset while Dick nibbles my neck and murmurs about our prenuptial contract. When he actually proposes, I shall be in the conservatory, dressed in a white frock and holding a red rose. The challenge is to find a conservatory which isn't crowded by the likes of Professor Plum and Miss Scarlet and their lead pipes and candlesticks."

The arithmetic was not challenging, especially to someone with a meticulous accountant like mine. "We'll worry about the conservatory when the time comes. Perfect men do not leap into an affair ten weeks after becoming widowers. The corpse may be cold by now, granted, but has he had time to clean out her closet and throw away her toothbrush?"

"I didn't examine the toothbrushes," Luanne said with only the tiniest glint of guilt. "There are a few things in her closet, such as an Imelda Marcos shoe collection, three fur coats, and enough clothes for an entire sorority house. The woman did like to shop."

I spotted youths with frizzy ponytails unloading instruments and amplifiers by the back gate. "I think you're out of your mind to get involved with this man, and I'll say as much in the eulogy. I need to relieve Caron at the store so that she and Inez can terrorize the mall." I finished the last swallow of beer and stood up, trying to disguise my annoyance with Luanne. She was in her mid-forties and more than old enough to date whomever she chose. If nothing else, he'd convinced her to stop smoking. I could only hope he wouldn't convince her to stop breathing.

She picked up her purse and we pushed our way through the throng and out to the sidewalk. Across the street, none of the pedestrians were streaming into

The Book Depot, my source of income and ulcers, but that was hardly surprising. The little man who'd sold it to me had warned me not to anticipate wealth within the millennium, but I was burdened with a daughter to support. At least once a week I was reminded that I was not doing so in a style she found acceptable.

"The captain may be hounding Dick because of his first wife's death," Luanne said as we seized a break in the traffic and stepped off the curb.

I froze in the middle of the street. "And there's a possibility that he murdered her, too? Luanne, you're safer standing here than allowing your neck to be nibbled by this pedodontist. You're hardly practicing safe sex if you're sleeping with Bluebeard."

"I think not," she said, shoving me into motion as a convertible filled with hooting fraternity boys bore down on us. "He didn't murder her, either. The only problem is that her death wasn't explained to Captain Gannet's satisfaction. As I said, he's anal retentive."

"You'd better pray he's not right."

We stopped under the portico that had once protected passengers as they awaited trains that would carry them to exotic places like New Orleans and Omaha. These days they'd have a futile wait, but they could entertain themselves looking at my very dusty window display of histories and mysteries.

I made a note to utilize the feather duster on a more regular basis, then said, "I am not your mother, and it's none of my business if you want to have a meaningful relationship with a homicidal maniac."

"He's a wonderful man," she said, her voice thickening and her eyes filling with tears. "None of this is his fault. When Carlton was killed, nobody came pounding on your doors with accusations and innuendos."

"Carlton died in a head-on collision with a chicken truck," I retorted, "and the culpable driver was standing there in a flurry of white feathers when the state police arrived. It's hardly the same situation—and it happened once, not twice. Or who knows how many times, to be brutally frank. This man could have buried a bevy of grade school sweethearts and fiancées along the way."

Luanne opened her mouth, then clamped it shut and stalked away without acknowledging the perspicacity of my remarks. I went inside, where Caron and Inez were entertaining each other by reading aloud from *Lady Chatterley's Lover.* Reminding myself the novel was a literary classic, if not precisely penned in hopes of sending fifteen-year-olds into paroxysms of snickers, I went behind the counter to make sure the contents of the cash register were not seriously depleted.

"Flowers in her pubic hair? That's gross!" shrieked Caron, who inherited my curly red hair and freckles but not one hint of my mild-mannered personality. She staggered out of sight behind the fiction rack, hiccuping with glee, and returned with a gardening book. "Pansies of passion? Dahlias of desire? Lilies of lust?"

As far as I can determine, Caron's every act is dictated by hormones. These last few years have been a series of Broadway theater productions, but I can never tell if we're to be drawn into a dark and brooding drama or a musical comedy. Or, more frequently, an Off-Broadway experimental piece that mystifies the cast as much as the audience. She has long since mastered the art of speaking in capital letters, and her lower lip sticks out most of the time to indicate her displeasure with someone who has patience, maternal acumen, and stretchmarks.

Inez Thornton is quite the opposite. She is limp and anemic but ever loyal. Her thick lenses disguise her occasional winces when Caron's volume rises to an unseemly level, and she keeps a judicious eye on the nearest exit. She is still in the throes of lower case, and at the moment she was turning pink. "Hello, Mrs. Malloy," she said as if my presence would have any damper on Caron's behavior.

"Snapdragons of salaciousness!" Caron shrieked before once again disappearing.

"Aren't you two going to the mall?" I said optimistically. "Everything's on sale, and you don't want to miss a minute."

"Zinnias of zest!"

If there'd been any customers, I might have felt obliged to put a stop to this litany of floral lasciviousness, but I was curious to learn the extent of Caron's vocabulary in such matters.

"Everlastings of eroticism!"

Inez had edged in front of the self-help books and was regarding me with the wide-eyed solemnity of a seal pup. "Actually, we're not going to the mall after all. Rhonda Maguire got her driver's license this morning and she's picking up everybody for pizza."

"Dandelions of depression!" came a groan.

"Afterwards, some of the football players are coming to Rhonda's to swim," Inez added. "Louis called her this afternoon."

"Wilderberries of wantonness!"

Inez frowned at this latest contribution. "I don't think there are plants called 'wilderberries,' Caron. His name is an anglicized version of whatever it was in German or Polish or something like that. His sister told me that at band practice."

Caron came around the rack. "Are you implying that I am botanically impaired? I know Perfectly Well that his name is German or whatever. I was attempting to make a point, not pass a course."

I shooed them away, locked the store, and walked back to our apartment, the second story of a white brick house across the street from the verdant lawn of Farber College. The Kappa Theta Eta house next to us was boarded up, and no longer were we treated to sisterly squeals at all hours of the night. I'd solved a murder for them, but apparently they'd not resolved their ensuing problems with the home office (aka National). I had not mourned the loss of a group that dressed in pink, coddled cats, and drank Tab and bourbon.

Peter Rosen arrived within the hour, looking less than dapper in a rumpled suit and unbuttoned collar. He has black hair, a jutting nose, and deceptively gentle brown eyes that have been known to narrow into unattractive slits when he's perturbed. Lately, our relationship had become as tempestuous as my daughter on a bad day. I wasn't sure if the source of tension lay in his muted but never absent arrogance or my unwillingness to make a commitment that would result in a division of closet space.

We also had intermittent confrontations when I went out of my way to assist the police when they were being bull-headed and blind. Peter, when caught up in his position as a lieutenant in the Farberville Criminal Investigation Department, takes exception to my invaluable contributions to truth and justice. He's been known to accuse me of meddling and threaten me with incarceration. Once he had my car impounded out of what I felt was nothing more than spite. Such things are not conducive to a harmonious relationship.

He accepted my offer of a beer, begged quite charmingly for a sandwich, and sank down on the couch. I provided him with said sustenance and then sat down at a marginally civil distance.

"My mother," he said with melancholy, "has decided she wants to spend at least a week of her final days on a cruise ship. If I allow her to go alone, they may well be her final days. She'll fall off the end of the ship within hours. I'll be stricken with remorse for the rest of my life."

"So go with her."

"I don't want to go with her. She'll pick up some pudgy condo salesman in the bar the first night, and then parade around with him as if they were the Duke and Duchess of Windsor."

"I thought you said she was going to fall overboard, not in love."

"Maybe it's one and the same," he said, no doubt thinking himself quite cryptic. He gave me the opportunity to ask what he meant, but I looked incuriously at him and then at my watch. "I don't suppose you want to come along and help me chaperon my white-haired seductress?" he added. "She has enough money to buy the ship. Surely she'll spring for a ticket so that her beloved son won't sulk in the bar while she plays roulette with her boyfriend."

"You suppose correctly. I've developed claustrophobia in my old age."

"Are you talking about a cruise ship or a relationship?"

"I'm too tired for profundities," I said as I finished my drink and again looked at my watch. "You'd better run along and call a travel agent. You're mother's getting older by the minute."

To what I suspected was mutual relief, he gave me a passionless kiss on the cheek and left. It was possible I was as crazy as Luanne, I thought as I tidied up the living room. I'd just turned down a Caribbean cruise with a man who had never been suspected of murdering an ex-wife, having opted for a routine divorce. He met all of Luanne's criteria: good-looking, rich, sensitive, virile ... and available. I doubted he could sew on a button or whip up a batch of pesto, but stress had never affected his performance in the sack. Peter was a man of many talents; regrettably, his most pronounced one these days was his ability to irritate me.

I heard from no one of any interest over the next few days, and on Saturday morning I was diligently dusting the window display (and sneezing explosively) when the telephone rang. My accountant had mentioned my second quarterly payment only the week before, and I was leery as I picked up the receiver.

Luanne bypassed the customary pleasantries. "Claire, I need your help! The most terrible thing has happened, and there's no one else I can turn to. I couldn't stop pacing last night, much less get any sleep, and now I—"

"What's wrong?" I asked in the voice that slows Caron down when she's describing Rhonda Maguire's latest incursion into perfidy.

"Captain Gannet came to the house at midnight and took Dick away for questioning. I called this morning, but all I got was a runaround from a simpering idiot who can't be old enough to shave, much less be issued a weapon. He told me not to bother to go to the office because they won't let me see Dick. If I knew the name of Dick's lawyer, I could at least call him. Should I hunt through his drawers for an address book?"

"Dick can call his lawyer himself." I paused to sort through her babbled words. "He was taken away for questioning, you said? He wasn't arrested?"

"What difference does it make?" she wailed.

"It makes a big difference, Luanne. Have they found new evidence to link him to his wife's"—I made myself use the word least likely to send her into more wails of desperation—"accident?"

"Gannet didn't say. He just showed up at the door, ordered Dick to get dressed, and then put him in the car and drove away. Dick has a rifle in the closet. I'm going to drive over there and demand that they let me speak to Dick."

"No!" I gripped the receiver and frantically tried to think how to deter my best friend from being gunned down in the doorway of the sheriff's office. "Under no circumstances are you to so much as open the closet door. Give me directions to the house. I'll leave here as soon as I can track down Caron so she can mind the store."

She gushed with gratitude, then rattled off highway numbers, county road numbers, turns onto roads that lacked numbers, and an admonishment to watch for deer during the last few miles. I reiterated my promise, hung up, and called Caron at Inez's house.

"I have plans," she said, unmoved by my plea. "It

was whispered last night that my body is the precise color of bread, which certain people found hilarious. The sun is shining. I intend to lay out and finish that book about pubic hair. I shall resemble toast by the end of the afternoon, and Rhonda can just take her tacky—"

"You'll have to do it tomorrow," I said, equally unmoved. "Luanne needs my help, and I cannot close the store on a Saturday. If you want to keep yourself in suntan oil, you'd better get over here in the next fifteen minutes."

Caron's compassion runs no deeper than her epidermis, but she is aware of the relationship between business activity and her own well-developed materialism. She and Inez arrived half an hour later. I gave one the feather duster and the other a lecture about not reading aloud from anything racier than Dr. Seuss, grabbed my scrawled directions, and left for Turnstone Lake, which was about forty miles from Farberville.

I followed the numbers easily, but once I left the pavement for a series of dirt roads, I became confused. Luanne had mentioned signs nailed on a post. There was no post. If I'd passed another car, or an inhabited dwelling, I could have asked directions, but as it was, I felt as though I'd abandoned society for some sort of primeval immersion. The sloping woods were dappled with sunlight. Orange hawkweed bloomed in the shadowy retreats, and black-eyed susans lined the ditches. A hawk circled high above a hilltop.

I might have enjoyed this incursion into nature, but I was keenly aware that I couldn't even find the lake. I wadded up the paper with the directions and tossed it into the backseat, gritted my teeth, and started turning left or right at each opportunity. My hatchback shuddered as I careened down and up the increasingly bad roads until I was on nothing better than a logging trail. The only water I'd encountered was a mushy puddle that left blinding brown splashes on the hood and windshield. I, a renowned amateur sleuth who'd uti-lized the smallest of clues to expose heinous crimes and unspeakable treachery (or an abundance of greed, anyway), was incapable of finding a large lake. Had my ego been more fragile, I might have found the ex-perience humbling.

I ran the wipers until I could see between the streaks, then took off once more. Several turns later I spotted a stout woman dressed in a wrinkled skirt, a baggy sweatshirt, heavy leather shoes, and a molded plastic pith helmet. As I stopped next to her, she turned and lowered a pair of binoculars.

"Good morning," she said, giving me a vaguely star-tled smile. "I'm on the trail of a hairy woodpecker. He is a shy fellow, and difficult to spot. I heard him only minutes ago, unless, of course, I mistook his hammer-ing for that of his cousin, the downy woodpecker." She cupped a hand around her ear and listened intently. "I don't hear him now."

"I'm sorry if I alarmed him," I said meekly.

"Ah, well."

"I'm lost. I've been driving around these roads for half an hour. Can you aim me in the direction of the lake?"

"The lake covers thirty thousand acres, my dear. We're on what is basically a peninsula, with water on three sides of us."

I hunted around in the backseat until I found my dis-carded directions. "I'm looking specifically for Dick Cissel's house on Blackburn Creek."

"Oh, you have strayed, haven't you? It's a good three miles from here. Let me fetch my bag and I'll ride there with you. My hairy woodpecker is much too shy to show himself anymore today." She took an enormous handbag from a branch and awkwardly climbed into my car. "I'm Livia Dunling, and you're a friend of Dick's. We stay on this road until the second turn to the right."

"I'm Claire Malloy. I've never met Dick. A friend of mind is at his house, and she asked me to come."

Livia rummaged through her bag and took out a plastic pillbox and a canteen. After she'd swallowed a pill, she returned the items to the bag. "While I was filling the feeders this morning, I saw your friend on the deck. She appeared very distraught. I considered going to the house to see if I could comfort her, but I began to feel fluttery and went inside to lie down. I have a most aggravating heart problem."

I wasn't sure what confidences I should share with my passenger. "You live near Dick?" I asked cautiously.

"Directly across the cove. My husband and I own Dunling Lodge. I wanted to call it Dun-Roaming, but Wharton does not appreciate whimsy. He'll be most displeased when he learns I've lost the Jeep again. I don't suppose you noticed it parked beneath a particularly fine specimen of wild dogwood?"

"No, I'm afraid not."

"That's the driveway," she said as she swung open the car door.

I jammed on the brakes in time to prevent her from tumbling under the tires to a certain death. "Thank you so much, Mrs. Dunling," I said between gasps. "Are you sure I can't take you to your front door?"

"No, no, I shall hike down by the gully where Wharton reported a hooded warbler only yesterday. He was certain he heard the distinctively flirtatious *tawee-tawee-tawee-tee-o*. Have a nice visit with your friend."

She limped across the road and into the woods, her bag thumping arrhythmically against her broad hips, her binoculars held aloft in one hand should they be called into immediate action.

Feeling inordinately guilty about frightening away the hairy woodpecker, I waited until she'd disappeared, then drove down the driveway and parked beside a forest green Range Rover. The front of the house was an unimposing expanse of native rockwork with only a few high windows. Landscaping consisted of neglected shrubs and a flagstone sidewalk. I had not yet seen the lake, but I heard the drone of a motorboat and deduced its proximity.

The front door opened before I could ring the bell, and Luanne gave me a radiant smile. "Oh good, you're just in time for a bloody mary on the deck. Dick is so excited to be meeting you."